The Boss

'I know it's a very important moment for a girl, her first spanking, which is why it should be done properly, by an expert. That means a bare bottom. Now, skirt up ...'

His words sent a powerful jolt through me, and I'd shut my eyes as his fingers took hold of the hem of my office skirt, lifting it slowly, up over the tops of my stay-ups and higher. I felt the turn of my bottom exposed, and more, the seat of my knickers, taut and pink over my cheeks, an image I could see so vividly it was as if I was standing behind myself rather than staring at a small area of orange carpet tile. Stephen gave a little chuckle.

'Pink, how sweet, and full-cut. I do hate thongs, don't you? Full-cut knickers are so much more feminine, and so much nicer to pull down.'

His hand settled on my bottom, big enough to cover most of the seat of my knickers, and I swallowed hard as he began to touch, stroking, exploring me, with a loitering intimacy that had me shaking my head in reaction.

The Boss
Monica Belle

BLACK LACE

Black Lace books contain sexual fantasies.
In real life, always practise safe sex.

First published in 2007 by
Black Lace
Thames Wharf Studios
Rainville Road
London W6 9HA

Typeset by SetSystems Ltd, Saffron Walden, Essex
Printed in Great Britain by CPI Bookmarque, Croydon, CR0 4TD

ISBN 978 0 352 34088 7

The Random House Group Limited supports The Forest Stewardship
Council (FSC), the leading international forest certification organisation.
All our titles that are printed on Greenpeace approved FSC certified
paper carry the FSC logo. Our paper procurement policy can be found
at: www.rbooks.co.uk/environment

1

I'd never felt so high as I went into my solo, striking the sticks in faster and harder to a crescendo that had the entire pub on their feet and screaming. I leapt up, kicking out at the bass, smashing one stick on the rim of my snare, letting go of the other and, as Josie's guitar cut back in, ripping the tear in my top wide open.

The yells of encouragement that greeted the sight of my bare breasts drove me higher still. I wrenched the tattered remains of my top off as the music rose to a metallic scream louder even than the human ones, then it faded, dying with a feeble whine to something approaching silence as the lights came up. A male voice called out from the back of the room, brash and authoritative.

'This venue is in breach of council regulations. You will leave quietly by the nearest exit . . .'

He went on quite a bit more, but I was already leaving by the nearest exit. Or I was trying to. My top was a write-off and I needed my coat anyway, from behind the bar. By the time I got it Josie and Dave Shaw where already in full flow with the Voice of Authority, only for him to turn on me as I tried to sneak past.

'You will remain here.'

The cheeky bastard had actually reached for my coat sleeve but I moved back out of reach. If he wanted witnesses or whatever there were plenty of other people who didn't seem to want to leave. Not me.

'I'm already gone.'

'You will remain here. I require your name and address as the one responsible for the breach of regulations.'

'Me? How?'

He stiffened, his face slightly red and his eyes protruding for all the world like a pair of boiled eggs before he replied in a voice even stuffier than before.

'The Dog and Duck does not have a striptease licence.'

It took a moment for what he was saying to sink in, and another one before I could decide whether to be outraged or amused.

'That wasn't a striptease!'

'According to council regulations –'

'I don't give a fuck about council regulations. All I did was take my top off!'

'An act of indecent exposure that may clearly be classified as an element of striptease, and therefore –'

'Bollocks! Striptease has to be slow, otherwise it wouldn't be a tease, would it?'

'The speed at which you undressed is not germane to the issue.'

'Yes it is.'

'No it isn't.'

'Yes it is.'

'No it ... Look, I am not going to discuss the matter. You performed an indecent act while hired to perform here at the Dog and Duck, and therefore I –'

'Christ, you talk a load of bollocks! I was paid to play the drums, not as a stripper, and it was just for a kick, not a striptease. If I was doing a striptease I wouldn't have been standing behind a drum kit, would I? And I'd have taken my clothes off nice and slowly, pretending I was going to show a bit more and then not doing it, all that stuff. I'd have worn some sexy gear too, not a ripped-up top, maybe a nice lacy bra and matching knickers, maybe stockings too. Do you like stockings? I bet you love stockings. Red or black? No, I know your sort, you're so repressed you're bound to be a pervert, so it's got to be white, maybe under a school uniform? Yeah, I bet that's your bag, tight white knickers under a pleated skirt, so tight you can see my . . .'

I couldn't help myself, because the dirtier I got the redder his face was going, and it was only because Josie was making urgent gestures at me over his shoulder that I stopped. He was making gulping motions with his mouth, a bit like a goldfish, but managed to pull out a little notebook and a biro.

'Your name and address, please.'

'OK, if you insist. Lisa Simpson, 742 Evergreen Terrace, Springfield.'

He'd written half of it down before he stopped, but this time I really was already gone. Maybe he called after me, maybe he didn't, but I was through the stores and out the back in just seconds. The night felt cool after the heat of the club, making the prickle of sweat on my skin feel chilly and rather nice.

Not many people had bothered to come out, just a scattering hanging around the front doors or their cars to see if there would be any fun. Hoping to cadge a lift, I made for the cars. You could tell which car belonged to the Voice of Authority. A blue Astra parked diagonally to the pavement. These people always like to think they're in the anti-terrorist squad or something.

He hadn't even bothered to close the window, and

the keys were in the ignition ... and the keys were in the ignition.

Well, what else could I do? I had to get home and the guy was a complete arsehole. Normally I wouldn't have done it, but I'm allergic to complete arseholes. Besides, he had acne.

I was in the car. I had the ignition on. I'd have run down Pete Manton if I hadn't looked over my shoulder. He stuck his head in the window.

'Hey, Fizz, new car?'

'It's not mine. It belongs to the council bloke inside, so get in or piss off.'

'I'm in.'

I was moving before he'd closed the door, with cheers and laughter following us as people realised I'd stolen the car. There was just a stab of apprehension before I was laughing too in wild exhilaration for what I'd done, and what I might be doing later. Pete was cute and I knew he'd had his eye on me, but that was to come. For now it was time to drive.

We were going to get reported, no question, so I hit out on the fen roads, touching eighty on the long straights, with Pete clinging to his seat and my head singing with adrenalin. I love to drive fast in a stolen car, a double thrill that lifts me high above all the dross of living on bugger-all in a small, boring town. It's as good as drumming, better than sex, mostly; the three things that have kept me sane over my teenage years.

I know I might get caught and I know I might get killed. But I don't care. Life must be for living. It's what people like the Voice of Authority can never see. They think we get pissed and joyride and fuck because we don't know any better. We know all right, and we know the life they want us to live, like a bunch of polite little state slaves. I'd rather crash and burn.

We nearly did, doing the ton on the long straight down to Brandon Bank when some prat on a push-bike appeared out of nowhere, no lights, nothing. He must have heard us coming, but he hadn't even had the sense to get out of the way. I hit the brakes and we hit gravel, then the bike, just one second after he'd thrown himself off into the ditch.

You do not know, cannot know, what one hundred miles per hour feels like until you lose control at that speed. I thought I was dead. I filled up with terror and self-pity and above all a ghastly sense of regret and helplessness, and then it was over. Mercifully, our wheels had taken hold again, because I'd been there before and had taken my foot off the brake. For maybe two seconds I was completely, calmly in control, allowing our speed to reduce slowly and shifting down a gear as soon as I safely could. Then the reaction hit me, like pins and needles in all four limbs at once while I was in desperate need of air.

I slowed and stopped, pulling off into a muddy gateway where tractors had been turning. My whole body was shaking and I lay back into the seat, my eyes closed, wanting to scream but not knowing if it was in fear or elation. I wanted sex too, to be held tight and fucked and fucked and fucked, in affirmation of my life and my existence. Finally Pete managed to find his voice.

'Jesus, Fizz!'

'Don't say another word. Just fuck me.'

I'd reached out to find his crotch, squeezing the full, soft mass through the denim of his jeans. He turned to

5

me with a look of amazement but he didn't stop me as I pulled him out and started to tug him erect. I wanted him on top of me, and inside me, quickly. He didn't need to turn me on, because I was there already, my feelings built up since the moment I'd taken my drumsticks in hand.

He needed a little help, his cock limp and bloodless, stirring only slowly in my hand as I played with him. Not that he was exactly resisting, just numb, but I knew how to deal with that. Leaning over, I took him into my mouth. His response was a whimper of pleasure, a little grunt of surprise as my fingers found the seat control and a long sigh as I began to suck him properly.

Now he was responding, his cock growing quickly as his fingers tangled in my hair, his other hand groping for the zip to my jacket. I let him, eager to be bare once more as his fingers fumbled open my zip and pushed within. A shrug and my jacket was off, sending a thrill of pleasure through me to be naked in the cool darkness of the car. I turned the light on to let him see, and to let me see him, his cock rising from his open jeans, wet and virile and exactly what I needed. He'd taken hold of himself as I rose, his eyes fixed to my chest as he pulled on his shaft. I love to watch a man grow excited for my body, to see all that desire just because I'm naked. I took my breasts in my hands, holding them out and stroking my nipples, to evoke a soft, urgent groan from somewhere deep in his throat.

He made a grab for me, pulling me down on top of him and pressing his mouth to mine. His hands were groping for my bum, so eager he didn't know whether to feel or try and get my knickers down. I gave him a helping hand, reaching back to guide him between my thighs as I straddled his body, using his cock to push my knickers out of the way and sliding him deep inside. He was thrusting into me immediately, far too urgent, but I needed it too much to slow him down; instead I wriggled on his cock in my need to get friction to my sex.

I heard him grunt and I knew he'd come, but I wasn't finished, not me. As he lay back with a sigh I was scrambling up his body, my legs cocked wide across his torso, and then his face. I could just see his eyes in the dim light, full of shock and surprise as he spoke.

'Hey, Fizz, no . . .'

'Don't be a pig, Pete. You've come. Make me.'

His answer was a muffled grunt as I pressed my pussy to his mouth. I was holding my knickers aside, making it skin on skin as I wriggled myself into his face, swearing at him and demanding he lick. He gave in, his tongue pushing out to lap at my sex, a heavenly feeling already close to orgasm. I began to grind my pussy into his face, my thighs locked tight around his head, one hand clawing his hair, the other the crotch of my knickers.

Lights burst in my head and I was coming, a hot, tight climax taken against his lips to fill me first with blinding ecstasy, then with a deep sense of satisfaction and a savage joy for my own behaviour. Only when I'd quite finished did I climb off, pushing the back door open so that I could step out into the cool of the night, both because I needed the air and to make it easier to adjust myself. Pete finally managed to find his voice.

'You play rough, Fizz!'

'That's what you get for coming so fast.'

I was laughing. I couldn't help it, mainly from the

expression on his face, but I stopped as I caught the purr of a motor in the distance. Pete had heard it too, and quickly we scrambled over the gate and into the field, running down along the hedge until we felt safe. The reckless thrill of joyriding was gone with my climax, and he seemed to feel the same as we crouched low and watched the lights approach.

It wasn't the police, just an ordinary car, and it didn't even slow down as it passed. I was wondering about the cyclist and how we'd get back, but neither of us even bothered to suggest taking the stolen car as we loped back towards it. Pete's door was still open, the light on, showing the crumpled pages of a magazine beneath the seat. I pulled it out, laughing as I saw that rather than *Which Parking Meter?* it was a porno mag, and a pretty smutty one at that. Pete chuckled as he took it.

'Dirty old bastard! Handy though.'

He'd begun to tear pages off, balling them up and throwing them into the footwell. I stood back, letting him get on with it and keeping my eyes and ears open for anyone approaching. There was nothing, the sky bright with stars but otherwise quite still, the only sounds faint and distant. A sudden flare of light and Pete was running towards me, ducked low as if he expected the car to go up like a bomb.

It didn't, the fire spreading only slowly, confined in the space beneath the seat we'd wound back for sex. Pete took my hand as we watched the car burn, an oddly sentimental gesture I thought, but I didn't mind. It was rather sweet, really, and I snuggled up against his arm as the flames licked higher, climbing the back of the driver's seat until within moments the entire interior was a flickering yellow glow. When the petrol tank went up there was a bang they must have heard in Ely. We felt the wave of heat but we were well clear of danger.

We watched for just a moment more, enjoying the fiercest of the blaze, then turned away. The fire was visible for miles and it couldn't be long before somebody came to investigate. Sure enough, we hadn't got halfway across the huge open field before we heard the distant sound of sirens and caught the flash of blue light among the trees towards Lakenheath. We ran, ducked low as we fled across the thick, clinging soil, both laughing, as much in nervous fear as in glee.

They couldn't see us, I knew that. They couldn't know which way we'd gone and they'd search the roads first, the way they always do. Unless we were really unlucky or did something incredibly stupid we were home free. Maybe, just maybe, my crime would catch up with me later. I won't say I didn't care, but it was worth it, the cost of all my heady thrills over a life of utter tedium.

We walked for hours, across Feltwell Fens and Hockwold Fens, jumping ditches and pushing through hedges, and talking all the while, about everything from music to mud – the fact that no matter how careful you are, the soggy bit always seems to manage to work its way up the insides of your legs as you walk. It was quite romantic, I suppose, and I'd seldom felt so at ease with a man.

Eventually we made it; exhausted, filthy, but triumphant. Pete dropped me off at my front door with a kiss and a squeeze of my bum, asking if I'd like to go out again. I hadn't really thought of what we'd done as a date, but I suppose it was, in a sense. He'd been fun, so I told him I would and kissed him back.

It was pitch black indoors, and I managed to sneak in without waking anyone. I was fit to drop and wouldn't have bothered stripping off if I hadn't been quite so muddy. There was a letter on my bed too, an official-looking one. My eyes were closing of their own accord as I pulled it open to see who was trying to screw me over and for what, but it was just an offer of an interview from some company called Black Knight Securities.

I'd only filled the form in to keep Mum happy. I'd certainly never expected to get to the interview stage, not with my qualifications. I was absolutely certain I wouldn't actually get the job, not in a million years. That sort of thing happens to nice, clean-cut girls with lots of A* GCSEs, not some retro-punk rock bitch with a bad habit of taking and driving.

What they wanted was a 'Management Support Operative', presumably some sort of glorified receptionist and general dogsbody, able to greet clients and show the less important ones around, probably also to make coffee, run errands for every Tom, Dick and Harry in the place and provide corporate bjs on demand. That meant blonde and neat and sweet, which is just not me. The company also specialised in CCTV systems, and while I like to think I have a fair bit of knowledge in that department it probably wasn't the sort of knowledge they were expecting.

I still had to make the effort: white face, black shirt, white socks, black shoes, black hair, Sweet Gene Vincent style, or almost. By the time Mum had finished with me I actually looked respectable, just not me any more, not Fizz, but Miss Felicity Cotton. I'd even let her destroy my hair, replacing the spikes and purple highlights with a predictable honey-blonde, so that on the way I was consoling myself with the thought of spikes with green and blue tips once I'd been turned down.

Black Knight Securities was on the new trading estate to the south of town, where the shoe factory Dad had worked in had been before it went bust. Just that was enough to make me feel resentful, although it wasn't their fault, obviously, let alone the way Mum and Dad had fallen apart afterwards.

Black Knight Securities were obviously just setting up. There was a showroom, with tall glass doors now wide open and a man in a white overall laying brick-red carpet tiles within. He didn't seem very likely to be the one doing the interviewing, so I stepped past him with what I hoped was a polite smile and through the door beyond into a warehouse piled high with crates and boxes. Two men were frowning over a clipboard, both suits, but otherwise very different.

One looked like a fox, fairly tall and very thin, with close-cropped red hair coming down across his fore-head in a point where he'd begun to go bald, while his features were pinched and suspicious. The other was equally tall, but dark haired and well built, his good looks spoilt only by the look of square-jawed, humour-less honesty projected in his face. They were just the sort of people I'd been dodging for years and I hated them both immediately. The last thing I wanted was their job, and I was sure they'd want a meek little thing behind the desk, so I stepped boldly forward, deliberately breaking into their conversation.

'Hi. I'm Felicity Cotton. I've come about the job.'

Foxy looked down, distinctly peeved. Square Jaw turned steel-grey eyes onto me and turned over a couple of pages on his clipboard before replying.

'Miss Cotton? Yes, eleven fifteen. Sorry, I didn't realise you were waiting.'

I hadn't been, I was late. I was almost tempted to say so too, but held back, telling myself it wasn't because of his air of natural command but simple common sense. He tapped his finger on the clipboard then spoke to Foxy.

'Would you interview Miss Cotton, Paul? I'll finish checking this in and join you in a minute.'

Foxy nodded and ushered me towards a wooden staircase which led up to an open office immediately above the showroom. He didn't look best pleased and I was sure I'd already failed, which brought an odd mixture of relief and annoyance. The office space was effectively a balcony overlooking the warehouse, with carpet tiles like the ones in the showroom and two desks each with its chair and computer. Everything looked brand new. I sat down without waiting to be asked while Foxy shuffled through various bits of paper before finally addressing me.

'Miss Cotton, right, here we are. You're twenty, you've lived in the area all your life, and this would be your first employment?'

He'd obviously written me off already and was only going through the motions, so I answered casually.

'That's right.'

'And how have you spent your time since leaving education?'

I almost answered that I'd been product-testing for companies like his, which was fairly true, but I wasn't feeling quite cheeky enough. Instead I shrugged, knowing full well that my complete failure to get a job for four years had already buried me.

'This and that. You know, moving around.'

'Travelling?'

I nodded. The trip down to Wiltshire with the convoy the year before counted as travelling, definitely travelling.

'Whereabouts?'

Wiltshire somehow didn't seem the right answer, but there were Steve's booze runs to Calais.

'The Continent, France mainly.'

'I see, and why did you choose to do this rather than start in full-time employment?'

I couldn't think of an answer other than the truth.

'I didn't want to get tied down, not straightaway.'

'So having soaked up a little culture you're now intent on starting on your career path?'

That sounded about right, even if it hadn't been culture I was soaking up.

'Yes.'

'And what made you choose the security industry?'

I hesitated, because it was a really stupid question. They wanted a dogsbody on the front desk, so it was hardly a career path, any more than taking a job flipping burgers is a career path in globalised evil. Foxy was looking expectant though and I had to say something, so snatched at something Pete had said when we were talking about speed cameras.

'It's the fastest growing industry in the country at present, with, er . . . unprecedented potential for expansion both on the national and international markets.'

'That's a very proactive attitude, Miss Cotton. Do you feel that's something you would bring to the company if we were to select you?'

I had no idea what he was talking about, but wasn't about to look a complete fool by asking what 'proactive' meant.

'Yes.'

He seemed to want me to continue, but I couldn't think of anything to say and eventually he looked down at his papers again, apparently scanning a list for another question to ask me. I waited, letting my eyes flicker around the big, white warehouse and the stacks of boxes. Most seemed to be cameras of one sort or another, which was really depressing. At last Foxy decided on a question.

'What do you have in your personal toolbox?'

Again I hesitated, not at all sure what he was asking, even if it was some sort of coded test to see if I'd show him my tits or something. Fortunately he spoke again before I could decide whether to slap the cheeky bastard or give him a flash.

'What skills will you bring to the job, that is, Miss Cotton?'

'Oh, I see, um ... Well, I know quite a bit about cameras, I suppose.'

He'd been going to ask another question but thought better of it, reaching across his desk instead and passing me a square black box as he spoke again.

'What do you make of this, then?'

From the picture on the box, it was obviously a surveillance camera, but only when I took it out did I realise it was one I'd never seen before, and seriously sneaky. It was black, no larger than my balled fist, and designed to be mounted high on a wall. Big Brother would have been proud. Foxy was waiting for my opinion.

'It's an external, wall-mounted surveillance camera, designed to be unobtrusive, while this shield would make it hard to break with a stone or something. The field of vision looks likes three-quarters of a circle, and the lens is a Zeiss, so high quality. It must be wired in and controlled from a base as there's a zoom facility. I imagine it's for use in shopping centres and stuff, anywhere with a security base. It says it's digital, so presumably it feeds back pictures to a computer? I've not seen it before though.'

'You wouldn't have. It's our new line, the ZX-4. After a lot of research, Stephen and I decided this was the best available, both in terms of money and technical merit. Last month he and I went to the Korean plant where they're produced, watched the demonstration and were given instructions on using them. What isn't obvious to the average person is that it can be used in conjunction with a facial recognition program, and automatically stores the images for future reference. With this baby you can pick a face from the crowd and it will retrieve every sighting of that individual going back as far as records have been kept. I'm sure you can see how powerful a tool that is, especially when linked to police or council databases.'

And they wonder why people wear hoodies. I turned the horrible thing over in my hand, looking for a weakness. It was clearly designed to be installed too high for spray paint to work easily, and was too tough and too small to make throwing things at it worth-while. I tried to think of anything I'd done wrong recently that might have been captured on camera. There was plenty, and I had to ask.

'Have any of these been installed yet, locally?'

'No, but we have an advisory team from the council coming over for a demonstration next week. In fact our primary marketing strategy is based on the supply of integrated systems including modules such as the ZX-4, and principally to corporate bodies. Assisting us with presentations would be an important part of your job, which is one reason we're keen to take on somebody with local knowledge. I take it you're aware of the high incidence of low-level crime in the Hockford area?'

'Er . . . yes.'

'The highest per capita rate of taking and driving in the country, for instance, which was a major deciding factor in locating ourselves here. We are an aggressive, forward-looking company, Miss Cotton, and by stamping down hard on street crime here, we aim to build a national reputation for our products. This is why we're looking for dynamic, proactive team members, perhaps like yourself. Furthermore, if you do work with us, you'll be taking on a fulfilling, real-time role in reducing street crime.'

That was true. I could reduce it by about half.

'So you're hoping the council will buy your system and you'll be able to catch the local scallies . . . sorry, I mean low-level criminals?'

'Exactly.'

'But won't they just move on? You can't put cameras everywhere.'

'Ah, but we can, just about. That's the beauty of the system. The ZX-4 is a high-cost, high-efficiency module, primarily designed to make the initial recordings for the facial recognition program. We have other low-cost modules, effectively disposable, which function as part of the integrated system to ensure close on one-hundred-per-cent coverage of the area for considerably less than the price of our competitors' systems.'

I had to say something.

'Isn't that a bit over the top?'

'At Black Knight Security we take a zero-tolerance approach. If they don't want to get caught, they shouldn't break the law. If you're not breaking the law, you have nothing to worry about. Simple.'

'But what about deterrence? Wouldn't it be better to put up a big, obvious camera, then maybe nobody would do anything in the first place?'

There was something almost conspiratorial in his voice as he answered me.

'You're not looking at the big picture. At this stage of the game we need the oxygen of publicity, and that means getting results. If we use big, obvious cameras, then the ... what was that word you used, scalies?'

'Scallies.'

'They'll be careful. We aim to get the full system installed without their knowledge, and to spend at least a week gathering facial recognition data before making our move. That should get us the attention we need.'

I was staring at him in horror, but he didn't notice, instead giving a dry cough as he realised he'd been getting carried away with his grand project. Once more he looked at the papers he'd been asking questions from before speaking.

'Right, er ... Miss Cotton, just one or two more general questions. Please could you give an example of a situation where you've used your own initiative to solve a problem?'

I could – bailing out of the old Beamer Dave Shaw had pinched before he decided to race the police down the M11 – but it didn't seem likely to go down very well. For a moment nothing else would come, before I thought of the way I'd managed to get backstage at the Bladders concert, but that wouldn't do either. I pretended to be considering several options, and finally decided to turn the whole thing around on him.

'I don't really see how you can solve a problem without showing initiative. After all, even if you go and ask somebody else to help, that's initiative, isn't it? But if you just stand there and do nothing, then you haven't solved the problem.'

He looked mildly perplexed for a moment, then went on.

'Do you feel you work best alone, or as part of a team?'

I knew the answer to that one, even it is was a total lie.

'Oh, as part of a team. I've always been a team player, although I can work alone if I have to.'

He gave a solemn nod, then continued.

'What do you do to relax?'

That at least I could answer.

'Play the drums.'

He looked a little surprised, but nodded once again. Mr Square Jaw was on his way up and gave me an affable smile as he leant against the banister. I smiled back, maybe a bit nervous, not because he was so good-looking, rather because the pair of them were freaking me out. I felt like a mouse between two cats, one scrawny ginger and one big, sleek black one.

I seemed to have survived the interview anyway, because Foxy stacked his papers and put them back on the desk as he spoke.

'Thank you very much, Miss Cotton. I'm Paul Minter, by the way, and my colleague is Stephen English.'

Square Jaw stuck out an enormous paw, which enfolded my own hand completely as I gave it a tentative shake. Foxy also offered a hand then I beat a retreat, complying with their final demand by sending up the next applicant, a woman older than me, smarter than me, and undoubtedly more suitable for the job in every possible way. She even looked as if she might have shown some proactive initiative in a team-based problem-solving scenario.

I went home, feeling distinctly depressed. Nobody was in, so I flopped down on my bed, thinking black thoughts. I obviously didn't have the job, not that I wanted it anyway, but much more importantly it looked like the entire town and maybe even the surrounding countryside was going to be swamped with Foxy and Square Jaw's horrid little cameras. Soon it would be impossible to have a snog without some closet perve peeping in to have a good leer and check that nothing happened to offend propriety, that or offer some thoroughly condescending advice on birth control.

Not even The Clash or Dag Nasty or *Fat Lip* could pick me up, but only succeeded in turning my thoughts to dark but ludicrously impractical ideas for putting a stop to the surveillance camera scheme. Yet at the very least I could warn everyone, so Foxy and Square Jaw might not get the bonanza scoop of scallies they expected. I knew what to look for too, which had to help, but with the sort of technology they were employing it was going to be very hard to hide.

I could of course give up my life of crime and become a model citizen, but I didn't want to, not with the punk blaring into my ears. Unfortunately it's one thing to sing 'Never Surrender', another to do it, and by the time I'd got to 'I Fought the Law' I found I couldn't get the lyrics out of my head. I thought back to my joyride with Pete just a few days before and wondered if it might be my last. It already felt distant in time, a lost moment of pleasure and excitement I would never know again.

That was nonsense. I'd just have to be clever, but there was always a way to beat the system. Foxy and Square Jaw would never control me. I'd be out again, maybe with one of those joke masks you can get of King Kong or the Queen. Let them put that in their facial recognition program. That made me laugh, and I began to daydream about the two men and how I could thwart their evil scheme, or their good scheme really, because I had no illusions about who the bad guys were, at least by most standards.

It was amazing how different they were to the men I knew, in some ways anyway. In other ways they were the same. After all, they were really in it to make money, just like Steve bringing the booze back from Calais, only legal. That was where the resemblance ended. Steve was full of life and emotion, always laughing, or angry, or dirty, filling my mouth with cold lager and then pulling my head down on his crotch because he liked the feeling on his cock. It was impossible to imagine Foxy doing that, or Square Jaw, who was definitely a Stephen and not a Steve.

There had been that one brief moment though, when Foxy had said that thing about my 'personal toolbox' and for one moment I'd really thought he was testing me to see if I'd be the sort of assistant who did personal favours. Not that I'd have done it for him, not in a million years. Square Jaw was a different matter, because he was undeniably good-looking, and I can sometimes be a bit of a sucker for a stern man, literally.

It actually made quite a nice fantasy, imagining Square Jaw interviewing me, with the same string of fatuous, newspeak questions, then all of a sudden a complete bombshell, something like 'And what would you do if I were to demand fellatio out of hours, Miss Cotton?' I'd tell him that I was no clock-watcher but dedicated to the success of the company and quite happy to work late, or that I fully understood the importance of teamwork and that if sexual tension was reducing his performance I would be more than happy to provide him relief in my mouth.

That was a deliciously dirty thought, and I made myself more comfortable on the bed, rucking my skirt up a little and letting my thighs come apart. For a moment the scene in my head changed, and I was imagining doing to Stephen English what I had done to Pete, straddling his face to make him lick me to heaven. Somehow it didn't work, but seemed inappropriate, even insolent. Stephen was too strong, too harsh to be handled so easily. If he licked me he'd have me on all fours, in a thoroughly exposed position, but it was much more likely to be me down on him.

I didn't want to admit to myself that he made me feel subservient, and I fought against what my body was telling me to do, but only for a moment. The idea was too sexy to hold back on. My hand went between my thighs, touching myself through the moist cotton of my knickers as I imagined the scene. It would be after hours, with both of us working late, and he would suddenly, casually make his demand, in a voice that allowed no possibility of disobedience – 'You will now give me fellatio, Miss Cotton.'

He would say it that way, very formal and stuffy, but the end result would be just the same, his cock fed into my mouth for me to suck him off. I'd be kneeling, under his desk, maybe with my smart little skirt suit –

the same one I was really in – disarranged to show my breasts and bottom. Men love that, to have a girl go bare while she sucks, and he would be no exception. I'd be playing with myself as his cock grew in my mouth, just as I was for real, with my fingers doing wonderful things between my legs and to one nipple.

Already I was on the edge of orgasm, but I took a last moment to strip myself, pushing down my knickers under my skirt and hauling my blouse and bra high to bare my breasts. That felt good, and as I began to touch again my mind focused on how he'd look in a similar dishevelled state, with his smart business suit still on, but with his cock and balls sticking out from his fly, huge and virile, ready for my mouth as I was ordered onto my knees to suck him.

I held the image as I came, my eyes tight shut, my body locked in ecstasy, clinging onto the moment for as long as I possibly could before slumping back on the bed with my mouth set in a wry smile for my own dirty behaviour.

2

Steve began to pick up speed as he pulled the van onto the M11, finding a gap in the traffic and drawing out into the middle lane before he spoke again.

'Remember, we're getting married and we need the booze for our wedding.'

'Yeah, yeah, yeah.'

'Fizz, get serious, will you? I've got a lot of money in this.'

'Yes, but, Steve, what if we get the same officer as last time, or the time before? Isn't he going to think it's a bit weird us getting married so often?'

'Nah, they get thousands of people coming over every day. They won't remember us. Anyway, you look well different. What did you go and do that to your hair for?'

'Mum made me change it, so I'd look respectable for a job interview.'

'A job interview? What d'you want a job for? I pay you something, don't I, and what with your social and Rubber Dollies.'

'That's not a lot, Steve, especially as the Dog and Duck are refusing to pay us because the council are on their backs. They've banned us too. I don't want the job anyway. I only went along to keep Mum happy.'

'Do you reckon you'll get it?'

'No. We're going to have to watch it though. They were these new people on the Hereward Trading Estate and they're trying to sell this security system to the council, hi-tech cameras, the works, and this program that records people's faces.'

'Nosy bastards! Still, I've got nothing to worry about.'

'No? What about when you make deliveries?'

'How do they know the stuff doesn't all come from the cash and carry?'

'Maybe, but keep an eye out anyway.'

'I will, thanks for the heads up.'

He'd pulled out to overtake a pair of lorries and I didn't answer, but settled down in my seat to watch the traffic and the fields beyond, with the perspective on a line of pylons slowly shifting as we moved beside and then beneath them. I always like to get out of town. It makes me feel free, or at least less trapped. I thought of how it would be working in an office, the same routine each day, the same places and the same faces, deadly dull, and obviously Stephen English wouldn't prove to be the dirty bastard of my fantasy but just another boring suit. I was best off out of it.

I began to flick through Steve's CDs, choosing Radiohead as the best of his somewhat motley and mainly 90s collection. He immediately began to sing along, his cement-mixer voice destroying all chance of my losing myself in the song. I didn't say anything, knowing that to let him realise he was being annoying would only make him worse. Finally he broke off to voice his opinion of an old blue Ford doing sixty in the middle lane and didn't start up again, leaving me to enjoy the journey.

Booze cruises are fun, especially if it's not your money that's at stake. I love the thrill of getting one over on the bastards, and that's what they are. Imagine taking a job where the main thing you do is make life unpleasant for other people? It's the same with traffic wardens and wheel-clamping firms and all the other little Hitlers. I don't know how they live with themselves.

The law is stupid anyway. Our taxes are way too high, anyone can see that, but do they reduce them? Do they fuck. They stick to every penny like glue and so you get the ridiculous situation where you can buy booze so cheap in France and Belgium that it's worthwhile for somebody like Steve to make a three-hundred-mile round trip to Calais, with the ferry and all, just to stock up. Not just worthwhile; he makes a living out of it. So he's a smuggler, big deal. Smuggling's not wrong, it's just a symptom of unjust taxation.

I would love to have been a smuggler. OK, well, I am, sort of, but I mean a proper smuggler, bringing gin in from Holland during the eighteenth century. I've got a book somewhere, which Nan gave me on my ninth birthday, which shows these guys in their big heavy coats and fancy hats, with pistols in their waistbands and knives in their boots. There even used to be women involved, including some really tough characters, and I used to daydream for hours about being one of them.

It was only years later I came to appreciate another virtue of smugglers. I've always loved rebels, and any man who just doesn't give a shit for the authorities has got to be at least a bit of a turn-on. That matters to me more than looks, more than how in he is, more than money or anything like that. A smuggler would be just perfect, some really big man with a devil-may-care attitude who'd fuck me bent over a barrel of gin while he held off three excise men with his pistols . . .

What I got was Steve, with his beaten-up Ford Transit and a penchant for risky blow jobs. Still, at least he wasn't likely to get hung, drawn and quartered at the drop of a tricorn hat, which was something. It's just not a very romantic image – jeans and a hoodie – although who knows, maybe in three hundred years' time girls will be daydreaming about the smooth, reckless lager and fag smugglers of the early twenty-first century?

We'd chosen a night run, because the ferries are so much cheaper and there's generally less hassle, or that's what Steve said anyway. I knew the real reason, which was producing just a little tiny tingle in the back of my mind. The knack is getting the timing right. You go over on the last ferry that lets you catch the hypermarkets, then mess around in Calais for a bit and come back at dead of night. That also meant I'd be driving back at least some of the way, so I closed my eyes and let my thoughts drift with the music, thinking of that huge smuggler, swearing defiance as he eased himself into me from behind.

By the time I woke up we were off the motorway and passing the complexes where the Channel Tunnel comes up. Steve had driven fast and we had plenty of time, allowing me to swallow a Diet Coke and a bag of crisps before we got in line. After that it was simple, a familiar but enjoyable routine. Through Customs, ignoring the temptation to tell them we were international terrorists on our way to a conference on hijacking techniques, onto the ferry and up to the highest deck to watch the sea while Steve stuffed his face with burgers and chips.

In no time we were in Calais and loaded up in not very much more, up to the limit of what the van could take but not another ounce. That's another problem – if you're too greedy. The police lurk on the A20 and pick anybody up if they're down on their axles, which is an offence. It makes them almost as big a risk as Customs. We didn't want to chance that, which was another good reason for coming back late at night, taking the back roads out of Dover and joining the motorway further up.

We ate at a French seafood restaurant, my choice, and Steve's second meal of the evening. It didn't seem to bother him, with his hands folded complacently over his stomach as we sat outside drinking coffee afterwards. He looked tired and I was wondering if he would just doze off, but I needn't have worried. No sooner had we returned to the ferry terminal than he slid the van in between a lorry and a big camper, and behind another van, so there was no possibility of anyone seeing into our cab unless they actually stuck their nose against the window. I knew what was coming and how I'd play it, pretending to be reluctant. He gets off on that, and I don't know why, but so do I. Even as the sound of the engine died he was turning to me, his face split by a big, dirty grin.

'How about my blow job?'

'You are a dirty pig, you know that?'

'What, because I like a blow job? Everybody likes a blow job.'

'Maybe, but not normally like this.'

'Aw, go on, Fizz, you gave me one last time.'

'As a special favour. That doesn't mean I have to give you one every time.'

'Well, I could do with another favour right now. I always get stiff when I wake up. Look.'

He'd pulled his cock out, holding it proud of his fly, already half erect. Immediately he began to pull on it, sighing in contentment as more blood pumped in.

Despite more than a little chagrin at the way he treated me, there was no denying my instinct: to take him in my mouth. I decided I'd shown enough resistance.

'OK, if you take your balls out too.'

'That's my girl!'

He complied, slipped a hand into his fly to pull out his balls. I love the look of a man like that, with just his cock and balls out of his trousers, otherwise fully dressed, or maybe with his top off if he has a good torso. It's so much hornier than naked. I bent down, using my fingernails to tease under his balls and up the long, thick shaft of his now fully erect cock. He let me do it for a moment, then gave a low growl under his breath.

'Get on with it, Fizz!'

'Pig.'

I just managed to get the word out before he guided my head down onto his erection, with his hand twisted into my hair. As I began to suck, so he began to play with the nape of my neck, which gets me every time. He chuckled as I grew more eager, and I could see his face from the corner of my eye, grinning down at me as I sucked on his penis, no doubt enjoying the power as much as the pleasure. I didn't mind. I'd have been the same, and he was turning me on by being firm with me.

That was part of the thrill; the other was knowing that it was just possible we'd get caught, maybe by a fellow passenger casting a curious glance in at our window as he passed, maybe by some official with a torch, maybe even by an illegal immigrant sneaking in among the lorries and vans. In any event they would get an eyeful of me with my mouth wide around Steve's erection.

Steve was trying to pull up my top and I let him, knowing it would make the view that much ruder. With my bra unclipped I slipped the cups up myself, relishing that delicious moment of exposure as I came fully bare. He began to stroke my chest, his breathing now hoarse with excitement as I tugged him into my mouth and squeezed on his balls. I was wondering if I dared go further, maybe to push my jeans and knickers down and play with myself as I sucked, making both my exposure and my pleasure complete. My hand had even gone to the button of my jeans when he grunted and came, too fast for me as usual, but I wasn't finished.

I pulled back, dizzy with sex and my mouth full of the taste of man. The side of the lorry was just a couple of feet from my window, blocking off any possibility of us really being seen. In a moment I had my jeans and knickers down, leaving myself nude from my ankles to my neck, deliciously, delightfully bare. I let my legs wide, drawing a grunt of surprise from Steve.

'I'd have fucked you if I'd known you were so horny.'

'You should have done. Now get down there.'

'You are one dirty bitch, Fizz.'

His hand went between my thighs, manipulating me. A finger pushed inside, and a second, making me sigh, but it wasn't what I wanted.

'Come on, Steve, lick me. I did it for you.'

'Yeah, but . . .'

'But nothing. Lick me, you chauvinist pig!'

He gave a doubtful grunt, or maybe it was supposed to be an oink, but he'd gone down, forcing me to slide forward on the seat and cock one leg high so that he could get his face to my sex properly. He began to lick and I settled back with a contented sigh, playing with my breasts as I went back to my thoughts of being caught. Obviously it would be no fun at all, not really, if it was by an official, but the officials of my imagination behaved very differently to real ones.

In order to let us off, they'd demand their fun with me. Steve, being a complete bastard, would let them, and I'd be taken into one of their little huts. They'd make me strip. They'd make me suck their cocks and balls. They'd bend me over and fuck me from behind. They'd make me suck them when they'd been inside me and come all over my face and breasts, leaving me so, so high I'd end up stark naked on the floor masturbating in front of them for the way they'd handled me.

I came, pushing Steve's head down at the last moment so I could get a finger where I needed it and the right rhythm to come. He didn't stop licking, his tongue still working on the inside of my thighs and across the curves of my bum cheeks as my body went tight in ecstasy and stopping only when I finally went limp.

Just a few minutes later officials began to walk up between the lines, asking us to move into position for boarding. I had trouble keeping a smirk off my face most of the way to Dover.

It had been a good run. Steve had been dropping by the time we came off the ferry and I took over driving. Customs was a breeze, with something going on at the other end of the docks and just two men dealing with us. I drove up through town, keeping to the back roads most of the way to Canterbury and only then joining the motorway. Steve stayed asleep until we were almost home and it was still dark when I got in. I collapsed into bed, thankful for the roll of notes in my pocket and still thinking sleepy, dirty thoughts as I drifted towards sleep.

I woke to the sight of Mum looking slightly disapproving and holding out a cup of coffee. I ignored the look and took the coffee, leaving her tutting as she picked up my discarded clothes from the floor.

'Honestly, Felicity, you didn't even put a nightie on.'

'I was tired. Sorry.'

'Well, at least you're all right. I worry about you, driving for so long, and all night.'

'We shared the driving, we always do.'

'That's something, I suppose, but I don't see why Steven can't take one of his friends. You'll injure your back with all that heavy lifting.'

'He prefers my company, and it's only a few beer cases.'

'Well, just you be careful. There's a letter for you, from that security company. Maybe you've got the job.'

I did my best to look interested and hopeful as I picked a large white envelope from the bundle she was holding. The back showed the Black Knight Securities name and logo, a tasteful gauntlet clutching a length of chain. Mum was hovering with intent so I took a sip of coffee and opened the letter, expecting to see the familiar words – 'Dear Miss Cotton, you are a dirty scally, so fuck off . . .' only perhaps phrased a bit more politely. I even began to read it out loud.

'Dear Miss Cotton, We are delighted to be able to offer you the position of Management Support Operative with our company . . . fucking hell! They're offering me the job, Mum.'

'There we are, I said you could do it if you tried.'

I braced myself to tell her I didn't want it, that I was going to turn them down, but then I saw how much they were offering me: £21,500 plus a performance-related bonus. That stopped me dead. It was enough to run my own car, something nice too. I might even insure it.

Only it was a complete betrayal of everything I believed in. I'd be working for the enemy. I'd be one of them. Or would I? Maybe I could subvert the company from the inside and wreck their plan. No, it was a ridiculous idea. I either worked for them or I didn't, and if I worked for them it meant becoming part of everything I hated. On the other hand, there were my catalogue bills, which were getting well out of hand, and Mum kept hinting that it was time I started paying something towards the house.

Maybe I could keep the job for just a few months, enough to get some money in my pocket and enough experience to let me move onto something else, something that paid OK but didn't compromise my principles, or rather, my lack of principles. Turning down the job wasn't going to stop the cameras going up anyway, and with me on the inside at least I could make sure everyone knew what was going on.

That had to be the best choice, surely? I was still feeling intensely guilty as I wrote out a letter of acceptance with Mum peering over my shoulder, a sensation that reached a peak as I pushed my envelope into the postbox at the end of the road. I'd done it, sold my soul in a way I'd told myself I would never do, had never even imagined myself doing. Me, Fizz, who'd always said that working as a check-out girl or flipping burgers was selling out, and I was a Management Support Operative with a security company. How was I going to tell my friends? What was I going to say to the girls in the band?

Not that there was much of a band, at least, not one with anywhere to play. Having been kicked out of the Dog and Duck there was nowhere closer than Thetford who were going to book us, let alone pay. Rubber Dollies was dead, to all intents and purposes, except possibly for winding up Josie's neighbours. In was no surprise either, because the council had had it in for us from the start, objecting to everything from the noise to us taking our tops off, as well as the general mayhem that tended to follow our gigs. Still, we'd never compromised, which was something.

I was going to have to tell Josie and Sam and as many other people as I could before they started talking about me behind my back, which was inevitable. It was tempting to put it off until after the weekend, but I was supposed to start work on the Monday and there really wouldn't be time. I had to get it over with and hope they'd realise that it was better to have me on the inside than somebody else.

As I walked over to Josie's I was dragging my feet, and the moment I saw her I was wondering if I could go through with it. She was outside the garage, messing about with her bike, in tatty jeans and a leather jacket, shades pushed up on top of her head and a cigarette sticking out from the side of black-painted lips. I hadn't seen her since the night at the Dog and Duck, and when we'd spoken on the phone I'd avoided any mention of my change of look. Inevitably it was the first thing she commented on.

'Shit, Fizz, what's with the hair? You look ... I don't know, like something out of one of those weird adverts where they drink bacteria.'

'Thanks, Josie, you're looking good too.'

I bent to kiss her, triggering the usual contradictory

emotions as her lips touched mine. However much I tried to treat her like any other friend it was impossible to forget that she preferred girls to men.

'I hear you've been to France. Got any vodka for me?'

'Yeah, but everything's with Steve. Look . . .'

'Great. Could you hold the bike while I sort this?'

I wasn't really dressed for oily motorbikes but I helped steady the thing while she bolted some widget or other back onto the engine. She was completely absorbed in what she was doing and I waited until she'd finished, only for her to speak before I did.

'I have got the best gig lined up, at the Yankee airbase at Hockwold.'

'You are joking? How did you pull that one off?'

'Easy. Sam's knobbing a fly-boy.'

'When did this happen?'

'After you fucked off with that council guy's car. We were all out in the street, and him and his mates came past. She stuck her thumb out, climbed on the lap of the one she liked best and now they're an item.'

'OK, so when's the gig?'

'Saturday week. You have to do something about your hair though, Fizz.'

'Never mind my hair. I let my mum do it so I could go to a job interview. You know she's always nagging me, only . . . only this time I got the job.'

'Cool. How much?'

'Twenty-one K.'

'Fuck me! What are you doing?'

'Oh, it's this new firm on the Hereward Trading Estate. They do security, that sort of stuff.'

'Cool. You'll be able to get a new kit, yeah?'

'Yes. I was thinking of a car.'

'Get a bike and a van. That way you can ride with me and we won't need Steve to haul our gear everywhere.'

'That's a thought.'

I'd meant to tell her more, but she didn't seem bothered and I decided to put it off, perhaps until the cameras started to go up. She'd been peering at the innards of the bike, then gave a satisfied nod and began to wipe her fingers on an already oily rag before she spoke again.

'So what're you doing tonight?'

'Going out, I suppose. I've got some money from the booze cruise.'

It was, maybe, my last chance for a really wild night out. From Monday I'd be working, and if the cameras went up I was going to have to be on my best behaviour. As I put the first ice-cold mix to my lips in Buzz Shack I was wondering what I could possibly do to top all the nights before. The only trouble was, it felt forced. Everything I'd ever done had been spontaneous, never planned, always the result of an on-the-spot, generally alcohol-fuelled decision. Now nothing seemed right; either childish, or tame, or not worth the risk. I was still thinking about it, brooding really, and had begun to play with my bottle on the bar top and pick bits off the corners of the label when a voice sounded from directly behind me.

'Felicity?'

I nearly fell off my bar stool. Nobody calls me Felicity, except Mum, and the voice was very definitely male, deep and gravelly, also familiar. Sure enough, there was Stephen English, looking faintly surprised in a smart pale-grey suit with a tie to match. Quite a few of my friends were around, and I found myself struggling for a suitable remark. He got in first.

'So it *is* you. I thought I saw you through the window. I'm a bit surprised to see you here.'

'I, um ... well, you know, just dropped in for a drink. Er ... would you like one?'

Somehow I was very sure he didn't drink premixed vodka and lime, let alone use the condensation on the bottle to wet the label and pick little bits off. I found myself blushing, then realised and my cheeks were getting hotter still as he glanced around the bar. Everybody was looking at us, including Pete, who'd already been flirting with me, and Dave Shaw, and what suddenly seemed like everybody I knew or had known in the last twenty years. Finally Stephen English decided to answer me.

'Not here, perhaps, but would you care to join me at Cuatro Cortado?'

It was a tapas bar at the other end of the High Street, Mum's favourite watering hole and not a place I'd normally be seen dead in, but at that moment I'd cheerfully have joined him at Croxton Landfill Site if he'd suggested it, anything to get out of Buzz Shack. I swallowed my mix with frantic haste, spent a moment choking while he gave me a couple of hearty thumps on my back, and we left.

I could feel their eyes on me and read their minds. What was Fizz doing with the suit? I knew the conclusion they'd come to as well, girls and boys both, their dirty little minds going straight down the one inevitable track: he was bonking me. My face must have been purple but Stephen English appeared not to notice, pausing on the pavement to glance up and down the street as he spoke.

'In a location like this you can easily appreciate the benefits of the ZX system.

'In fact, it's ideal; one principal street with the nuisance bars concentrated into a small area, which acts as a focus and allows the faces of those out on any particular night to be recorded. We'd then have smaller units covering the dispersal zone and any potential hotspots outside town, which would allow us to map the activity of any individual we chose to target, with the data remaining on file for an indefinite period.'

He was nodding as he spoke, well pleased with himself and in full view of the bar window. I began to move up the street, not at all sure what to say in the face of his enthusiasm for total control. After a moment he followed, still pointing out features as he went.

'... and if installed carefully, the ZX-1 and ZX-2 modules will be invisible from street level, while the automatic facial recognition feature on the ZX-4 and ZX-5 will be able to record the faces of people actually inside the bars, thus avoiding what we like to call the hoodie problem. You don't usually drink in that dreadful place, do you?'

'No, no, I'd er ... just been for a walk ... along the river, and I was thirsty.'

'The river walk is beautiful, isn't it? I jog up as far as the B road and back every morning as part of my workout.'

'Up to the road? That's miles.'

'Ten K. You should join me sometime.'

'Er ... right. Well, here's Cuatro Cortado.'

We went in and I was immediately struck by the smell of the air, warm and fruity yet somehow old, making me think of Nan's kitchen when she was cooking a Christmas dinner. The lighting was a dim amber glow and there was no music, only a low buzz of conversation from the customers, most of whom were twice my age or more. To my relief Mum wasn't among them, but I still felt distinctly out of place as Stephen led me to the bar.

'What will you have?'

'I don't really drink sherry. It's too sweet for me.'

'No? Then you're missing a treat, and real sherry is dry, never sweet, with the exception of Pedro Ximenez which is probably a bit specialist for your first time. Essentially, there are three styles of real sherry, according to the amount of a mould called flor that forms –'

'A mould?'

'Yes, but it doesn't produce a mouldy taste. Just the opposite in fact. A lot of flor keeps the sherry fresh and light, which we call fino and is generally considered the high point of the sherry maker's art. I am perhaps something of a philistine as I prefer the darker, richer amontillados and olorosos, in which the flor does not develop in the same way.'

'There's less mould?'

'Exactly.'

'I'll try that.'

He spoke to the barman in Spanish but perhaps not very good Spanish as it took quite a bit of gesticulation to get his point across. At last two small dark-brown bottles, two small glasses and some bowls of nibbles were loaded onto a tray which he carried to a table directly opposite the bar. I obviously wasn't supposed to neck the stuff from the bottle but otherwise wasn't quite sure what to do, so waited while he twisted the cork loose from his own bottle, poured a small measure into his glass and put it to his nose, inhaling the scent with his face set in deep concentration.

'Splendid! I could almost be back in Cadiz.'

I attempted to follow his procedure and was surprised to find that the sherry smelled quite nice. Unfortunately it tasted like a mixture of old socks and battery acid but a handful of olives and nuts helped with that. I continued to sip at my glass and listen politely as he went into an explanation of how sherry was made, all of which seemed unnecessarily complicated. Finally he stopped and sat back.

'But I'm sure I'm boring you. Tell me about yourself. Paul says you've travelled on the Continent. Have you visited the vineyard areas at all?'

'Um ... only in passing.'

'Ah, you should stop. Champagne is the most convenient. It's only a hundred and fifty miles in from Calais, on autoroute the whole way. The Avenue de Champagne is wonderful, and of course Rheims is one of the finest cities in Europe, although sadly spoiled now.'

'Yes, I thought that. Is it much cheaper than buying over here, or in Calais?'

'That rather depends what you want. For the Grand Marques, not really, no, and Calais is certainly cheaper for ordinary brands, but if you want the finest, from individual growers, there's no substitute for visiting the area. By my reckoning, a purchase of ten cases made in the region rather than here will save enough money to cover the cost of the trip, including hotels and meals of a respectable standard.'

'Sounds good.'

'You should come ... although of course as your employer ...'

He'd gone slightly pink, and trailed off. I hastened to reassure him.

'That wouldn't bother me. Who cares anyway? You're the boss, aren't you? You can do whatever you like.'

He gave a nod, still somewhat guarded, and would have spoken again but the door had opened and he was distracted. My heart sank as I saw who the newcomers were: Mum and her latest admirer, Archie Feltham. Both looked surprised to see me but there was no choice but to make the best of it.

'Hi, Mum, this is Mr English, my boss.'

The three of them immediately went into a sort of British fit, assuring each other they should use first names and being delighted to meet. Mum at least wasn't faking, but looked well pleased with herself to discover that my boss went to Cuatro Cortado, and that I was there with him. It was just the sort of situation she'd wanted me to be in for years.

I gave in. I was obviously stuck for the evening, drinking sherry and making polite conversation when I should have been out on the razz. Soon I'd begun to clock-watch, wondering what I'd have been doing otherwise, what time I'd have left Buzz Shack, or been thrown out, what time I'd have committed some outrage against public decency, what time Pete Manton would have been pulling my knickers down . . .

The answer was, not for ages, because time seemed to have slowed to a crawl. The three of them had a wealth of subjects to choose from, few of which I could add to. Even Stephen's weird but strong appeal didn't help because there was nothing I could do about it in front of Mum. At least there was plenty to drink and nobody seemed to expect me to pay, Archie providing one bottle and Stephen another. The sherry didn't even seem quite so nasty either, and I made the best of it, that and the roasted cashew nuts. Otherwise I'd switched off, with a 999 drum beat running through my head over and over and my eyes moving between my glass and the lines of Stephen's face and body.

It was only ten o'clock when Mum started making noises about getting home. She normally stays until closing time, so I knew she was just trying to find an excuse to leave me alone with Stephen English, but it was at least a small improvement. I could feel the sherry getting to me too, and was even wondering if he'd want to snog me, but not sure if the idea was revolting or compelling.

Another half hour and I'd decided it was compelling. There was something about him, the way he was so certain about everything, that made me feel weak. It put my back up too but just at the moment the weak feeling was winning. Maybe it was just the alcohol but I didn't care. I wanted to be snogged, and touched, and maybe even have his cock slid inside my body as I lay open and naked beneath him.

Only when I tried to stand up did I realise just how drunk I was. The sherry had gone straight to my head, leaving me unsteady on my feet, and just at that stage where everything seems like a good idea, no matter how stupid. I felt I wanted more too but the bar was closing. Stephen had already put his coat on and was offering me my jacket, but I turned to the bar.

'Excuse me ... hey you, could I have another bottle? The dark stuff we had last. That's the one, yes, cheers.'

The barman passed it to me and I paid, Stephen giving me an indulgent smile as he held the door. Outside the air was cool and fresh, making my head spin. I took his arm, no longer really caring what happened, so long as I got my snog, at the least, and preferably a good, hard fucking. I wasn't in the mood to play word games either.

'You can take me home if you like.'

'Of course. I'd be delighted.'

I smiled. It was that easy. It's always that easy. Maybe he was a stiff, but stiffs are OK as long as they're stiff in the right department. He began to steer me up the road and I let myself melt into his side, already imagining the feel of his cock in my hand, in my mouth, in my pussy. I opened the sherry, taking gulps from the bottle as we walked, and only when we reached the end of my road did I wonder if he might not have got the wrong end of the stick.

'Hang on, Stephen, this is my road.'

'Naturally.'

'But I thought ... and how do you know my address? Of course, it was on those form thingies, wasn't it? How silly of me, I forgot you were a nosy ... Sorry, I mean you ...'

'Let's get you home, Felicity.'

'Yeah, yeah, but your place ... mine's full of little sisters and stuff, and Mum'll be back ... once Archie's bonked her brains out.'

He didn't answer but continued to steer me along the road until we'd reached my gate. I knew I was drunk and that he was turning my offer down, which filled me with all sorts of emotions, mainly self-pity, and I found myself looking up at him through hazy eyes.

'You're not really going to go, are you, Stephen? I thought you liked me? I thought you were going to take me home and bonk me.'

'I really think you should go to bed, Felicity. Sleep it off, that's the best thing.'

'Aw, come on, what's the point of getting pissed if you can't have some fun? You can bonk me, I don't mind, really ... And you're my boss, you ought to bonk me, don't you think, or at least make me give you a bj?'

I was running my fingers down his chest as I spoke and felt the hard muscles move as he swallowed, encouraging me.

'Oh, you do want to, don't you. Come on, do it here. Nobody will see if we go in the back garden. Come on, let's have your cock out, I bet you've got a lovely cock. I'll suck you, shall I? I'm a good little cocksucker, Stephen. I'll show you, shall I?'

'Felicity!'

I'd moved in close, sliding my hand down to his crotch. Whatever he was saying, he was ready for me, his cock a hard bar in his pants. I went down, meaning to take him out so he'd have to come into the back with me, but he detached my fingers and stood away.

'Felicity, really, you're very drunk, and I'm sure you'll regret this in the morning.'

'No I won't, and you do want me, don't you?'

'Yes, of course I do, but look, really ...'

'Oh, come on, please? I'll lick your balls. I bet you like that?'

'I ... I'd better go. Goodnight.'

He'd gone back through the gate and set off quickly down the road. I stood there for a long moment, swaying slightly, and wondering what the matter was. He'd been ready and so had I, more than ready. Maybe he was just nice and didn't want to take advantage of me, and yet that was exactly what I wanted, to be taken advantage of. When I finally moved it wasn't indoors but around the side, to the back garden where I'd planned to take him. It was perfect because only my room and the kitchen overlooked it, while it was far too dark for any of the neighbours to see, especially under the trees.

I went to sit on the swing, drinking sherry with my legs cocked well apart to balance myself. My head felt hot with alcohol, my body sensitive and urgent, both because I was horny and because I felt so sorry for myself. He should have fucked me, maybe bent over the swing. Yes, that would have been dirty, with me bent over and my skirt turned up, my knickers pulled down to get my bum bare and his cock eased in up me from behind. It would have felt so nice.

Before I really knew what I was doing I'd stood up to push my knickers off under my skirt. It felt good, and better when I'd sat my bare bum on the seat. I began to swing, keeping my legs spread wide to let the cool air touch my pussy and wishing he was there to watch me play dirty and to fuck me. I pulled my top and bra up, imagining him cajoling me into stripping while he got hard over what he could see. Again I began to swing, now nearly nude, and when I picked up the sherry bottle for another swig the feel of the cold hard glass decided me on what I would do.

I began to rub it on myself, first pressing it to my nipples and tummy, then lower, rubbing the width of the bottle between my thighs, to bump the raised letters saying whoever had made the stuff right onto my clit. It felt good, so deliciously rude, so naughty to be swinging near nude in the cool night air, my clothing dishevelled, my titties and bum and pussy all nice and bare as I used the bottle to bring myself high, and higher still, to a gasping, shivering orgasm that left me feeling weak and, for some reason, very close to tears.

3

What had I done? I'd got drunk and propositioned my boss. I'd asked him to fuck me. I'd offered to suck his cock. I'd offered to lick his balls.

It didn't bear thinking about, only I didn't have much choice. On the Monday I was going to have to go into work and face him, unless of course he had already decided to sack me. My headache didn't help either.

The rest of the weekend passed in a blur. Every time the phone rang I expected it to be him, with a curt instruction that I needn't bother to come in after all. I tried to tell myself it was exactly what I wanted, but not only had I already spent my first year's salary in my head, but deep within I badly wanted to see him again and for him not to be cross with me.

Even Mum's roast chicken dinner seemed to turn to ashes in my mouth, but no phone call ever came. I went to bed early, making the excuse that I wanted to be at my best in the morning, but in reality still feeling a little tender after the sherry.

Monday morning was not good. From the moment I woke up I was filled with apprehension, also self-reproach, telling myself that it would all have been OK if he'd accepted my offer. I hadn't felt that way since waiting outside the headmaster's study after driving a hockey ball through his window while he was talking with the chairman of the Board of Governors, only worse. At least I hadn't offered to lick the headmaster's balls.

I'd made sure I was immaculate, in a navy skirt suit over a white blouse, with stockings and a ribbon tie, my hair up and just a touch of make-up. Why looking respectable was supposed to make it better I didn't really know, only that it seemed the right thing to do. I'd turned up a little early too, keen to seem as efficient as possible, but the big glass doors were already open onto the now finished interior where Stephen English was standing at the desk – my desk. He greeted me with a smile, perfectly friendly if maybe a bit stern, but I was stumbling my apology out before I could stop myself.

'I . . . I'm really sorry about the other night, that is, I shouldn't have drunk . . . and . . .'

He put a hand up and I stopped.

'Don't mention it, please. Least said, soonest mended, and it was my fault anyway. I don't suppose you're used to sherry? It's strong stuff.'

I managed a nod, feeling embarrassed and also pathetically grateful. He gave me another of his smiles and gestured to the desk.

'This will be your work station. Your primary function is to receive potential clients and enquiries, in person, on the phone and by email. Anything technical should be passed on to Paul, anything else to me. With time you can also handle sales to private customers, although this is not a key part of our marketing strategy. For now, I'd like you to familiarise yourself with our computer system.'

As he spoke my head had been going up and down like one of those nodding dogs you get in the backs of cars, and he finished with a beaming smile. As I turned towards my desk, he gave me just the gentlest of pats on my bum to send me on my way. It was like an electric shock, a gesture at once so assertive, so condescending and so casually intimate. I felt outraged but at the same time pleased, because he'd shown me affection after rejecting me before, a reaction that provoked further outrage, at myself.

He'd turned me on with one touch like a switch. As I sat down, I couldn't help but wonder if he'd make a habit of it. Because I'd shown my true feelings he would now take casual control of my body, touching me when he pleased and where he pleased. The thought sent a shiver through me, even as I was telling myself it was an appalling way for him to behave.

To make it worse, he'd ducked down next to me to explain the workings of the computer system, which meant I could feel the firm muscle of his upper arm pressing against me, and smell his skin and some very masculine lotion he used. It was intoxicating and I had to force myself to concentrate as he showed me how to check the stock list and a dozen other functions.

I soon had the hang of the computer and was left to my own devices for a while. Paul was in the back, tinkering with bits of their equipment, and Stephen had joined him, only coming back to me when he wanted a coffee. I'd already guessed I'd be coffee girl and it shouldn't have been a big deal, but as I went through the motions it was impossible not to feel that I was serving him, personally.

That just isn't me. I've always held my own in relationships, more often taken the initiative. Now I was feeling grateful to have my bum patted and to be allowed to make coffee, and for a man who had rejected an open advance from me. Worse, he was a suit. Mum even approved of him. It was appalling, but I couldn't help it, and even found myself giving him a little curtsey as I passed over the coffee.

He didn't notice, reacting only with a distracted 'thank you' as he studied a diagram Paul was holding up, which only served to make my feelings worse. Just being there was bad enough, because for all my desire to see myself as a spy, I felt more like a captive. To be in love with my boss was almost too much. Part of me wanted to run screaming from the room, but it was an impulse I was unable to follow.

I'd gone back to my desk to drink my own coffee and continue to familiarise myself with the mysteries of their computer system, but I'd barely sat down when Stephen's head appeared through the inner door.

'Can we borrow you for a minute, Felicity?'

'Sure.'

I hopped down from my chair, which was quite high, and as I reached him he spoke again.

'This is a minor point, but I do think we will gain by projecting a professional image at all times, during office hours that is, so that it becomes second nature in the presence of clients.'

'I'm sorry, how do you mean?'

'Well, for instance, although naturally I wouldn't expect anything of the sort outside hours, I think it would be best if you addressed me as Mr English, and Paul as Mr Minter.'

'If you like.'

'I think it's best.'

So he got to call me Felicity while I had to call him Mr English. Why didn't he just put me in a French maid's uniform and give me a feather duster while he was at it?

We'd come into the warehouse, where Paul was now standing high among a bank of gadgetry, with all five camera models set up on a gantry and a spaghetti of wires running up to his computer. He gave a thumbs-up signal and Stephen spoke to me again.

'If you could walk forward, towards the cameras, then turn left and continue a little way.'

I was facing the cameras so it was already too late as I realised the significance of the act. They were on, recording me, putting my face into the recognition program. I flinched but there was nothing to be done, only walk on as instructed, just like a good little dolly-bird receptionist should. Stephen continued to talk, oblivious to my stolen image or the gross invasion of my privacy his act represented.

'This is just a test, of course. Once we're sure of the system we'll repeat it somewhere more picturesque.'

'With me?'

'Of course. It's a curious thing but marketing studies repeatedly show that better results are achieved by visually pleasing presentations. Thus, while it makes no difference whatsoever in terms of demonstrating our equipment, sales can be predicted to show a significant improvement if our presentation shows you walking along a woodland path, rather than, say, me walking between a row of packing crates. It's an entirely subconscious reaction, but that's true of so much of advertising.'

'So your computer can now recognise my face?'

'I certainly hope so or we've wasted a great deal of money. Could you go out of the room and come in again, please?'

I obeyed, praying the whole thing would cock up and that the system would either fail to recognise me completely or decide I was somebody else. It didn't. Almost on the instant I stepped back into the warehouse Paul's system gave a self-satisfied ping. He clapped his hands in approval.

'Perfect! That took less than a second, and at a different angle to her initial approach.'

Stephen beamed. 'That's good. Now we know the Koreans haven't sold us a dud and the system can recognise a face, but there are still tests to be done to make sure it's able to pick your face from among others.'

Paul called down, 'It knows she's not you or me, but we'll need a much bigger sample before we can get an idea of percentage efficiency.'

Stephen gave a reflective nod. 'Bit of a chicken and egg situation there. We have the original Korean data, of course, but buyers like to see these things working on the ground, and of course we can't gather our own data until we have a system installed.'

He wandered off, looking thoughtful. They were evidently done with me, so I returned to my desk. A few clicks and I had my face up on the screen, labelled not as Felicity Cotton, but as 0000003. The thing had reduced me to a number, which was no big surprise, and also seemed to be capable of storing ten million faces. It had even captured me in 3D, allowing me to examine my head from different angles, including from above and behind, which was bizarre. I could also play back the video, making my machine beep and display my code number every time it recognised me.

I had to admit there was a certain fascination to it, and it also gave me that uneasy feeling which had been creeping up on me in the last few years, that the sort of illegal things I liked to do were in fact wrong and that I should stop, or in my darker moments, that I should be punished. Not that I was going to be confessing to anything in a hurry, but I did seem to be developing an adult conscience, which was all very depressing.

Stephen's voice cut through my reverie.

'The council advisory team is coming on Wednesday. We need to have something to show them, and that means getting the video done today. As I was saying, we want it to look visually appealing, but I think you should look slightly suspicious too, otherwise we risk creating the impression of intrusion rather than valid surveillance. Perhaps if you put on some old jeans and a pair of trainers, and would you mind wearing one of those awful hooded tops?'

'Not at all, no.'

'Good girl. We'll pick one up in the High Street.'

He had obviously decided I couldn't possibly own a hoodie, and the way he said 'good girl' seemed almost as condescending as having my bottom patted, but again he was oblivious to his own behaviour. Stephen's car was outside, a flashy silver Saab. He held the door for me, but somehow even that came across as a gesture of control rather than courtesy. Paul took their van, along with the equipment, and they already seemed to know where they were going, driving off separately.

Being alone with him in the car was worse than before, as without Paul around I kept wanting to say something about what had happened between us. If he was aware of my discomfort or felt any himself it didn't show, his manner as bland and affable as ever as he turned on the sound system.

'I imagine you like music?'

'Yes. Shall I choose a CD?'

'No need. I can choose from six, already preloaded. Shall we have a little Albrechtsberger?'

It sounded like some weird Goth band, which gave me hope, but turned out to be church organ music. As with the sherry Stephen simply assumed that his taste was definitive, and I kept my thoughts to myself as we drove into town. He gave me a tenner to pick up a black hoodie at one of the market stalls and we drove on to my house, where he waited while I changed into jeans and trainers. I wasn't sure if they'd want me to change back later, and didn't want to have to ask to go back via the house, so I carefully folded my work clothes into a bag and took it with me.

Stephen made no comment, and took the Lynn Road, still humming along to Albrechtsberger as he drove. I couldn't help but notice that he was well over the speed limit, and slowed for the camera at Weeting just like everybody else. Whatever his attitude to lawbreakers it clearly didn't extend to driving too fast, or perhaps he simply felt that such things didn't apply to him, which wouldn't have surprised me in the least.

He came to a stop at the mouth of one of the logging tracks, where the van was already parked. It was a place I knew well, not the best spot for parking up because there were often peeping Toms in among the bushes, but I had happy memories of coming under Dave Shaw's fingers as he whispered filthy things into my ear. There was also a smear of rust and char on the ground at one side, evidence of a yet more discreditable episode in which I'd been involved. Paul was already out of the van, looking down the path that led into the woods.

'This should be ideal. We'll go a little way in to avoid

traffic noise and I'll fix the camera at about five metres.'

The path was certainly pretty. No timber had been taken out of that part of the wood for years so the sides of the track had grown in, leaving just a single grassy path running between banks of ferns and long grass, then well-grown bushes with big oaks rising beyond them. We walked in, the foliage quickly closing until I needed to push the taller ferns aside to stop them tickling my face.

We stopped where the oaks gave way to a pine plantation, now mature, so that thick trees rose in ranks with open space below them, while the path was considerably more open. One of the younger oaks looked ideal, and Paul had quickly pulled himself up into the branches. Stephen passed him the camera and set up the power source while it was fixed in place. Just as they'd predicted, it was hardly noticeable from ground level unless you knew it was there. Stephen thought the same.

'We could leave it for a while, Paul. A field test would be useful.'

'Who's going to come past?'

'A few people use the track, dog walkers I suppose.'

'I'd rather stay close in case anyone notices it and decides they'd like a camera.'

'Fair enough. Once we've done the take of Felicity we'll wait nearby for a while. OK, Felicity, we need you to start out of range so the camera can track you.'

I walked further down the track. Here was my chance to test the camera and see just how little of my face it needed to see to recognise me. Just walking away from Stephen restored something of my determination, and when Paul called out for me to stop I pulled the hood around my face and slouched forward, deliberately looking at the ground. Ahead of me, Stephen was crouched at the base of the oak tree, peering at the laptop they'd rigged up to the camera, and he didn't speak until I'd almost passed him.

'I don't think you have to look quite that suspicious, Felicity.'

'Sorry.'

I'd looked around as he spoke, dislodging my hood, and at that instant the laptop pinged. It had recognised me, with maybe half my face showing and from above and behind, which was far too good for my liking. Not for theirs, as Stephen confirmed.

'Positive ID. Excellent. Right, if you could just run through that again, Felicity, and don't overplay it.'

I went back, this time with my hoodie open. The laptop signalled its triumphant ping when I was only halfway there. It was far too good and almost hoodie-proof. Both of them were well impressed, Paul speaking down from the tree as I went out of camera shot.

'Excellent, and that last take is easily good enough to use. That should impress them.'

Stephen agreed, at least in part.

'Yes, but we need a bullet point, something to really catch their attention. Felicity, you brought your office clothes with you, I believe? Would you mind changing into them and perhaps putting your hair up, to make you look as different as possible? That way we can demonstrate how the system uses facial indexing and can ignore minor changes.'

'OK, but how does that work?'

'A lot of systems simply take an image and compare it with others to get a match, in which case a new haircut or even putting on glasses will fool them. With the ZX it establishes a series of readings based on the bone structure of your head, which as you can imagine is far harder to fool.'

I gave what I hoped was an understanding nod. We were finished, done and dusted, or to use Steve's favourite phrase, buttered and buggered. Nor was I particularly happy about changing my clothes. It was a simple enough thing; I've always rather liked showing off, and they'd didn't have to see anything anyway, but somehow it seemed to be one more act of sub-mission. I'd be undressing close to Stephen English. To all intents and purposes he'd ordered me to take my clothes off. The fact that it wasn't for sex didn't matter – it was going to turn me on.

To make matters worse, I couldn't even flirt, not that I was going to do anything obvious, not after last time, because Paul was there and I very definitely didn't want him getting the wrong end of the stick. I caught myself biting my lip as I retrieved my bag from the car, and spent ages choosing a quiet place in among the ferns to undress. Even then I was so carried away with the idea of Stephen ordering me to strip that I had my knickers half down before I remembered that it was completely unnecessary.

It was just as well that I'd gone well in among the trees, because somebody passed with a dog while I was changing and would definitely have got an eyeful if I hadn't been careful. Just hearing them pass made me blush and hurry to pull my skirt up, and immediately wonder what was happening to me, Fizz, who'd play topless in the band and flash my knickers in the street for the hell of it.

They were waiting, Stephen with his full attention on Paul's explanation of how the camera tracked movement, as if making me strip to my undies in the middle of a wood was of no consequence whatsoever. I knew it shouldn't have been either, but I couldn't get it out of my head. I found myself smiling and hoping he'd say something as I waited for them to finish talking. He did, sort of.

'Felicity, splendid, you look human again. Now if you could just walk through as you did before.'

I went through the same simple routine and, as before, the laptop pinged long before I'd reached the oak tree. Stephen gave me a thumbs-up as if I'd done something clever and I continued until I was sure I was no longer in shot. Paul was the first to speak.

'Perfect. You're a natural, Felicity.'

'That was hardly difficult.'

'You'd be surprised. A lot of people can't help but keep looking at the camera, or just appear self-conscious.'

'Are we done then?'

Stephen had closed the laptop and glanced at his watch as he spoke.

'Just about. We should wait for a few more people to pass to see how the camera reacts, and then I don't know about you two, but I could do with a bite of lunch.'

He was so utterly indifferent to other people's privacy that I just had to say something.

'Might people not object?'

'I don't see why. Besides, they're unlikely to notice.'

His arrogance really was breathtaking, but he was right about nobody noticing. In the time we spent waiting three people passed, two just minding their own business and the third walking her dog. Stephen decided that was enough for the time being, and we left, first for lunch at the Green Man and then back to the office. They were very confident about making money, casually putting an expensive lunch on the company accounts, including a bottle of strong red wine which left them in an easygoing mood for the afternoon.

I didn't seem to have anything to do, so I played with the computer, first pretending to study the system and then looking at the images they'd downloaded from the laptop. As with my own and theirs, each had a number, first a jogger, the man who'd passed while I was dressing, then a shifty-looking man who might just have been going for a walk, or not. Enough gay guys cruise the area to make me wonder, but there was only a slight nervousness in his manner to suggest his intentions were anything other than completely inno-cent. Next came the jogger going the other way, and last an elderly and prim lady with her dog. I couldn't help but smile at the way the camera had reacted, recording not only her face, but that of the dog, which was a big old mastiff with huge jowls and a bad case of doggy drool.

Stephen and Paul were impressed with the results, and immediately decided to install a more carefully hidden camera and get some more. I was left to mind the shop, first trying to be good by sitting attentively behind my desk, then playing minesweeper on the computer. I almost gave into my curiosity to explore, but it occurred to me that a pair of control freaks like Stephen and Paul probably had the entire warehouse wired, and I had no intention of providing video evi-dence of me going through their things, or even scratching my bum for that matter.

Instead I began to play with the database, first

looking at my own head and Stephen's from different angles, then exchanging his for the slobbery mastiff, only to quickly set things straight for fear I would leave some sort of electronic trace. It was a terrible feeling, not being sure if I was being watched or tracked in some way, and I knew it would be worse once their system was set up in the town. There would be no escape, nowhere I could be sure I wasn't observed except the deepest woods, and then only because I was likely to know where the cameras were.

The thought made me feel tense, adding to my unease at the reactions Stephen English provoked in me. I've always hated men like that, who think the whole world should dance to their tune, and it wasn't just his general attitude either. He was a condescending bastard to me personally, so why did I have such a strong urge to go down on my knees to him, naked, and pay court to his cock and balls until he'd satisfied himself in my mouth.

When they got back they were well pleased with themselves. They'd put up six cameras in various locations in the Breckland, and I at least had a chance to see the map they'd made before I left. Two lay-bys were covered, along with four sections of logging track, all quiet, likely places for the sort of mischief I love. I'd decided to fight my emotions and tried to be cold and formal, but as before Stephen appeared completely oblivious, behaving towards me exactly as he had earlier.

My head was full of contradictions as I walked back home. It was a beautiful evening, tempting me to go out, but I couldn't help but think of those cameras, and that I had to be up for work in the morning. It was as if something had taken up residence in my head, like a prissy guardian angel chiding me for my behaviour and providing instructions on how to correct myself. After tea I began to feel tired as well, and it would have been all too easy to slump in front of TV and give up, only for a white knight appearing in the extremely unlikely form of Dave Shaw, who rang for me, greeting Mum in his usual suave manner.

'Fizz in?'

'One moment, I'll call her. Felicity, it's your friend David.'

My angel was telling me I had work in the morning and that Dave was a bad influence, and that he was a spotty little oik unworthy to tie the laces of Stephen English's immaculate black brogues, but I went to the door. He was as lanky, red-haired and scruffy as ever, the complete scally, and behind him, parked right across our driveway, was an ancient, rusting Rover 800. Mum had gone in.

'Where did you nick that? Why did you nick that?'

He sounded genuinely hurt as he answered.

'It ain't nicked. It's mine. I got it down Reardon's Scrapyard. It's a 2.7. You coming?'

It was a death trap, but I was coming. I had to get out.

'Sure.'

He was grinning all over his face as we ran out to the car. I knew what he wanted, and I knew that he knew I'd turn him down too, but we'd enjoy the drive anyway. Sure enough, he headed out on the Lynn Road, exactly the same route Stephen English had taken that morning, and with more stopping places per mile than any other I know. Like Stephen he drove fast, only instead of the muted purr and effortless power of the Saab there was a gravelly, complaining rumble to the

Rover's big but ancient engine. Only when we'd passed the Weeting did he pay any attention to the way I looked, and then he tried to make it a compliment.

'I like your new hair.'

'Same hair, different colour and style.'

'Yeah ... right, you know what I mean. You look right smart too. Been to a funeral or something?'

'Thanks a lot, Dave. No, I've got a job.'

I told him, using the same explanation as I had before. He accepted it, desperate to please as ever, but I could see he was surprised. I changed the topic of conversation.

'Why not take this heap of junk off-road?'

'This is my car, Fizz, I ain't wrecking it.'

'How much did you pay for it?'

'Twenty-five quid.'

'Right, and how long do you reckon you'll keep it with no tax, no insurance, no MOT and a suspended licence? We might as well have some fun with it before the police get you.'

He made to reply but didn't, putting his foot down instead as if that would answer my question. There was a sulky look on his face, one I knew only too well, and I was about to say something to try to put off the inevitable when he spoke up.

'Tell you what. I'll go off-road, and you can drive if you blow me?'

'You're a dirty little boy, Dave, you know that?'

'A hand job then?'

'Dave, shut up.'

'Aw, come on, Fizz. I need you so bad.'

He was whining, and there can't be many bigger turn-offs than a whining man, especially when he was such a weedy specimen next to Stephen English. Stephen wouldn't have whined ... no, he'd never have asked. It was so frustrating, and so typical, to have one man wanting me and wanting another myself, especially when Stephen was so wrong for me. Dave chirped up again.

'How about giving us a titty show then, like you do when you play?'

'That's part of the act, you pervert.'

'Yeah, but you look so fucking good. You give me blue balls, Fizz, you do.'

'Turquoise? Ultramarine?'

'What?'

'Never mind. Look, can't we just go for a drive?'

'Yeah, but ...'

'Just drive, OK, and maybe I'll think about it.'

'Yeah!'

I'd only said it to shut him up, but as he slammed his foot down on the long straight into Methwold I realised that there was more to it than that. Stephen English had made me feel small, and if I showed off for Dave it would make me feel powerful again, to have him grovelling and begging for the least little favour while he pulled on his cock in desperate need. It would also be an act of rebellion against the creeping need to behave myself I'd been suffering from all day.

'Turn right. You said you'd go off-road.'

'You got it.'

He swung back into the forest, fast at first, then slowly, glancing to the side each time we passed the end of a logging track, and turned sharply the moment he found one where the gate was open. They'd been working there, maybe earlier in the day, leaving the ground scarred with lorry tracks and showing bare flints, which he sent up in a spray as he brought the Rover to a skidding halt. He spoke immediately.

'Don't fuck it up, yeah? And remember, I get to see your titties.'

'Here's a hint, Dave, for free. When you want sex, it's best to play it by ear instead of negotiating every detail in advance.'

'Oh ... right ... but I get my titty show, yeah?'

'You get what I choose to give, if anything. Now get out.'

He was looking seriously sulky, no doubt thinking I was going to trick him, but he got out. I don't actually mind guys who ask for stuff if I'm in the mood, but this was different, because I didn't want to admit what I might do. He shifted into the passenger seat as I walked around the car, and I spent a moment going over the controls. There was a lot of power, raw, loose power, poorly controlled and just great to play with.

I hurled the car down the logging track, throwing up a shower of flints and a great cloud of yellowish dust. The track was arrow straight, but a fully loaded trailer had been left half in the woods, making me swerve. One wheel hit a patch of mud, sending up a spray of water and losing grip just long enough to give me a hit. My hands were tingling with the familiar pins and needles as I swung the car around where a turning circle had been made for the lorries, now riding a high as I had so many times before.

Dave was clinging to the seat in fear and excitement, adding to my thrill, especially when he gave a yelp of alarm as I threw the car into what was supposed to be a spectacular skid turn but ended in a bang as one of the rear tyres blew. There was an ear-splitting screech, a juddering shock as the wheel rim jammed into the ground, and we stopped. I was shivering in reaction and laughing too, but Dave didn't seem to be amused.

'Shit, Fizz, you've blown a tyre!'

I'd done rather more than that, tearing the off rear tyre to shreds on a patch of jagged flints. We examined the damage together, Dave quickly giving his considered opinion.

'It's fucked.'

'Bollocks. You've got a spare, haven't you?'

'No.'

I shrugged. He looked shifty.

'How about my titty show then?'

'I didn't get much of a drive.'

'You blew the fucking tyre! Now I've got to go to Reardon's and get another, and get it out here.'

For once there was a hard edge to his voice, and suddenly I wanted to do it. I'd been driving for maybe five minutes, but it had left me tingling with adrenalin, while it was a lot easier to give in to what was only a fair demand rather than his wheedling.

'OK, come on then.'

All the aggression went straight out of him at my words, and he followed like a puppy at my heels as I walked in among the pines. The loggers had cut a big swathe of clear ground, but where they'd stopped work two felled trees still had their top foliage on, creating a near perfect shelter for my rude little show. I didn't waste time, pausing only until Dave had sat down on the trunk of one of the fallen trees before opening my blouse and pulling up my bra.

'Here you are, you little pervert.'

He was staring, his mouth a little open, his eyes riveted on my bare breasts. I put one hand on my hip and stuck my chest out a little, looking down on him with a great feeling of power as I spoke.

'Is this what you wanted?'

He gave a weak nod. I couldn't help but smile, but tried to make it look contemptuous, and put as much scorn as I could manage into my voice as I spoke again.

'Go on then. You can toss off in your hand.'

'Thanks, Fizz. You are lovely . . . I do love your titties . . . I . . .'

'Shh. Come on, do it then.'

Again he nodded, and his hands were trembling badly as they went to his fly. I was loving his helpless excitement, but I did want to see his cock too and watch him come because he couldn't control his excitement over my body. He took it out, long and pale in his hand, already close to full erection, and his eyes had gone back to my chest as he began to masturbate.

I smiled down at him, now thoroughly enjoying myself and tempted to tease him even more. Cocking one leg up on a branch, I took my breasts in my hands, lifting them and running my fingers over my nipples to make them pop out. He gave a whimper and said something about puppy-dog's noses, his hand now hammering up and down on his fully erect cock and his face set in an expression of worship. I leant forward, cupping my breasts and squeezing them together to show him what cleavage I had, and as I did so I stuck out my tongue and waggled it at him.

That was too much for him. He gave a single muted grunt and he'd come in his hand, thick white semen running down over his fingers as he finished himself off with a final crescendo of hard tugs. I couldn't help but laugh, just at the expression on his face and at how much he'd been prepared to sacrifice – both his car, wreck that it was, and his dignity – for the sake of seeing my breasts. Only his shamefaced look as he put his cock away changed my mind, making me feel sorry for him.

'I don't mean to take the piss, Dave. I did enjoy that.'

'Yeah? Like you act it.'

'No, really. It was fun. I . . . I like to see your cock.'

'What, for real?'

'Yes. I promise. You've even turned me on a bit.'

It was true, sort of, if only because it was quite a naughty situation, and I do like to show off, but what he asked for took me completely aback.

'Why not do it in front of me then?'

'Do what?'

'You know, touch yourself off. You did it for Pete, and stuff.'

What is it with men? They think because you get off with one of them it means you're up for everything and with everybody. They can't keep their mouths shut either. I knew what he meant by stuff too, which sent a little shiver between my thighs as I answered.

'Pete is Pete, you're you.'

'Yeah, but . . .'

'Oh, allright. You're such a fucking pervert, Dave.'

I just wanted to put him in his place, because I was already tugging my skirt up. It felt good, to be bare and dishevelled outdoors, the sun warm on my naked breasts, and on my thighs and bottom as I pushed my knickers down. Now I was enjoying showing off, fully, and the look of worship in his eyes as I let my thighs come wide to show him exactly what I was doing.

His mouth had come open like a goldfish as I began to masturbate, with my pleasure rising quickly, the thrill of being naughty outdoors mixing with the thrill of my power over him and the sheer physical joy of playing with myself. I knew I could make him lick me if I wanted. I knew I could make him do anything if I wanted.

Only it wasn't what I wanted. As I stood there, bold and in control, showing myself off because a man had begged for me, so as my orgasm began to rise up new thoughts pushed unbidden into my head, thoughts I'd had earlier, of me grovelling on my knees, stark naked as I licked and sucked on Stephen English's cock and balls, begging to be permitted to let him satisfy himself in my mouth.

I tried to fight it, thinking of how Dave had begged just to see me bare, but it wouldn't work. It was Stephen I wanted, and I knew he'd never beg. He'd have me bare though, naked on my knees while he was fully dressed in his smart suit, only with his cock and balls rising proud and virile from his fly, for the pleasure of my mouth, for me to worship him, to lick and suck and kiss until he gave me everything he had full in my open mouth.

As I came I cried out in ecstasy, making a thorough, uninhibited exhibition of myself, but I didn't care. In my mind I wasn't even there, and Dave mattered not at all. In my mind I was on the floor of Stephen's office, kneeling in the nude as I sucked on his cock and rubbed myself to ecstasy for the privilege.

4

I really did not want to go into work on the Tuesday morning, and it had nothing to do with walking back across the Breckland and not getting home until well after dark. It did have a little to do with my dislike for my job, but mostly it was because of Stephen English. Not that he was to blame, as such, but that only made it worse.

As it happened, it wasn't as bad as I'd expected. With the men from the council coming the next day all three of us were too busy for me to brood, and the worst of it was having to call him Mr English, because every time I said it I got a little jolt and the memory of how I'd come the day before. He was as oblivious and as condescending as ever, but I was at least distracted.

Wednesday was the meeting, which had me nervous as I walked in, and also seriously conflicted. On the one hand I did feel a sort of loyalty to Black Knight Securities and I had put a lot of work into the presentation, but on the other it was firmly against my interests for us to be awarded the contract we were after. Nevertheless, I was there on time, smart and attentive in my skirt suit with my hair pinned up and a fixed smile on my discreetly painted lips.

The arrival of the council advisory team wiped the smile right off my face. There were three of them: a middle-aged woman in tweeds whose face registered disapproval of everything, a large man with a red complexion and watery eyes and the Voice of Authority from the Dog and Duck. I just froze, standing there like an idiot with my presentation folders held out, waiting for him to denounce me. He came close, looked straight into my eyes, and spoke.

'Thank you.'

It took me an instant to realise that he had absolutely no recollection of me whatsoever, and then I'd gone into automatic, handing him a folder and reeling off the little speech I'd prepared like a machine.

'Good morning, and may I welcome you to Black Knight Securities. My name is Felicity Cotton. Please may I introduce my colleagues, Mr Stephen English and Mr Paul Minter.'

Both Stephen and Paul had appeared through the door on cue, beaming and extending their hands. The big florid man responded much in kind, introducing himself as Mr Burrows, while the woman, Mrs Shelby, accepted Paul's hand with what seemed every evidence of distaste. The Voice of Authority was the last to introduce himself, as Mr Phelps, and he too remained very formal. I was still terrified he'd recognise me, and I was sure I could feel his eyes on my back as I left the room, Stephen having told me to make coffee.

By the time I came back they were seated and Stephen was in full flow, expounding on the virtues of the ZX system. Mr Burrows seemed blandly welcoming, Mrs Shelby sceptical, Mr Phelps interested. I handed out the coffees and took a seat at the back, listening to Stephen's now familiar presentation of how the system worked and how he was going to catch every scally in a ten-mile radius. When he finally finished it was Mr Phelps who put the first question.

'Let us take a hypothetical example, Mr English. I myself have been a victim of street crime recently. My car was stolen and later found burnt out. There seems to be little or no possibility of catching the culprits, despite our system of street cameras. Could you improve on that?'

Stephen's voice carried a wealth of assurance as he answered.

'Certainly. Number plate recognition is an option with the ZX system, so you would need only to identify your car on a single camera image to call up all those on which it had been recorded. As you have seen, our proposal includes plans to install cameras in a wide range of black spots. Therefore we would be able to trace the progress of the car. As long as you were able to report the theft quickly enough, the information would be relayed to the police, preventing any criminal damage and allowing the perpetrator to be apprehended. Failing that, the system would have stored a record of the theft, the car's progress and almost certainly the features of the perpetrator, who could either be identified from our existing database, or caught by automatic back reference if added to the database at a later date.'

Mrs Shelby posed a question.

'How reliable is this?'

Again Stephen was completely confident as he answered.

'Both the manufacturer's figures and our own tests indicate an exceptional degree of reliability. Indeed, so far we have enjoyed a one-hundred-per-cent success rate. Felicity, if you would be kind enough to play the video.'

There was nothing I could do but comply and pray

that if Mr Phelps hadn't recognised me in my work clothes then he wouldn't recognise me in my jeans and hoodie. At least my hair was different, which made me deeply grateful to Mum as the DVD began to play. I appeared, the image crystal clear as I made my way down the path, looking highly suspicious and immediately triggering the camera. Then came the captured image, showing my head in detail on the screen, rotating slowly and with my name now in place of the code number. Mr Phelps said nothing, nor as I appeared again, now in my office clothes, and once more triggering the camera to identify me correctly on the spot. As the video finished Stephen was looking immensely proud of himself.

'There we are, Mr Phelps. As I have explained, the facial recognition program works on the individual's bone structure and requires only a small area of the face for accurate recognition. Yes, I think we can safely say that had Felicity been the one who stole your car, you would now have the satisfaction of a prosecution pending.'

He finished with a dry chuckle, amused by his own wit in suggesting that I might have been the thief. Mr Phelps was looking right at me, but still with no hint of recognition and as he spoke again I began to let myself relax.

'Very impressive, Mr English, if all you say is true. However, the price is considerable and we will need to study the matter at length. Meanwhile, would it be feasible to install a pilot scheme with which you can make good your claims?'

'Absolutely.'

It was as much as we'd expected, and more importantly I seemed to have got away with it, leaving triumph and relief as my main reactions, so much so that I had to actively remind myself that I was supposed to be against the scheme. There were more questions, but even Mrs Shelby seemed moderately impressed, and by the time they left Stephen was rubbing his hands in satisfaction and talking earnestly with Paul about the details of the pilot scheme.

'What we need are concrete results, something to show them we'll really make a difference. If we are to test the entire system they'll need to allow us significant freedom of operation, and hopefully they'll allow us to choose our own testing ground, but the question is: where? Felicity, you know the area, where do you think we should set up the pilot?'

I hesitated, desperately trying to decide what to say and asking a question as inspiration struck me.

'It depends who you want to catch. I suppose the more serious the crime the better, and you'll want to keep public support?'

Stephen frowned.

'Public support only really matters in so far as the council represent the public, which frankly isn't much. But yes, that might ward off any protests from idiot liberals. As to serious crimes, we have to bear in mind the probabilities involved. Murderers are few and far between.'

He made it sound like it was a pity.

'Maybe not murderers, but how about dirty old men? Nobody has any sympathy for them, and I bet you'd get some if you put the cameras along the river behind the path.'

It was true, and I was earnestly hoping that Mr Phelps might prove to be one of them.

* * *

I'm all for catching dirty old men, the nasty sort, along with murderers, rapists and any other dangerous psychos who happen to be about, but the pilot scheme had to fail, otherwise life would soon be unbearable, and not just for me. I know I'm a bad girl, and maybe I do deserve to be caught and punished, at least for some of the things I've done, but most of the time I haven't hurt anybody. OK, so maybe I did deserve it for my joyriding activity, or maybe not, but where does it stop? If the full ZX system was installed soon people would be getting photos of themselves dropping a bubblegum wrapping through the post, accompanied by a £50 fine. I don't claim to know the answers, but I don't want that.

The trouble was: what to do? Maybe I could somehow sabotage the system so that it failed, but if so I was going to have to be very clever about it. Anything technical and I was sure to be spotted, but it was hard to see what else was possible. Also, just thinking about it made me feel guilty and I couldn't bear the thought of Stephen English catching me.

So I brooded over it, moving between hare-brained but satisfying schemes to a state of deep guilt, all the rest of the day and that evening. The next day both Stephen and Paul were extremely busy preparing equipment and software so that they could move fast and show how efficient they were when they got the go-ahead from the council. Stephen had also been out early to retrieve the cameras they'd set up in the woods and came to me with the discs shortly after I'd made the second coffee of the morning.

'Felicity, these are the discs from our test. Could you look through them and flag up anything that might be of interest?'

'Sure . . . I mean, certainly, Mr English.'

He grinned.

'I rather like the sound of that.'

I felt my tummy flutter and an immediate flush of irritation at my own reaction. He put the discs on my desk and went back into the warehouse, whistling a classical air which I'd learnt meant he was both busy and happy. I put the first DVD in, one from a static ZX-2, and began to search for action. The camera had been positioned about three metres up a tree, and showed a section of logging track much like any other, only rather more overgrown. There were dense stands of young pine to either side and ferns and brambles in the middle with just a narrow path between. The first living thing I saw was a large fly, and for a moment I expected a huge and hideous head to appear in the window displaying the recorded data. It didn't, fortunately, but after a moment a deer strolled into view. That was labelled as 0000014 and clearly a candidate for a fine or some community service as it relieved itself at the side of the path.

For a while I watched the deer browse, only for it to suddenly take fright and bound off among the pines. Again I was left looking at the empty path, and about to move the disc forward when a man appeared. He was in his twenties, fairly tall, with a receding hairline and dressed in sports casuals. I also recognised him, but it took me a moment to place him as the younger of the two men who ran the bookshop where Mum had worked briefly the summer before. He was duly recorded as 0000015 and moved on, once more leaving the path empty.

Nothing more happened and I ran the disc on, only to stop at a flicker of movement. Twenty minutes of disc time had passed and 0000015 was back, only this time with a companion, who was promptly added to the data base. 0000016 was another man, older but in good condition and dressed in tight running shorts and a vest top. They were talking earnestly together and it wasn't about jogging.

I watched in fascination as the younger man gave a nervous smile and sank slowly to his knees, his face at the height of the older one's crotch. The older man had set his legs apart and now put his hands on his hips as he looked down, a pose suggesting dominance and not a little contempt as he watched his thick, white cock being extracted from his shorts. I was about to witness a gay blow job.

I felt a regular little peeping Thomasina as I watched, but I was not going to stop. It was too good, too rude, watching one man's cock grow slowly to erection in another's mouth, also the way the young man handled his lover's balls, stroking beneath them and occasionally sticking out a finger to stimulate the anus. He was so dirty about it, so uninhibited, licking and sucking as if in worship of what was soon a towering white erection, just as I'd imagined myself doing with Stephen, or worse. The older man took it as I'd imagined Stephen doing too, calm and poised, cool and amused as he watched his cock being sucked.

Gazing at it was making me shake and wishing I'd been there, peeping guiltily from among the ferns as I played with myself over what they were doing. Better still, they might have caught me and made me join in, helping the young man as he kissed and licked and nibbled and sucked at his lover's wonderfully virile manhood. I knew it was ridiculous, that they wouldn't want a woman anywhere near them, but that didn't stop me fantasising, and if I hadn't been in full view of the big glass window my hand would have been down my knickers before they'd finished.

It was quite some finish too. The young man had got his cock out around the side of his shorts, tugging rapidly at the shaft until he was erect, then slowing down. All the while the older man was completely cool about it, holding his pose until the last moment, when he suddenly took hold of the younger man's head and thrust his cock deep. I saw the young man struggle to swallow and some of the come escape from his mouth, sending a jolt of mingled excitement and disgust through me, and with that he'd come too, bringing himself off in his hand even as he got his mouth filled.

That was it, but I was still staring at the screen long after both of them had left, at once revolted and utterly enthralled. They'd been so open about it, and so casual, each taking pleasure in the other to his own taste and then simply walking away. I couldn't imagine doing that, and thought of the negotiation and mind games between myself and Pete, or Dave, even Stephen. I'd always thought of myself as bold, but I just wasn't in their league.

It left me feeling seriously flustered as well, with my head full of images of erect cocks and my fingers trembling as I changed the DVD. None of the others were nearly as interesting, with just a few dog walkers and runners, along with one or two people with no obvious purpose but presumably just enjoying a walk. In all we had recorded seventeen new faces, including the deer, an assortment of dogs and a large ginger tomcat. I was still watching the last one when Stephen came back.

'Anything to report?'

I found myself blushing as I answered.

'Er ... yes. The system seems to work very well, although it records animals as well as human beings.'

'Yes, that's a glitch that didn't show up in the manufacturer's tests, either that or they neglected to mention it. How many did we get?'

'Seventeen new ones, ten men and women, five dogs, a deer and a cat.'

'Did we get any recognitions?'

'Yes, the cat came back, one of the walkers and her dog, and, er ... two of the men. It works very well.'

'Good. No criminal activity then?'

'Um ... not really, although the two guys ...'

He was looking puzzled and I could feel my face going gradually redder, my voice coming out as a whisper as I finished.

'... they were cruising.'

His eyebrows rose.

'Having sex in public? Rather a grey area in my view, but definitely illegal. Which one is it?'

'This one. Are you going to do anything about it?'

'No, not for that. We only supply the equipment. It's up to the council and the police to decide how best to make use of it, although obviously if we happened to capture a murder or something ...'

He trailed off, manipulating the controls so that the picture on the screen jumped from the path, to the path with the deer browsing and several times more before he stopped, leaving the screen filled with the image of the two men, the older standing above the younger, connected cock to mouth. Stephen laughed.

'Tut, tut, what naughty boys. Oh well, I dare say they'll learn to be more careful once the full system's installed.'

'Only when some of them have been caught.'

'That's a risk they take. In fact, I expect the risk is part of the thrill, and besides, it's pretty antisocial. Wouldn't you be scared if you came across two men doing that?'

'Not really, no. They're gay, so they're no threat to me, are they?'

'That's a very forthright attitude for a young woman, but I suppose you're right. We're going to take your advice, by the way, if the council give us the go-ahead we'll install a system along the river path using all five models. There's plenty of graffiti along there, especially under the bridges, so we should get something there . . .'

I thought of Dave's little brother, a nice kid but with a habit of expressing himself with a spray can. He'd grow out of it like everybody else, and giving him a criminal record wouldn't do anybody any good at all.

'. . . and maybe the odd flasher, if we're lucky.'

I thought of the horrible greasy man who'd flashed me near Chale Farm. He'd run away when I'd yelled at him, but it had left a sick feeling in my stomach for days. There were pros and cons.

While Stephen had been talking, the cock-sucking scene had continued to play, and as it reached its climax he gave an amused chuckle.

'Very macho. Does that shock you?'

'Um . . . a bit. I'm not really used to watching two guys get off.'

'I imagine not, but you don't object?'

'I'm not homophobic, if that's what you mean. I think everyone should be allowed to express themselves the way they want to, so long as they're not hurting anybody.'

'A most enlightened attitude.'

He walked away, and as he went I found myself wondering if he himself was gay. It certainly explained the way he'd turned me down, and I was pretty sure he wasn't married and he didn't seem to be with anybody. He also seemed pleased that I took a tolerant attitude and in no hurry to report the two men.

I couldn't be sure, but it helped me to relax a little as I went back to work and to think more clearly about the problem of the cameras. Obviously I'd have to tell Dave, who would make sure the news got passed around his brother's friends in double-quick time.

With that thought, I had the solution.

The rest of the week passed quietly enough. I found myself settling into the routine of the office, answering calls and doing the post and making the coffee, generally behaving as dogsbody to Stephen and Paul. I still felt put upon, but telling myself that Stephen was gay made life a lot easier. It was fun to imagine him in the role of the older guy who'd been so assertive about getting his cock sucked, even if I couldn't help but imagine myself as the one on my knees.

We had the gig at the American airbase on the Saturday, which meant a major change of image. I looked far too wholesome and different clothes would only go so far. That meant food dye and a serious gel attack. It took me most of the afternoon, with endless disapproving looks from Mum, and the others getting in a state because I was hogging the bathroom. By the time I was finished my hair was a riot of tall blonde spikes, each tipped with brilliant green, which looked great. I also felt like me, really for the first time since joining Black Knight Securities.

I was already drumming out beats as I finished getting ready, all in black with an insanely short mini-skirt, a carefully ripped top, fishnets and big clumpy shoes. A wide metal belt and some black and green make-up and I was ready, and so utterly different from the prim and proper girl I'd been all week it made me want to shout in triumph.

Steve was taking us, and had already loaded my drum kit into his van by the time I got downstairs. He was leaning against the bonnet, smoking, and threw me an appreciative glance as I came out.

'That's the Fizz I know. You've not got a bra on, have you?'

'No.'

'Nice. You know you're going to have to suck me for your lift, don't you?'

He clicked his tongue on the word 'suck', sending a little shiver through me as I imagined myself going down for him at the end of the night, but I simply stuck my tongue out and climbed in. I knew he could see up my skirt but I didn't expect him to take a handful, and had to quickly slap his hand away.

'Steve, not here! Mum might see.'

'She's knows I'm just kidding about.'

'Groping my bum is hardly kidding about. Now come on.'

He laughed and walked around to the driver's door. I stuck the new Tortured Souls CD on as we set off and twisted the volume up, following the fast aggressive beat and ignoring Steve's continued efforts to tease me. He left off when we'd picked up Josie and Sam, and we were left with the music as we drove out past Hockwold.

I'd known the base since I was a toddler, but only

really as a towering wire fence beyond which uniformed men marched up and down while huge aircraft lifted off and set down again. It had always seemed like an alien world, and the feeling was reinforced as the rough heathland and woods gave way to neatly trimmed verges and great white concrete road obstacles.

We had all the necessary passes but their security guys were fanatical, checking and double-checking our identity and then making us wait for what seemed like an age with armed men standing to either side of the van. Finally we were cleared to go in, and parked the van in an open area to one side of the gates, where it was unloaded and given a second more thorough check.

For all their vigilance they were extremely friendly, joking with us, flirting and tripping over each other to help us with our kit. After Stephen's attitude that was just what I needed, and I found myself responding, cheeking them back and being deliberately bossy as they carried everything into what I at first thought was an aircraft hangar.

It wasn't, just a mess of sorts set aside for entertainment, with ranks of chairs already out and an impromptu stage at one end. We began to set up, searching out power sockets and making sure everything worked, with half a dozen Americans helping us and wolf-whistling every time one of us bent over or did anything to show a little leg. Sam's boyfriend was there, a lanky corporal who was soon in earnest conversation with Steve as they set up a makeshift bar at the far end of the room.

I was already feeling high when we began to practise, and a bit drunk. There seemed to be an infinite supply of beer and plenty of people willing to press bottles into my hands. I prefer playing drunk, if not completely plastered, because that way the beat of all the songs I know comes by instinct and I don't even have to think about what I'm doing. It gives me a better high too and just makes it all work.

Sam had made Josie promise not to play anything anti-American, but I don't think it would have mattered if we'd put three chairs together and played pattacake. They loved us, clapping and yelling for more even while we were practising, and the room was packed long before we were due to start. I was in my element, lapping up the attention and showing off as I played, and I already decided my top was coming off, not at the end the way I usually did, but early on so I'd have to play the rest of the gig topless and drive them absolutely nuts.

Just knowing I was going to do it felt good, and when Josie called for 'God Save the Queen' I really threw myself into it. Of course it's the one everybody recognises, and they lapped it up, yelling and stamping and calling for more, especially when I stood up to salute at the end. We gave them some *Fat Lip*, then *Ever Fallen in Love* as loud as we could play. That was enough for me. The entire crowd whistled and cat-called, obviously far more into us than the music, and as Josie picked out the opening bar for our own title song I stood up and stripped off my top in full view of maybe two hundred cheering Americans.

They went wild, yelling for more, and I stayed on my feet, letting all of them see. I was struggling to play properly, but I didn't care, and that's pure punk, noise and show and being rude for the sake of it. If all two hundred of them had stormed the stage and just had me then and there I'd have gone for it, and I was already determined that I'd be getting mine before the night was through.

Somebody had pushed a beer close to me from behind the stage and as the song finished I picked it up, lifting it to my lips to let the chilly liquid slide down my throat, then higher, to pour the full contents out over my face and down my chest, to run down my tummy and drip from my stiff nipples as I posed with my hands behind my head and my chest thrust out, making a deliberate show of myself. Immediately more beers had been thrust towards us and I did the same again, this time shaking my wet tits to spatter the stage with droplets. Sam was no better, her thin cotton top plastered to her chest to leave her nipples showing through. As more yells of approval went up she'd tugged up the front of her skirt and pressed the bottle she was holding to her knickers, rubbing it slowly and provocatively up and down to send the audience into a screaming frenzy.

I thought they'd stop it, because somebody, surely, had to object to our behaviour, but I didn't care. The worst they could do was throw us off the base, and except for one thing that would be a triumph. That one thing was that I wouldn't get the stiff fucking I so badly needed, and as Josie called out the next song I was praying the authorities would hold off long enough for me to get taken care of.

Billy had come up on stage, singing the words to 'Homicide' with Sam, and I knew the whole thing was going to fall to pieces anyway. Sure enough, they ended up snogging to the delight of the rest of the audience and, as another beer was pushed my way, I saw that my provider was a big young man with the blackest skin I'd ever seen and a come-on smile, which was all the encouragement I needed.

I abandoned the drums and came down into his arms, kissing him immediately. He slid a hand under my bottom, so strong he lifted me bodily down from the stage with one arm. I clung on, wriggling myself against him where I could feel the bulge of his cock through his trousers and a moment later I'd been taken in behind the drapes and turned with my back to the wall.

He was still supporting me under my bum, his smallest finger pushed in between my cheeks to tickle my anus. I managed to call him a dirty pig as he went inside, but that didn't stop him and I didn't want it to. He began to wriggle his finger about as he freed his cock, hot and hard between my open thighs as I wrapped my legs around his powerful body. My knickers were pulled aside, two firm thrusts and he was inside me, fucking me with my body pushed against the wall as I clung onto him, kissing in furious passion and wriggling myself onto his cock and his finger too.

I never even realised anything was wrong until the last moment, when I'd just managed to tell him not to come in me. He'd whipped his cock out, pushing me down so quickly I ended up sat sprawled on the floor with my legs apart even as he fed his erection into my mouth. I could taste myself, and I took his balls in my hand as I started to suck, eager for what he had to give me, and to come myself while he was still in my mouth. He was too quick, thrusting himself deep before I could even get my hand down my knickers, and I was forced to swallow as best I could as he came in my mouth.

By then I'd realised we were being watched, with several grinning faces peering around either end of the curtains. I really thought they were going to take turns with me, maybe bend me over the back of the stage and fuck me from behind while I kept the next one warm in my mouth. Unfortunately they seemed to have decided that the big black guy had taken charge of me, and he was the same, helping me tidy up and pushing yet another beer into my hand.

The gig was plainly over, and despite wanting to come I contented myself with sitting on my lover's lap, still topless and with his hand up my skirt, the centre of a ring of men. It felt particularly good to be near nude when all of them were in full uniform, and I didn't mind being fondled at all. If anything I'd have been ready for more, but before Martin, my black airman, was ready some bunch of pushy types arrived to announce that it was time to go home.

I felt frustrated but there was nothing to be done, with the lights up and no chance for more than a quick grope and an exchange of mobile numbers before we were being hustled off the base. It had been good and I was telling myself I should be content, but I hadn't come, and I wasn't. There was only one thing for it. As soon as we'd dropped Josie and Sam off I told Steve I needed him and that he could have what he liked in return. I got masturbated, brought off under his fingers as I sucked lovingly on his cock, thinking of how easily Martin had handled me and trying not to wish it had been Stephen English.

5

I know women are supposed to be romantic creatures who fall deeply in love with one man and reject all others with a haughty sniff, or at least with one man at a time, but it really is bollocks. Maybe my day will come, although I've had some pretty intense relationships as a teenager and it's never once stopped me being rude with Steve, or indulging myself when I know it's not going to get back to the boyfriend. If that makes me a bad girl or a slut or whatever, then fair enough, but men are no better and I refuse to accept that the rules are different depending on which sex you are.

I'd enjoyed Martin, and I wouldn't have missed the fucking he'd given me for the world, while not getting it quite perfect had only left me eager for more. It had also left me feeling a great deal better about myself, because his desire for me had been so strong. That didn't change my feelings for Stephen at all, except to give me renewed confidence and determination to either find out if he was gay or work it so that he got me into the sack, or up against the wall, or over his desk at the office, according to circumstance.

A good deal of Sunday was spent washing my hair out so that I'd be able to be Miss Felicity Cotton again on the Monday morning. Steve was around too, for lunch, teasing me about how eager I'd been the night before and eventually cajoling me into a blow job before he went home. It was risky, with him sitting on my bed as I knelt between his legs and the door shut but not locked, which had my heart hammering at the possibility of Mum walking in on us.

Monday morning I was back in my work clothes and thoroughly respectable, walking through town to work with all the other busy bees. Stephen was already there, and I was immediately told to make coffee, which seemed to be a bit of a power trip for him. He asked about my weekend in a perfectly casual way, but I couldn't resist a little test to see if I could get any interest out of him, one way or another.

'It was fun, thanks. I went out to the big American airbase at Hockwold.'

'Did you? I'm surprised they let anybody in.'

'We had passes. One of my friends' boyfriend is stationed there. In fact it's full of good-looking young men.'

He chuckled.

'Anyone special?'

'Sort of. I met someone, Martin. Not that it's serious.'

'An officer, I trust?'

'No.'

His eyebrows rose slightly.

'Not an officer? Tut, tut, Felicity, that will never do.'

He was joking, but it was the most bizarre reaction, neither the jealousy I might have expected if he'd been interested in me, nor the sort of response he might have given if he'd been gay, but a peculiar and unexpected snobbery. I couldn't help but be defensive.

'He's very nice.'

'I'm sure he is. Now, we have a representative from the local police coming over this morning, so you're to be on best behaviour.'

'I'll be sure to be, Mr English.'

His words had sent a little involuntary shiver through me, as had my response, which had come out before I could stop myself, leaving me feeling excited and ashamed of myself as usual. I was even half hoping he might apply his hand to my bottom as I turned from his desk, but he restrained himself.

The rest of the morning was busy, first with the policeman, who had an endless string of questions and wanted to examine the entire system in detail, then with the owner of one of the other industrial units on the estate, who was considering protection for his premises. Shortly before twelve o'clock, I answered the phone to Mr Phelps. He had called to give the go-ahead for the pilot scheme and had quickly agreed to the installation of a system along the river path subject to plans being submitted.

There was an immediate frenzy of activity, Paul dealing with what technical details remained while Stephen had me ringing around to find a company who could supply techies to help with surveillance at the council offices. By the time I'd succeeded Stephen had the full plans printed out, a detailed map of the river path showing where each camera would be placed. It was on the computer as well, and once he'd gone to show it to Mr Phelps and the others at the council offices I was left to examine it.

They were going to have the entire length of the path covered, from the edge of Grim's Fen to Sariton, about five miles in all. It was sneaky too. The larger, highest quality cameras were to be mounted in obvious places, set on poles or walls, where they could record people's faces, but the smaller, simpler ones were hidden and it was those that would catch anybody up to no good. Everybody would get recorded, even those merely passing by, but they wouldn't know it. Then, when they thought they were safe to indulge in whatever skulduggery took their fancy, they'd be caught and recognised by one of the hidden cameras. The only thing the police and council would need would be the names of the local scallies, most of which they had.

It was a huge file, much too big for a floppy, so I burnt it onto CD, all the while with my heart in my mouth and praying Stephen wouldn't return unexpectedly or Paul emerge from the back. Neither did, and I'd soon slipped the CD into my jacket pocket, feeling both guilty and triumphant. Nicking it was crucial to my plan, and the least scary part of it.

I'd barely sorted myself out when my phone went, which made me jump. It was Martin, who was off duty in the evening and wanted to see me. I agreed, accepting his suggestion of the Blue Boar, which I knew was popular with American servicemen. It was also easiest to reach by following the river path, which I wanted to do in order to get a look at it before the cameras went up.

Stephen didn't get back until very nearly five and needed me to sort out various bits of paperwork he'd picked up at the council offices, so it was half an hour after my normal knocking-off time that I found myself outside the unit, wondering if I had time to change before meeting Martin. He was going to get a shock anyway, so I decided against it and walked straight up to the river.

It was a beautiful evening, very warm and still, with the water barely moving and everything sleepy. Any painter would have loved it, and was a place I'd known since childhood, but it now seemed sinister and I continually found myself glancing from side to side, trying to work out where the cameras were likely to be installed and who they might catch. For a start there was the graffiti under Town Bridge, which always got moaned about but was more colourful than anything. They'd catch the younger boys that way, landing them with criminal records before they'd had a chance to grow up. Then there was the long stretch beside Foulds' sawmill where the elderberry bushes pushed out and made ideal places for snogging. I could clearly remember the thrill as I let Ed Gorton slip a hand down the front of my knickers and put a finger inside me for the first time in my life, and a dozen other incidents, most of them a lot steamier. All of that would be gone, leaving the world a greyer, duller place.

We'd never hurt anybody, beyond shocking the occasional old granny, perhaps, and just about everybody I knew had got up to something at one time or another, but I didn't know anyone who'd had a nasty experience. Perhaps in a city, it might have been a dangerous place, but not in Hockford. The only really nasty things I knew about had all happened behind closed doors.

It was hard to shake my mood as I walked on, despite the beautiful weather and the prospect of seeing Martin. Everywhere I looked brought back memories, and while I had to admit that I'd been a right little brat as a child and a bad girl among bad girls as a teenager, I still felt a sense of injustice. Only when I got to the Blue Boar did I brighten up at the sight of Martin sitting outside, a bottle of beer in one hand and his face painted in a big, sloppy grin.

'You look different.'

'Work clothes, I'm afraid, sorry.'

'That's OK. What are you drinking?'

'A vodka mix, lime if they've got it.'

'Coming right up.'

He disappeared into the pub, allowing me to admire the breadth of his shoulders and the easy power of his walk. I remembered how casually he'd lifted me, with just one hand curled under my bum as if I weighed nothing at all, and how dirty he'd been with me. I like men to be that way, to get a real kick out of me and not be embarrassed about it, and he'd done it beautifully, not even caring that other people were watching.

By the time he came back with the drinks I'd already decided that I wanted him again, and where. I let him talk for a while, content to listen as he described his home in Arizona, showing a touch of homesickness. He wouldn't let me buy the next round, which I accepted as a gesture of masculine pride. We ate there too, steaks topped with sauce and big fat chips before he bought me a huge chocolate dessert that left me feeling pretty full. I was more than a little drunk too, while the day was fading to a warm twilight.

I suggested we walk, taking his arm and steering him towards the river path. He didn't push, perhaps because he knew I'd be willing, and it was left to me to choose the time and the place, at the back of Foulds', the same place I'd first allowed a man to enter my body, only this time much more of a man, and much more in the way of entry.

He was wonderfully big, his cock full and meaty first in my hand and then in my mouth as I went down on him among the bushes. I was determined to get my own climax this time, but to fully enjoy him as well, and spent an age just paying court to his cock and balls with my lips and tongue and mouth, until his breathing had begun to grow deep and his fingers were tangled in my hair to hold me in place.

I'd been going to take him all the way, and play with myself while I did it, but I'd no sooner eased my work skirt up than he'd taken me under my arms, lifting me without appreciable effort and, as before, holding me under my bum while he pulled my knickers aside and slid me down onto him. I clung on, our mouths open together as he fucked me, both hands now on my bottom, holding me wide to the night with one fingertip tickling the tight little hole between my cheeks.

We were well in between two bushes, in deep gloom, but anyone who came by and peered in was going to get a full view of my open bottom with his cock moving inside me as he lifted me up and down. That alone felt wonderful, helping my excitement rise higher as I wriggled myself onto him and begged him to pump me faster and harder between passionate kisses. He obliged, and I'd been reduced to panting breathlessness a second later, only to be lifted free once more and set back down on the ground.

He just manipulated me, so strong I barely had time to react as I was spun around and bent over, now with my bottom pushed out to him. I just had time to brace myself against the wall before my knickers had been pulled down and his cock eased back inside me, now from behind with the hard muscle of his belly pushed to my cheeks as he began to fuck me. Again he was hard, setting me gasping and clutching at the rough brick of the wall, and again his massive hands were on my bottom, holding me and spreading me wide.

I really thought he would come in me, but at what must have been the last moment he pulled out, grunting a demand to suck him as I had before. Down I went, but this time I wasn't letting him get there first. My hand was already between my thighs as I squatted down, snuggling my face against his cock and balls, so hot and so virile against my skin. It was an act almost of worship, yet more for my pleasure than his, as all the while I was rubbing at myself harder and faster. He gave a soft grunt of complaint and took me by the hair, forcing me to take him deep in my mouth once more, but that gesture was enough to tip me over the edge. I was coming, my body locked tight in orgasm even as he gave me everything he had full in my open mouth with perfect timing.

It had been my last opportunity. Stephen now had full permission to install the ZX system, and the next day we began to put the cameras in place. The area where Martin and I had been was one of the first to be covered, with a big ZX-5 mounted high on the wall to scan the river bank and three of the sneaky little ZX-1 models across the water so that there was nowhere left to hide.

I spent the entire day running backwards and forwards between the river path and the warehouse, carrying gear and generally helping to seal my own fate as well as that of so many of my friends. Inevitably what we were doing was noticed, and I even had a chance to exchange a few shamefaced words with Pete, apologising for my involvement but promising I'd be doing my best to make sure the installation wasn't permanent.

By the evening we'd covered nearly half the river path, and two days later the system was complete with all the cameras in place and feeding data back to the council offices. That meant Paul had to be there to keep an eye on the equipment and train various techies in the operation of the system, and so on the Friday morning I found myself alone in the office with Stephen. He was whistling one of his classical airs, clearly well pleased with himself and for once didn't demand coffee the moment I'd come in.

'Ah, Felicity, there you are. We're up and running as of now, but I want to make a quick test if you wouldn't mind walking down to the river path with me to make sure the system recognises us.'

'Of course.'

'Splendid.'

He actually smacked his hands together in glee and was going over the details as we walked up towards the river, all of which I knew already. There were twin ZX-4s positioned on poles to either side of Town Bridge, big and obvious, their lenses moving back and forth to cover the movement of people as they came down to the path or climbed up to the roadway. Stephen chuckled.

'There we are. Now that should make the naughty boys and girls think twice, shouldn't it? There, it will have us both now, so just as well you're not one of the naughty ones, isn't it?'

He laughed and I found myself returning a nervous smile, only to have him push the point, as if he wanted an answer.

'You wouldn't be naughty, would you, Felicity?'

I hesitated, not about to admit to anything but wanting to see if he had any loyalty to me.

'I might be. OK, I'm not, but let's say I was. Let's say

the cameras caught me doing something wrong and you saw the image before the council had got to it. What would you do?'

He laughed.

'Well, unless you were actually murdering some-body, I'd delete the image and then smack your naughty bottom.'

It took a moment for what he'd said to sink in, and then the blood was rushing to my cheeks from a sense of embarrassment beyond anything I could remember, only not so much for the appallingly inappropriate suggestion but because it had given me that same involuntary thrill his domineering words always did, only far stronger. For a moment I was dumbstruck, contemplating the idea of surrendering myself to him and having my bottom smacked as if I was a baby. He meant it too, I was sure, completing my outrage as I managed to croak a reply.

'What, really?'

'Oh, I think a little spanking would do you the world of good, if you were a naughty girl, that is.'

He chuckled, a sound at once so dirty and so authoritative it left me blushing hotter than ever and thoroughly confused. What he was saying was utterly outrageous, the sort of thing only the grubbiest of dirty old men would want to do to a girl. Yet with his cool authority it came across as the most natural thing in the world, for me, younger than him and his junior in the office, to have my bottom smacked as a punishment for being naughty. No, not me, not Fizz, I would never submit to such an appalling degrada-tion, but on the other hand, Miss Felicity Cotton just might . . .

'We should certainly catch these graffiti artists,

that's for sure. Would you mind going in under the bridge and we'll see how the ZX-2 picks you up.'

My head had been full of hideously embarrassing yet highly erotic images of me across his knee with my bum stuck up for a spanking, and it took me a moment to adjust to the change in the topic of conversation.

'Um ... of course, although it would probably be dark if they were doing it.'

'That's not a problem. The ZX-2 can pick up infrared.'

'Oh, yes ... I remember you saying.'

I went in under the bridge, to where some blocky letters almost as tall as me spelt out the word 'WILD' in vivid orange and black. Wild was Dave's little brother's tag, which he'd left all over Hockford, but this was his masterpiece, the one he always repainted if anyone went over it. I faced the wall, then turned around slowly, trying to pick out the lens of the hidden ZX-2. I knew where it was, hidden in an angle of the big cast-iron beams supporting the bridge, actually over the water and almost impossible to get at. It was also almost impossible to see, let alone recognise for what it was. Stephen spoke again.

'Come back, then go in again as if you were trying to conceal your face.'

He meant as if I was wearing a hoodie and I used my jacket, taking it off and holding it around my head so that my face was deep within the black material. Again I stepped up to the big orange and black tag, peering to either side as if checking that the coast was clear, then turning to rejoin Stephen at the bottom of the steps.

'Thank you. That should give us an idea of how the integrated system functions. Let's walk a little further, then check the results.'

We moved on along the path as far as the end of Foulds', and I found myself glancing in among the bushes where Martin and I had had sex. I hadn't heard from him since, making me wonder if I was just a conquest to him and if he'd moved on, which hurt a little despite my determination to keep any relationship between us casual.

Twice more Stephen had me do things to check if the cameras would capture my image, then we headed back to the warehouse. He went immediately to the office, sitting down in front of his computer and apparently quite happy for me to join him instead of staying at my desk.

'OK, let us see what we have ...'

He trailed off, manipulating his mouse to bring up the relevant image. The picture was absolutely clear, a section of roadway and the steps leading down to the river path. Each time somebody passed a ping announced the capture of a new face, which would then come up in a separate window along with an identification number. When we appeared two windows came up immediately, correctly identifying us from the database, but as we drew close to the camera our voices grew audible and embarrassingly clear. First was Stephen's.

'You wouldn't be naughty, would you, Felicity?'

Then my reply.

'I might be. OK, I'm not, but let's say I was. Let's say the cameras caught me doing something wrong and you saw the image before the council had got to it. What would you do?'

I heard his laughter, then he spoke again.

'Well, unless you were actually murdering somebody, I'd delete the image and then smack your naughty bottom.'

Our voices faded as we moved on, leaving me staring aghast at the screen. Stephen just laughed and shook his head, speaking as he once more began to move the cursor across the screen.

'I think we had better delete that bit, don't you? It wouldn't do to have the council thinking we cheat, or that I spank you when you're naughty.'

I found myself going red again, but he seemed as oblivious as ever, quickly deleting the offending section and then moving on as I voiced a worry.

'Might not Mr Phelps or somebody already have seen that bit?'

'Very unlikely, given the sheer volume of data that's coming in. Also I doubt they've got the hang of the system yet, and Paul would certainly delete anything he thought might be difficult. In fact . . .'

He trailed off, frowning in concentration as he brought up a new window and tapped a code into a box. A list of numbers appeared, some of which had names besides them, followed by little square boxes. I watched as he ticked the first three boxes.

'This is to remain strictly between us, Felicity, and I do mean strictly. You're not even to tell your mother. Do I have your word on that?'

'Yes . . . of course.'

'The original Korean system is designed to pick out faces in large crowds, a group leaving a factory, for instance, but there is also a facility to ignore certain faces. This is hidden, as only senior operatives need know about it, in this case, me. I've now adjusted the system so that in future you, myself and Paul will be ignored.'

'Thank you.'

'My pleasure. After all, imagine how embarrassing it would be if you were, say, to get caught short on the way back from Cuatro Cortado and be caught on camera too.'

He gave his dirty chuckle and I found myself blushing again, unable to fight down my instinctive response to his intrusive comments. If it had been Steve or Pete, let alone Dave, I'd have smacked him playfully, but hard enough to make my point. With Stephen I found myself tightening my thighs and imagining myself squatting down between the bushes beside Foulds' wall to pee, with him standing watching. First he'd suggested I be spanked, and now he'd made me think of peeing in front of him. Was there nothing too intimate for him to mention?

Despite that, it was impossible not to feel grateful for having my details taken off the database. I might still be caught on camera, but presumably I'd come up as an unknown, or simply missed in the crowd. It would still be dangerous to do anything really blatant, but otherwise I was safe. I also felt Stephen had made me one of the team, extending protection of a sort when he hadn't had to at all, which added a great deal of guilt to my feelings. He'd closed the window and spoke again as he sat back in his chair, now pensive.

'Speaking of Cuatro Cortado, I er ... do hope you didn't take my actions the other night in the wrong light. It was, um ... simply that you were very drunk and I didn't want to take advantage of that, especially as you are my employee.'

I found myself swallowing as I answered, and wondering what he was getting at.

'That's OK. In fact, I appreciate it. It was nice of you.'

'Not at all, just what any gentleman would have done, but, um ... I hope you won't be offended if I admit to a great deal of regret?'

'No, not at all.'

Suddenly I was filled with hope. He wasn't gay at all, just rather shy beneath his brash, confident exterior. I waited for him to speak again, knowing it was one of those crucial moments that can lead either way. It was obvious what he wanted, but he seemed oddly hesitant, although after the way I'd propositioned him he could hardly think I was too innocent to cope with him making a move on me. The temptation to simply reach out and ease his fly down for him was considerable. Most men love a bold move and I was sure he'd let me, but with him I wanted it to be different, for him to take control. I could even guess what he wanted to do to me, and for all the feelings of embarrassment and resentment it brought it was impossible not to feel that it was exactly what I deserved. Finally he spoke again, suddenly intense.

'May I ask if your feelings were genuine?'

'I ... I never fake it, not for anyone ... that is, I hope you don't think I was coming onto you just because you're my boss or something, but ...'

It was not easy to say, not easy to give in to all those contradictory feelings, and I could feel my face growing hotter as I went on.

'... but, if you wanted, maybe, to be a bit ... a bit stern with me, that would be OK.'

I'd done it, admitted my feelings, admitted how I wanted him to handle me, and from the look on his face I had a suspicion it might cost me rather more. He had nodded, very slowly, and when he spoke again all the old confidence was back in his voice.

'I know what I'd like to do, Felicity. I'd like to spank you. Do you think that would be appropriate?'

He didn't know how appropriate, but even as he spoke I could feel my guilt draining away and my tummy starting to flutter. I managed a feeble nod, with one motion surrendering myself to what would have been an unthinkable indignity in any other circumstances, and to pain, but I simply couldn't stop myself. He smiled, perhaps understanding my emotions better than I did myself, because something told me this was not the first time for him, not by a long way. Not that he understood me completely, or the extent to which I deserved what I was about to get. He patted his lap.

'Come along then, my girl, over my knee.'

His tone had changed, sterner still and yet somehow playful. It was a game, in a sense, I knew that, a little ritual to express our emotions for each other. But that wasn't going to make my feelings any less genuine, only to make that essential change, to make the utterly unacceptable be acceptable because we both knew it was sex.

I stood up, my hands shaking badly as I folded them in my lap, wanting to make him happy by behaving the right way but unsure what to do beyond showing my submission. I hung my head, letting my hair swing down around my face, and my voice was soft and contrite as I spoke, words I could hardly accept I could say.

'Yes, Mr English, sir. I'm sorry.'

He didn't know what I was sorry for, but it seemed to work, his answer as stern as before but with every word infused with erotic relish.

'Sorry isn't good enough, I'm afraid, Felicity. What

you need is a good spanking, and I'm just the man to give it to you.'

As he spoke he had taken my arm, pulling me gently but firmly towards him. I came, unable to resist as he laid me across his knees, positioning my body so that I was forced to put my hands on the office floor to keep my balance. My whole body was trembling, with a part of me screaming to get up, to tell him what a pervert he was, to slap him or kick him even. I didn't. I lay mute and shivering across his knee as the tail of my jacket was turned up to leave my bottom pushed out into the seat of my skirt, the highest part of my body and feeling very vulnerable indeed. He took me around my waist, pulling me closer and holding me in place, then spoke once more.

'I'm going to bare your bottom. I hope you realise that is necessary?'

I didn't answer. I couldn't answer. My head was far too full of emotion, of burning shame and an overwhelming excitement, of fear of the coming pain and amazement at what I was allowing him to do to me. He seemed to understand too, or perhaps he could just feel me shivering against his leg, because as he went on there was a trace of sympathy in his voice as well as lecherous, sadistic glee.

'I know it's a very important moment for a girl, her first spanking, which is why it should be done properly, by an expert. That means a bare bottom. Now, skirt up . . .'

His words sent a powerful jolt through me, and I shut my eyes as his fingers took hold of the hem of my office skirt, lifting it slowly, up over the tops of my stay-ups and higher. I felt the turn of my bottom exposed, and more, the seat of my knickers, taut and pink over my cheeks, an image I could see so vividly it was as if I was standing behind myself rather than staring at a small area of orange carpet tile. Stephen gave a little chuckle.

'Pink, how sweet, and full-cut. I do hate thongs, don't you? Full-cut knickers are so much more feminine, and so much nicer to pull down.'

He really was an utter out-and-out pervert, but I found his words filling me not with disgust, but with desire, albeit coupled with a vast sense of resentment. His hand settled on my bottom, big enough to cover most of the seat of my knickers. I swallowed hard as he began to touch, stroking, exploring me, with a loitering intimacy that had me shaking my head in reaction. Again he spoke.

'Very pretty, and you do have a beautiful bottom, but enough messing about. Down they come.'

A sob broke from my throat at his words, so casual, as if pulling a girl's knickers down for a spanking were a perfectly ordinary, acceptable thing to do. Not for me it wasn't, my emotions rising to a near unbearable peak as he took a pinch out of the waistband of my knickers and slowly, deliberately began to pull them down. God knows, enough boys have taken my knickers down, but this was different. He wasn't just getting an inconvenient barrier out of the way, he was exposing me, baring me, to add to the pain and humiliation of my punishment.

I'd closed my eyes, unable to stop myself from concentrating on the feeling of having my knickers slowly drawn down over my cheeks and settled around my thighs. Now my bottom was bare, showing nude to a man, that man fully dressed as he held me down across his knees, as he held me to spank me. Another sob escaped my lips at the thought of how I would look, with the sure knowledge that the lips of my pussy would be showing from behind to add one more thoroughly rude detail to my exposure.

Stephen made a final adjustment to my knickers, pulling them out from between my thighs so that he could see absolutely everything, then gave a satisfied sigh as he once more laid his big hand across my bottom cheeks, now flesh on flesh. He gave me a quick wobble, chuckled to himself at the sight and his hand lifted. I braced myself for the pain, trying to tell myself I'd be brave, but sure I'd bawl my eyes out.

It never came. His hand came down, but gently, little more than a pat, delivered full across my bottom but with surely no more than the tiniest fraction of the force he had to be capable of. It still gave me an immense jolt of shame and resentment and unstoppable erotic pleasure, just to know that I was actually being given a spanking for the sake of a man's pleasure, but that was all. Again he smacked, no harder than before, and again, setting up a slow rhythm, in time to the bouncing of my bottom cheeks, but never hard.

I still took it trembling and gasping, the thought that I was being given a spanking running over and over in my head, to provoke a dozen contradictory feelings, but above all, arousal. My bottom had begun to glow, in the most extraordinary, delightful way, making me feel dirty and desperately horny all at once. There was no inhibition either, the very fact that he had me bare bottom over his knee removing any trace. If a man could do that to me, it didn't matter what I showed him, how far I'd let myself go.

As he continued to spank me I started to stick my bottom up, sighing with pleasure and giggling. I let my thighs apart, stretching my knickers out and showing off between my legs and cheeks, my pussy and the tiny star of my bottom hole too. Still he spanked, a little harder now, making my flesh sting and filling me with the most glorious glowing sensation behind, but cool and collected despite having me writhing and wriggling my bare bottom across his knee.

He wasn't all that cool though. I could feel the lump of his cock growing against my side, his excitement rising at the pleasure of spanking me just as mine was rising at the pleasure of being spanked. Already I wanted him, to suck his cock while I was punished, or to have him put me over the desk and fuck me while he continued to smack my cheeks. I tried to wriggle back, eager to play, but he merely tightened his grip and began to spank harder, calling me a naughty girl as my cheeks began to bounce under slaps.

It was hard now, but it didn't hurt, my bum too warm and my excitement too high. I was laughing as he applied himself to my bottom, and by clutching the leg of his desk I'd managed to get my hand to his fly, burrowing for his cock even as my spanking continued. He told me I was a naughty girl again, but he didn't try to stop me, just the opposite. Letting my body slide a little lower down his legs, he changed the way he was spanking me, alternately slapping my cheeks and stroking my hot flesh.

I pulled down his zip and allowed my hand in to find his cock hot and hard within. Even as I pulled him out he was still spanking me and groping me more intimately, touching between my thighs as I pulled at his cock. I was lost, completely enthralled by the warmth in my bum and the idea of being spanked by a man and then made to toss his cock off because he'd got excited over having me bare.

Not that there was any coercion in it, none at all. I was more than eager, pulling on his lovely thick erection as he spanked me and touched me up, now teasing between my sex lips and around my bottom hole. I tried to wriggle off again, eager to take him in my mouth or sit in his lap with his cock inside me. Again he held me firmly in the spanking position, telling me off for being so wanton even as he slid a hand under my belly. His thumb went inside me, his fingers pushed between my lips, and he began to masturbate me even as he told me, calmly, casually, that he was going to bring me off.

I screamed out at his words, my emotions as overpowering as the feel of his fingers on my clitoris. He'd got me bare, he'd spanked my bottom, and now he was going to bring me to orgasm under his hand as I writhed and squirmed across his lap, in helpless ecstasy and clinging desperately to his erection. I'd have done anything for him at that moment, any dirty thing he wanted, even let him try to put it up my bum, but he was just going to masturbate me, at least first.

A moment later I was there, wriggling in his grip as wave after wave of blinding ecstasy flowed over me, utterly uninhibited, with my hot, smacked bottom wide open, showing everything and glad of it, still tugging on his cock, and as a second equally exquisite peak hit me I felt hot, slippery come running down my hand.

6

I had been spanked over my boss's knee. It was impossible to get it out of my head, that awful, mind-numbing
truth that not only had I allowed a complete suit to
put me across his knee and smack my bare bottom, but
that I had thoroughly enjoyed it. In a sense it was
worse than having it done against my will, because at
least I'd have been able to tell myself I'd put up a fight.
I hadn't, far from it. I hadn't even made a fuss about it,
or pretended to be unwilling the way I do with Steve.
I'd revelled in it.

He'd taken me by surprise too, which was really
unfair. I'd expected it to be painful, and hadn't even
fully understood why I wanted to accept it, aside from
guilt. Only he hadn't done it to hurt me or even to
punish me. He'd done it to turn me on, and he had
succeeded in a way that had anybody suggested to me
how I'd react beforehand I'd have laughed at them, or
hit them.

Despite all that, I knew full well I'd be coming back
for more. After he'd finished with me, Stephen had
given me a cuddle, holding me for as long as it took to
get over my emotions. Even after that the glow in my
bum had kept me on a high for hours, full of nervous
energy like a kid who's been overdoing it on artificial
flavourings. A part of me still felt deeply humiliated,
but the physical sensation was too good to resist, like a
drug.

The other reason was the one that had helped me accept punishment in the first place: the fact that I had misbehaved to Stephen, and that if ever a girl had deserved her spanking, it was me. I'd always suffered a bit from my conscience, and more so in recent years, thoroughly enjoying being bad but with an underlying sense of guilt and a conviction that I should be punished. Beforehand I'd always managed to fight back that feeling, easily in fact, because what society deemed appropriate consequences for my behaviour went far beyond what I'd have accepted as just. Now it was different. I'd misbehaved and I'd paid with a smacked bottom, which counted for me even if the man who'd spanked me didn't know.

I was about to earn myself another spanking. Just because Stephen had taken me off the database hadn't changed my conviction about what I should do. That would have been selfish. It had made it easier, while the remainder of the test we'd done under Town Bridge showed that a tightly held hoodie was adequate protection against the facial recognition program, if not necessarily old-fashioned human observation. My face had been absolutely invisible from the ZX-2, but my office clothes had made me unmistakable.

My plan was based on the idea that councils hate to lose money. They love to spend it, but only on the things they want to, like sixty grand on the weird-looking arty thing in the middle of the roundabout by the station. Surveillance cameras definitely come in the same class, especially when they allow fines to be issued and make more money than they cost. That was what Stephen and Paul were relying on to make their profit: that however much they charged the council it would never be more than the resulting fines brought in. However, if the cost of the pilot scheme far exceeded the amount made in fines, the council would, I hoped, decide against it. I was going to vandalise the cameras.

At first I'd wanted to get as many people as I could to help, but when I'd looked at what that would actually mean I'd changed my mind. Once the likes of Dave and Pete got involved it was sure to be a disaster. There were enough problems as it was. For one thing the cameras would be recording people's faces, and anyone who was about was sure to look suspicious. That meant waiting until the early hours of the morning, and I had to be very careful not to get recognised by Stephen or Paul.

I also wanted an alibi, but I couldn't think of a way of making people think I was in two places at once. Instead I accept Stephen's suggestion that he take me to dinner at Cuatro Cortado on the Saturday night. Mum was also going there, with Archie as usual, and was delighted to hear Stephen was taking me out. I already knew that as far as she was concerned he and I were the perfect match, but it was amusing to wonder what she'd have thought if she'd known what a pervert he was.

Mum's matchmaking at least meant that Stephen and I got a table to ourselves, and he was really sweet all evening, which made me feel a complete bitch. I pretended to knock back the sherry, but managed to pour most of it into an unfortunate pot plant next to my chair. Stephen completely failed to notice, in full flow on a dozen subjects, including Spain, cathedral architecture and classical music. We left only when the bar finally closed, and he had his arm around me as we walked back.

I was acting drunk, but I was genuinely amorous,

turned on as always by his sheer presence and despite my feelings. Outside my house he took me in his arms to kiss me and I responded, not even bothering to kid myself that it was part of the act as I allowed my hand to slip down to his crotch. His response was to suggest returning to his flat instead, a problem I solved by slipping his cock out of his fly and into my mouth.

He protested, not surprisingly as we were in view of several houses, but allowed me to lead him into the back, where I indulged myself in the fantasy I'd had about him since we'd first met, down on my knees as I sucked and licked at his cock and balls. Despite being well in among the shrubs he was nervous, and hurried, pushing himself deep and using a hand to finish himself off before I'd really got into it, but I didn't mind, too tense to fully enjoy myself and pretty sure there would be a next time.

It was gone midnight when he left. The house was completely dark, with Mum doubtless getting hers from Archie, a thought that always made me wince. Everybody else was asleep, and I sneaked quietly upstairs after a jolt of Pepsi Max from a bottle in the fridge. I was still feeling a bitch to Stephen, and more nervous than ever as I changed into black trainers and black jeans, a T-shirt and a black hoodie, with my hair wound up into a bun.

I was shaking as I left the house, feeling very lonely and not a little scared, with a hundred reasons why I should abandon the scheme running through my head. I ignored them all, having been through the whole thing a thousand times, and convinced myself it was for the best. The map showing the positions of the cameras was in my pocket, along with a torch and various other bits of equipment. My route was even planned out, keeping the chances of me being seen, let alone recognised, to a minimum.

Nobody seemed to be about, although my heart was jumping at even the tiniest noises as I made my way along the footpath beside the church, and when I mistook the outline of a decaying tree for a man standing motionless by the side of the path I was very nearly sick. I had to go slowly too, because of poor light, despite a bright half moon only occasionally covered by slow-moving clouds.

To get beyond the line of cameras meant taking a wide loop and coming back across fields, but I finally reached the river path just a hundred yards from the ZX-4 mounted on a pole beside a group of river cruisers moored along the bank. Bushes gave me cover until I was directly beneath it and out of sight, but it was much too high to reach, forcing me to squeeze myself up between the pole and the wall behind it until I was close enough to aim a spray can at the lens, putting the camera out of commission and, I hoped, wrecking it completely.

I'd done it, one anyway, filling me with both triumph and guilt as I climbed down. Nobody had seen me, I was sure of that, and that the camera wouldn't have caught me either, or if it had, merely as a black figure moving among the shadows. Again I felt a strong urge to turn back, mission complete, but again I resisted. One was not enough.

With the ZX-4 out of action I could get behind a fixed ZX-2 positioned to cover a gloomy alley mouth which led from the river path down between the buildings of the Hattersley Estate. It was across the river, and I'd never have noticed it if I hadn't known it was there, but a few minutes later it had been spray-painted and pushed down so that lens was no longer even aiming straight.

Two down. As I moved towards the next one I heard voices and ducked in among the bushes. A couple passed within inches of me, completely unaware of my presence. He called her Malteser, a pet name so silly I had to put my hand across my mouth to hold back a giggle. I was gaining confidence, so much so that after levering a ZX-1 clean off the wall I had to stop and make myself slow down. There was a sort of manic energy inside, similar to the way I'd felt driving stolen cars or after my spanking, but now I knew I had to keep myself under control.

My fourth was the main one covering the long straight stretch of path opposite Neal's Boatyard, my fifth a sneaky ZX-2 designed to catch graffiti artists on the same stretch. That I managed to detach completely, an effort that drained more than just physical energy, and with that I decided to call it a night. I knew how much the things cost and I was sure my efforts would make the council think twice before buying any. Not that I was finished, not by a long chalk.

I went out again on the Sunday night, using spray paint to ruin the set of cameras covering Foulds' and a little further along. The ones by Town Bridge were too risky, but I'd now done eight in all. That had to at least attract attention, although as I walked into work on the Monday morning I was as tired as if I'd played a gig and then sat up drinking for most of the night. I was worried too, imagining that Stephen would catch me out despite all my precautions and dreading the prospect of a confrontation.

He was already there, just opening up, and the look

on his face made me go cold, a sensation only partly relieved as he spoke.

'Good morning, Felicity. We've had trouble, I'm afraid, several cameras vandalised along by the Hattersley Estate, it seems.'

'Oh dear. Do you know how much damage there is?'

'No, only that eight cameras are out of action. We need to get this sorted out, and fast.'

'I'll help in any way I can, of course.'

'Good girl. For a start, let's see what we've got on disc.'

He opened the door and went straight to my work station, taking the seat. In view of the way we'd parted on the Saturday night I'd expected at least a welcoming kiss, but he seemed completely focused on the problem I'd created. So was I, largely because I was terrified I was about to be revealed as the culprit.

I moved close beside him, peering at the screen as the first image came up. It showed the river path from the ZX-4 I'd done first, a set of pools of dull orange light from the streetlamps with shadows between and a frame of absolute black. Stephen moved the image forward in time until it suddenly vanished, then back, and my heart was in my mouth as it began to play.

Nothing showed, not a flicker of movement, not so much as a change in the shadows. I could make out the bushes I'd used for cover, just, but nothing more, until a black gloved hand appeared, holding a spray can pointed directly at the lens, then a blur, then nothing. Stephen hissed in vexation.

'Bastards!'

'How did they get up the pole?'

'Not too hard, I dare say, for a kid, but anti-climb paint will soon put a stop to that.'

'How do you know it's kids?'

'Bound to be. Who else would do that? Anyway, look at the size of his hand.'

He moved the image back, freezing it on the gloved hand. My thick black glove made it impossible to pick out any details, but you could certainly see it wasn't a grown man holding the can, or almost certainly not.

'It could have been a dwarf.'

'That's hardly likely.'

'I was joking.'

'This is no time for levity ... Sorry, Felicity, as you can imagine, I'm not particularly happy about this.'

'Of course.'

I kissed him, to which he responded with a smile before moving on to the next camera. This time there was nothing to be seen at all, just the fixed image of the alley mouth looking ghostly in the infrared, then nothing. I began to allow myself to relax, just a little, as Stephen moved on through the cameras, the five I'd done on Saturday and the three on Sunday. Not once had I given anything away, beyond the appearance of my gloved hand and once the edge of my hoodie. Stephen had obviously been hoping for more, and grew increasingly frustrated, finally banging the mouse down.

'The little bastards are damn good at locating the cameras, I'll give them that. Right, I want the entire system up and running again by lunchtime.'

'Can we do that?'

'I certainly hope so. It will be easy enough with the ones they spray-painted anyway. The others we may have to replace.'

He'd marched into the main body of the warehouse as he spoke and I was left at my desk. I spent a moment flicking back and forth between the camera images, just to make absolutely sure I hadn't given myself away. There was nothing, but it was interesting watching what else had been going on that night, and more than a little scary.

I saw the couple who'd been sweet-talking each other, both as they'd passed my hiding place and earlier, coming down the steps of Town Bridge and pausing for a snog among the shadows, blissfully unaware they were being recorded and identified. Then there was the bit next to Foulds', where a middle-aged man in a heavy greatcoat passed not five minutes before I put the camera out of action. His face showed clearly, angry and morose, his mouth twitching with strong emotion. Most likely he was harmless, perhaps somebody who'd gone out for a walk after an argument with his wife, but I was glad I hadn't bumped into him, a thought that gave me fresh qualms about what I was doing.

When Stephen emerged from the warehouse he was carrying a large box. I held the door for him and helped him put it in his car, but he didn't explain until he was locking up.

'I've got everything we need here. Paul's at the council offices, calming Phelps down, and they don't even know how much of the system is down. I aim to keep it that way. If we can put it down to a few kids with spray paint and show how easily we get back in operation this might actually do more good than harm.'

'Won't we have to replace the cameras?'

'No, that's what's great about this system. It seems that only two are badly damaged, so yes, we have to put new ones up there, but that's all.'

'Oh. I'd have thought the spray paint would mess up the works?'

'No. That's one of its great beauties. You'll see.'

He didn't tell me any more and it didn't seem sensible to ask too many questions, so that was all I got as we drove out to the Hattersley Estate. He parked and we got out, Stephen looking doubtfully at a patch of scorched concrete where a car had been burnt out sometime before; nothing to do with me for once. I was praying nobody I knew was about and eager to move on, but very aware I wasn't supposed to have seen this set of cameras except on the map.

Stephen finally shook his head and started down the alley towards the river. I followed faithfully behind, doing my best puppy-dog imitation and keeping my eyes firmly on him. He stopped beneath the pole supporting the ZX-4, most of which was now Glitter Box purple instead of Ministry of Nosy Parkers black. It was at least a metre above his head. He sighed.

'If only they'd put all that energy into something productive.'

I declined to comment, waiting as he put the box down and took out a transparent bag with something inside that was obviously a camera part. Once he'd pulled open the bag he held it up to show me.

'This is how we get around spray paint. This housing covers the front section of the camera, including the lens, and can be replaced in a few seconds, although it looks as if the entire casing is solid. They're so cheap it's hardly worth cleaning up the vandalised ones. Clever, don't you think?'

'Yes, very.'

Well, it had fooled me, but replacing it wasn't as

easy as Stephen might have liked. He could climb the pole, but he couldn't hold on securely enough to remove the old housing and replace it. After watching for five minutes while trying to keep a straight face I made a suggestion.

'Maybe if I sat on your shoulders?'

'Would you mind?'

'No, of course not.'

He climbed down and picked me up with that easy strength I always like in a man, lifting me onto his shoulders. I had to bunch my skirt up, pressing the crotch of my knickers directly to his neck, a curious sensation and oddly embarrassing after what we'd been up to. I knew he'd be able to feel the heat of my pussy, but in typical Stephen fashion he didn't comment, concentrating on the work by giving out completely unnecessary instructions as I twisted the old housing loose and replaced it with the new one. Just as he'd said, the expensive and delicate parts of the camera were completely untouched, while it was obvious that the housing could not only be spray-painted but hit quite hard without doing any damage at all. Removing the housing and then using the paint was going to look highly suspicious.

The ZX-2 across the river he simply took hold of and bent back into the right position, then replaced the housing as before. So it went all along the path, with only the two cameras I'd managed to pull right off needing replacing and the whole job done in roughly the same time I'd taken in the first place. He was still cross about it, and looked far from happy as he dumped the purple-painted housings on the warehouse floor, voicing his opinion of the perpetrators.

'Little bastards! You'd think even a child would realise that security cameras are for their own protection, wouldn't you?'

'I suppose they see them as intrusive.'

'Oh, right, so they can vandalise phone boxes and burn cars and spray their graffiti over every available surface. Why do these people do these things?'

'I don't know. Maybe they're just bored?'

'Bored? There's a community centre, isn't there? Or they could just read a book.'

I shrugged, not wanting to get any deeper into the argument. There was a community centre, it was true, run by a church association and avoided by every self-respecting scally in Hockford. I'd never been there. Stephen went on.

'I mean, you've lived in Hockford all your life. What did you do to keep yourself amused as a teenager?'

The answer was that I'd vandalised telephone boxes, burnt cars and sprayed graffiti over every available surface, along with drumming for Rubber Dollies, indulging myself with boys, getting blind drunk and helping Steve smuggle booze into the country.

'This and that.'

'No, but really?'

It was not a line of conversation I wanted to get into, and I found myself looking for a distraction. He was making me feel guilty too, because he was really upset over what I'd done. Again I shrugged. I knew what I wanted to say, but there was a hollow feeling in my stomach and it was hard to get the words out.

'You seem really angry, Stephen ... Mr English. Would it help at all if you were to take it out on my bottom?'

He obviously hadn't been thinking of anything of the sort, because for a moment he simply looked blank. Then he smiled and laughed.

'That would be extremely unfair!'

'Maybe, but ... but I really quite like the idea of being punished by you.'

'And I like the idea of punishing you, believe me, Felicity, but the mood I'm in it might be rather more than you could handle.'

'I'll be OK, as long as you stop if I say to. You can pretend it was me who vandalised all the cameras.'

He frowned, glanced at his watch, then smiled and spoke again.

'Actually, that's an offer I can't refuse. Come along then, over you go.'

I was already shaking badly as I stepped forward, and he didn't even bother to take me upstairs but simply sat down on the nearest packing crate to haul me bodily across his knee. Helpless excitement, fear, humiliation, all the emotions I'd known before came flooding back as he lifted his knee to push my bottom higher, speaking as he took hold of the hem of my skirt.

'Right, skirt up, knickers down. I'm going to enjoy this.'

As before, his voice was full of relish at the prospect of stripping me, but this time my exposure was brusque, allowing no time for my feelings to sink in but making me gasp in shock as my skirt was tugged high and my knickers whipped smartly down. I bit my lip, afraid of the pain but wanting it all at once, wanting punishment too but still screaming at myself inside for allowing such a gross indignity to be inflicted on me when I was in the right all the time.

He cocked his knee up higher still, to draw a second gasp of shock from my lips as my pussy was put on show from behind, and a third of pain as his hand smacked across my bare cheeks. I cried out, astonished by how much it hurt compared with before, and again with the second smack, too breathless to protest as he laid into me. It stung crazily, his big hand cupping almost my entire bottom and setting both cheeks afire, a firm, no-nonsense spanking that had me writhing across his lap in an instant, with my legs kicking in my knickers and both my shoes already off.

I tried to protest, but all that came out was a sob, and even as I squirmed in my frenzied pain one part of me was still saying I was getting only what I deserved. It was true too, my actions more than deserving of an over-the-knee spanking, and the more he spanked the more I felt I deserved it, until at last I gave in to my emotions and burst into tears. He stopped immediately, his hand resting on my blazing bottom, his voice full of apology as he spoke to me.

'I'm sorry, Felicity, I shouldn't . . .'

'No. It's OK, I . . . I'm just a bit emotional. I'll be all right now, carry on.'

He didn't start immediately, perhaps doubtful, but with my bare bottom hot beneath his hand and the tears streaming down my face, I was undergoing a really intense experience, all my feelings flooding out, although I could still barely accept what I was saying as new words tumbled from my lips.

'Go on, Stephen, do it, spank me . . . spank me hard. I want to be punished, Stephen, by you.'

I thought he'd stop, unable to cope with my emotional outburst, but I was wrong. After just a moment his hand lifted from my bottom and came down again, not as hard as before, but a firm, purposeful smack, and another, applying my punishment the way a naughty girl ought to be smacked, or at least how I felt I ought to be smacked.

My legs had come wide, showing everything, in that same state of absolute surrender he'd got me into before. I'd never understood before how it felt to be completely exposed in front of a man when, instead of being in charge, I was his to do with as he pleased. I felt sheer joy, knowing it didn't matter what I was showing to him because he was giving me a well-deserved punishment.

I'd given in, my toes braced wide on the ground to lift my bottom as he spanked me, still delivering those same firm swats full across my cheeks, but it no longer hurt, each smack now provoking a jolt of pleasure to my sex. He had me ready for entry, which was just as well because I could feel the hard lump of his cock pressing to my side and I knew I'd soon be accepting him inside me.

He took his time, perhaps exhausting all his ill feeling on my bottom before his arousal finally got the better of him. First he began to smack lower, pushing up under my cheeks to increase the sensation to my pussy, which quickly had me gasping and shaking my head. I was no longer crying, but my vision was hazy and my mouth wide, completely abandoned to my emotions without thought for dignity. After all, how undignified can it get, turned over a man's knee to be spanked and ending up turned on?

At last he slowed and began to alternate the smacks with touches, first stroking and petting my burning cheeks, then more intimate still, his fingers stealing between my thighs to find how wet I was. The answer was that I was soaking, and he gave a low chuckle of satisfaction as he slid a finger deep inside me. Immediately I was pushing my bottom up to meet the pressure, allowing him to enter me deep. He began to play with me, exploring my sex and stroking my bottom, applying the occasional smack and then doing something exquisitely rude, holding my cheeks wide to inspect my bottom hole. A sigh escaped my lips at being so blatantly exposed, and again as he touched me, tickling the tiny hole until he'd got me whimpering and jerking in reaction.

Only when he'd really had his fill of my bottom did he finally let me up or, at least, let me off his knee. He kept his hands on me, guiding me gently but firmly to the stairs and speaking in a low, firm voice, quite clearly a command.

'Put your feet well apart, Felicity, and brace yourself on the steps. I'm going to fuck you.'

The way he said it sent an extraordinary jolt of emotion through me, as if entering me, fucking me, was not a mutual thing at all, but part of my punishment. I still obeyed, setting my legs wide just as I'd been ordered to, with my knickers stretched taut between my thighs and my bottom on full show. My hair fell down around my face as I bent over, the same way it had been while I was spanked, so as I looked back it was through a curtain of golden strands.

Stephen was standing behind me, his eyes fixed on my exposed, vulnerable body, his hand on his crotch, squeezing. For one moment I wondered what the hell I was doing, bent over the office stairs with my bottom all hot and red from spanking, waiting for my boss to enter me from behind. Then he pulled his cock out and I forgot my dignity once more, eager only to have him inside me.

He gave a pleased nod, perhaps reading something of my lust in my expression, and he came forward. I felt him touch me, his hand on my bottom, holding me open for his cock, then the hot, round tip, pushing up inside me, and deep-filling my body with that blissful sensation that comes no other way. He took me by the hips and began to do just what he'd said, to fuck me. I tried to think of it as a punishment, because it was turning me on, to imagine myself spanked across his knee and then bent over and fucked.

I had to come, just like that, with my bottom all hot and his cock deep inside me, fucking me as a punishment. My hand went back, leaving me supported almost entirely by his grip on my hips, down my half-lowered knickers and onto the warm, wet bulge of my pussy. He realised what I was doing and gave a knowing chuckle, but made no effort to stop me. My fingers found the crucial place and the right rhythm, rubbing myself to the motion of my fucking.

His hard belly was smacking onto my bottom, his cock driving deep, helping to take me high as I thought of what he had done to me, taken down my knickers and spanked me, punished me, then made me bend over and fucked me too. I'd asked for it, and I'd got it, punished the way I so thoroughly deserved, and by my stern, suited boss, spanked and fucked with my bare bum sticking out from my smart little office suit and lowered panties.

I came, and I screamed, unable to hold myself back due to the sheer power of my orgasm. Like all the best, it was as much in my head as my body, the thought of what Stephen had done to me and the motion of his cock inside me, still pumping deep and hard as I wriggled and shook and stamped my way through the most glorious climax. He even gave my bottom a last hard smack at the perfect moment, adding a final touch to my ecstasy as I remembered how I'd been spanked.

Spent, I collapsed down onto my knees, my bottom still raised and open. He'd slipped out, and I stayed as I was, completely open to him as he finished himself off all over my smacked cheeks.

7

All my effort and I'd got exactly nothing for it. Well, I'd got a smacked bottom, but that wasn't strictly speaking relevant.

In fact I'd done more harm than good, as I quickly discovered. Mr Phelps and his cronies where immensely impressed both with the rapid repair to the camera system and the low cost of doing so, leaving Black Knight Securities very much in favour. Only then did I discover that we had not one but two rivals for the contract, the firm who'd supplied the small existing system and were offering to expand it and another who wanted to put in something very much like our own but apparently less cost effective.

Stephen was well pleased with himself, and with me, both for my willing assistance and my desire to indulge him in his little perversion. I was rather less happy, both because of the failure of my plot and because I could feel that his little perversion was rapidly becoming mine. Before, I'd been amazed at how I'd accepted that I would let somebody spank me, but there had been no denying my enjoyment and despite my mixed feelings it had been intensely erotic from the start. I'd not only been given a painful punishment and still got off on it, but I'd wanted more almost before my bum had cooled down. I was in danger of growing addicted.

I could just imagine what it would be like having to persuade people to spank me. Some I wouldn't even be able to ask. Dave, for instance, because it quite simply wouldn't work. Steve I could ask, and I knew he'd do it. He'd also laugh at me, but I had a nasty suspicion that would just turn me on even more. Fortunately Stephen seemed more than capable of looking after my needs, and very keen to do so.

He was extremely attentive, and also friendly, taking me to lunch and dinner several times during the week and always talkative and considerate. I'd been worried that he might treat me badly after I'd given in to him so completely and in a way that left no doubt whatsoever that he was my boss in more than just the employment sense. Nothing could have been further from the truth. He was more intimate, kissing me and allowing his hand to stray to my bottom, but not in front of other people, while he was a great deal more polite and less arrogant than before. On the Wednesday morning he even made me coffee.

I also got my third spanking, just a playful one, applied to the seat of my skirt and supposedly for making a spelling mistake in a letter I'd typed, but it made it very clear how things stood between us. As long as there was to be physical intimacy there would be spankings, and I knew that for all my low-key resentment of what he was doing to me I could not resist. That resentment would have been the only problem in my life had it not been for the cameras.

My plan had failed and I was completely stuck for what to do next. Further sabotage was clearly pointless, as the best I could do would be to ensure the contract went to another firm. If it did, then I'd have no chance of changing anything at all, and no inside knowledge of how the system worked either. Possibly if I could destroy the entire system it might have some effect, but I didn't have the time or the ability, while the specialist knowledge needed would surely mean I got caught.

It would have been so easy to just give in. There were lots of good reasons. For a start my relationship with Stephen and work, which together were taking up all my time and keeping me out of mischief. Then there was the security the cameras undoubtedly provided, even if Hockford was short of maniacs, and the fact that my face wasn't going to be recognised either. Lastly I could warn people, and if that meant everybody had to behave themselves perhaps it really wasn't the end of the world after all.

I still didn't feel right about it. Some of the things I'd done in the past now seemed pretty unacceptable, and I could understand people wanting to put a stop to it. I could also understand the feelings of boredom and dissatisfaction which had led me to do them in the first place, and nothing was being done to remedy that except the same old platitudes. Other things were just too trivial, or offences only to those with stuffy, old-fashioned morals, but authoritarianism seemed to be all the rage.

Then there was Mr Phelps and his colleagues, who came round occasionally. They were unbearably smug and superior about the whole thing, also immensely self-satisfied about all the poor sods they were going to land with criminal records for really very little, and even talking openly about the revenue they expected to raise from the fines. When he joked about taking an expenses-paid trip to Korea on the money, I'd have gladly planted my shoe up his saggy backside, and I had no regrets whatsoever about burning his car.

I went back to brooding, generally late at night

when I could lie in bed and let my mind run onto increasingly impractical schemes, such as swapping all the images on the database around so that every scally was automatically identified as Mr Phelps, or all my friends came up as the various dogs and cats the system was still recording. Sadly neither would have been more than a temporary solution, while the search for the perpetrator would have led straight to me. I couldn't get into Stephen's private editing facility either, as I didn't know the password, but even that would only have been a partial solution.

On the Friday I got what I'd been expecting all week: an invitation to Stephen's flat. It was for the Saturday evening, and for me it felt like a confirmation that our relationship amounted to more than just a boss taking advantage of his employee. Had he merely wanted me physically he could have just kept me at the office, while his invitation also removed my sneaking suspicion that he might actually be married.

I accepted, although in ways it seemed like the final surrender, especially if he expected me to be faithful. Playing the field is fun, and I never did understand all this bullshit about my body being a temple at which only my one true love should be permitted to worship. Sex is special, sure, but for me it's always been something I do with my friends if I feel like it. I like the way Steve cajoles me into sucking his cock, and I like the way that boys like Pete and Dave get so hot over me they end up grovelling for the slightest taste of honey. I hadn't forgotten about Martin either, but I'd assumed that for whatever reason he was no longer interested in me. Inevitably that stung my pride, but I tried to tell myself it was just as well, because if my relationship with Stephen was going to get serious then the fewer complications the better. It was still a pity, because Martin was even bigger and stronger than Stephen; he also seemed to like my bum, and it would have been very interesting indeed to see how he reacted to my new-found love of spanking.

When I saw Sam with Billy in the High Street on the way home it was Martin I immediately thought of, only for my curiosity to take a new turn as Steve appeared and accepted two large bags. They'd seen me, Sam giving me a teasing smile as she looked my skirt suit up and down.

'Hey, Fizz. How's Miss Goodie-Two-Shoes?'

I stuck my tongue out at her and turned to Steve.

'What are you up to?'

There was no hesitation at all in his reply.

'It's great. Billy's been getting me stuff from the base. They have this shop, right, with all American gear, really cheap.'

'You're going to get locked up one day, Steve, or shot.'

'No, it's all above board, so long as I don't take the piss. Isn't that right, Billy?'

'Sure. Once we've bought it we can sell it to who we like, and why not? It's our private property, ain't it?'

'If you say so. So you're not doing Calais any more, Steve?'

'Yeah, I'm doing Calais, this is just a bit extra. I'm going tomorrow if you want to come?'

'I can't. I'm going out.'

'Oh yeah?'

I knew if I admitted to the details they'd be taking the piss out of me for months. Then again it had to come out sometime.

'Yes, with Stephen English, from where I work.'

'Your boss?'

Sam laughed.

'Fizz is knobbing her boss!'

I had immediately gone scarlet, not because of the sex but because of the spanking, which was something they very definitely were not going to find out about. Sam saw immediately and I got the inevitable reaction.

'Oh my, it's not serious, is it? Not you, Fizz?'

'Yes it is, sort of, and who are you to talk? You two go everywhere together now.'

'Sure, but my man's not a suit.'

She'd put her arms around Billy as she spoke, and for once I couldn't find an answer so I contented myself with sticking my tongue out at her again. She just laughed, but there was a serious note in Billy's voice as he posed a question, almost accusing.

'I thought you were hot on Martin?'

I shrugged, immediately defensive.

'I like Martin, yes, but he hasn't called me or anything.'

'He's in Afghanistan.'

'Oh ... well, he might have said something.'

'He's not allowed to. What am I going to tell him when he comes back? He thinks he's got the second sweetest girl in the UK waiting for him when he comes back and you're off with some guy from your work.'

'It's not like that. Martin and I only went out once ... well, twice, sort of, and he didn't ask me about being his girlfriend or anything.'

'You fucked, didn't you? Don't that make it plain enough?'

'No it does not! I'm sorry, but just because I choose to go with a man does not make me his fucking property!'

He was going to reply, but Sam got in first.

'Leave her, Billy. She didn't know.'

'Yeah, but . . .'

I wasn't leaving it, not like that.

'Look, when Martin comes back you can tell him this. I like him, and I would like to go out with him again sometime, but I am no man's property, and if he thinks I'm his he can go and fuck himself with his oversized prick. Got that?'

Billy looked shocked, maybe not used to women a foot shorter than him shouting at him in the street, and there was no mistaking the implication of his answer.

'Yeah, I got that, and I'll be sure to tell Martin, just like it is.'

I'd have said more, but Sam was already hustling him away and I was left fuming in the street. Steve looked bemused by the entire incident, and spoke as soon as Billy was out of earshot.

'What's his problem? Anyone would think he's the one you cheated.'

'I didn't cheat anybody! Jesus, Steve, not you too . . .'

'Hey, be cool, Fizz, I didn't mean it like that. I just don't see what his beef is.'

'I suppose he thinks he's sticking up for his mate, but I never said anything about being faithful to Martin, and he didn't ask. Now even if Martin was OK with me Billy's going to fuck it up. Bastard!'

'Come and have a jar, yeah?'

He put his arm around my shoulder, not in a sexual way at all, but just affection. I let myself be steered into Buzz Shack, where he put an ice-cold lime mix in front of me. My temper was still running high and I swallowed more than half of it in one, which helped me to relax at least a little. Steve already seemed to have forgotten the incident, spreading himself out on the bench with his pint of lager in one hand as he spoke.

'Shame about Calais. It's not the same without you.'

'Dave will go, won't he?'

'Thanks a bunch, Fizz.'

'I'm sorry, anyway. Next time, I promise.'

'OK. So what's with these cameras? Have they got the go-ahead?'

'Not yet, but it looks like they will.'

'So what do I need to know?'

'Your face will be recorded and memorised, so there'll be a record of you wherever you go. Some of the cameras are small and easily concealed to deliberately catch you out. The bigger models pick up sound too.'

'What about deliveries and stuff?'

'I don't know. Who's to say that you didn't get what you're taking from the cash and carry? I don't think even the ZX-5 can zoom in close enough to read the small print on a can of beer, but they might be able to put together a case based on your movements.'

'Shit. But you're going to know where these things are, right?'

'Yes, but you know what Town's like. There are only five roads they need to cover.'

'Yeah, but I was thinking. If you fixed it so the camera on the Bury Road is in the right place I could cut through the country park.'

'That might work.'

He began to enlarge on his plan, suggesting ways in which I could help him and others cheat the system. At first I felt a little guilt as well as appreciation for his ideas, but by my second mix I'd decided that I wouldn't be betraying Stephen or Black Knight at all, and I felt no loyalty whatsoever to the council. Just as many cameras would be sold after all, and we weren't being paid by specific results.

My bad temper died down slowly as we talked and drank. Soon Josie had joined us, then Pete and others, until it was the usual crowd all laughing and joking around the biggest table in the bar, just like old times except that I was in my work clothes. I called Mum to say I wouldn't be in for dinner and treated myself to a big plate of sticky cheese nachos, which left me feeling full and mellow.

I was on my fifth mix by the time Steve left, intent on getting an early night before his Calais trip. Both Pete and Dave were hitting on me, and I was drunk enough to want to torment them, not giving in to either but never rejecting them flat out either. Zoe was snogging with her new boyfriend in the corner, one tit peeping out from under her top as he felt her, which made the boys worse and ensured that I got my drinks for free.

By the time they kicked us out my head was spinning. Pete was no better, staggering, but determined to stick close to me, which only made me worse. Dave still had his old wreck of a car too, pulling open the door and jerking his thumb at the inside in an effort to look cool.

'Get in, Fizz, we're going for a drive. See ya later, Pete.'

Pete immediately piled in, starting an argument and leaving me laughing by the side of the road. It felt good to be in control, but I didn't want them fighting over me and climbed in the back, snapping my fingers at Dave as he tried to push Pete back out of the car.

'Drive, chauffeur.'

He glanced back at me, and I could see the need in his eyes, close to desperation. Full of mischief, I put my fingers to the top button of my blouse, pushing it slowly open. He just stared, but Pete let out a howl like a demented wolf. They began to argue again, but I quickly put a stop to that.

'Hey, shut up both you or I'm getting out. Just drive, Dave.'

Pete put on a triumphant grin, Dave his sulky face. Both wanted me, that was obvious. I wasn't sure what I'd do – maybe just tease them until they were ready to explode and leave them like that, or maybe let it go further if I felt like it. I was still smarting over the business with Martin and, despite a touch of guilt for Stephen, keen to show that nobody held me down.

We pulled out into the traffic, my senses too full of alcohol to care about whether Dave was too drunk to drive. I just lay back, watching the lights flicker past and the faces of the people spilling out of the pubs. As always, I recognised half of them, including a young man just getting into a taxi outside the Bull, clean cut, muscular, and last seen on his knees to an older man on our surveillance disc. I laughed at the memory, and suddenly a really evil idea had come to me.

'Hey, boys, have either of you ever had a threesome?'

Dave nearly left the road. Pete spun around, staring right at me.

'What? You saying you're up for it?'

'I might be, if you behave yourselves.'

He let out another ear-splitting whoop as Dave finally found his voice.

'What, like both of us at the same time?'

'Something like that.'

His answer was a wordless expulsion of breath. Pete was still staring at me, his eyes nearly popping out of his head. I gave him a lazy smile and casually undid another button of my blouse. His tongue poked out to wet his lips, and as he spoke his voice was a croak.

'Show us then, Fizz, go on.'

'Uh-uh, not here. Keep going, Dave. Park up well out of town.'

He'd reached the turning for the Lynn Road, and sped up. I could hear his breathing, while Pete was staring at me as if he'd never seen a woman before despite the time we'd gone together. It was too good to resist and I undid another button, and a fourth, leaving my blouse wide open and my bra showing. Dave swallowed and I poked my tongue out, licking my lips as I took hold of the bottom of my bra.

'Peek-a-boo, Petey.'

I jerked my bra up, spilling my breasts out into the flickering light from the street lamps overhead. Pete shook his head, staring wide-eyed as he spoke.

'Fuck me!'

'Maybe, if you're lucky.'

Dave could see in the mirror, his eyes as wide as Pete's and a single bead of sweat forming on his forehead. He put his foot down as he pulled away from town and the lights, leaving the interior of the car in near darkness save for the faint glow of the instrument panel. I began to play with my breasts, knowing Pete could barely see as I teased my nipples and stroked underneath to show off to him. Dave drove faster still, only to suddenly slam the brakes on and pull us in.

'This is a good place. Fuck me, will you look at that!'

He'd turned the inside light on and craned around, both of them now staring at my chest as I toyed with myself. They looked fit to burst, and I was having trouble keeping the laughter out of my voice and sounding sultry instead.

'OK, here will do. What would you like to do first, boys, spit-roast me?'

'Yeah, great!'

'What's that?'

'When one bloke has her each end, you prat. A lot of footballers are into it, when they get groupies and that.'

'Nice, we're going to do it like footballers.'

He began to scramble into the back, but I wagged a finger at him.

'Uh-uh, not so fast. You boys always tell. This time I don't want you to.'

'Yeah, yeah. We promise, right, Dave?'

'Right.'

'Uh-uh. I want to make sure, and I want to have fun too . . .'

'Yeah, I don't mind doing that stuff you like, that's cool.'

'Good, let's see your cocks then.'

They hesitated, wary of doing it in front of each other, which made me smile as I craned forward between the seats. Pete had his out first, already hard from watching my little strip show. Dave had quickly followed, but he was still limp, pleading as he spoke.

'Give us a tug first, Fizz.'

I reached out immediately to take him in hand, enjoying the meaty feel of his penis, which quickly began to grow. Pete didn't know where to look at first, but quickly decided to take advantage of my bare chest, slipping a hand down the back of the seat to cup my breast. He was pulling at himself as he did it, already urgent, so I gently detached his hand.

'Calm down, Pete. If you're in such a hurry we won't get any fun, will we?'

'I need it, Fizz, I tell you.'

'Just take it easy, will you? Right, boys, who wants to fuck me first?'

I said it slowly, savouring the words, and both of them were demanding the right immediately, even though Dave was still only half hard in my hand. I went on, feigning surprise.

'Both of you? That's a bit difficult. I tell you what, if you want to have me, you've got to suck the other guy's cock first, OK?'

Neither of them answered, both staring at me as if I'd suggested a cannibal feast. I burst out laughing, unable to hold it back and Pete finally found his voice.

'Fuck that. That's gay, that is!'

I shrugged, leant back and began to toy with my nipples as I answered.

'It doesn't have to be gay. You liked it when I let Josie feel my tits at the Dog and Duck that time, didn't you? Don't deny it.'

'Yeah, but ... I mean, Josie's a dyke, ain't she?'

'Yes, but I'm not.'

'Yeah, but you're still a girl. It's not the same for blokes.'

'Why not?'

'It's just not, it's ... I don't know ...'

'It just ain't right, Fizz. Come on, you ain't being fair!'

Both of them had gone limp. I shrugged, enjoying myself immensely as I went on.

'Come on, just for me. It doesn't mean you're gay, it's just to turn me on, and I promise I won't tell anybody.'

'No way!'

'Come on, Fizz, quit joking.'

'I'm not joking. If you want to have me, I want to see you suck each other's cocks. You can do anything you like, I promise.'

I meant it. I was drunk enough and horny enough to try anything, but only if they went along with it. Dave had started to sulk, but Pete gave me a calculating look.

'Like what?'

'You tell me.'

'What if you, like, let us watch while you piss?'

'OK, if that's what you want.'

'Through your knickers.'

'You're a little pervert, do you know that?'

He didn't bother to answer, but bit his lip. I was willing, more than willing, because I'd found the perfect game, indulging my cruel streak while at the same time allowing myself to get into things I wouldn't normally have dared do. It's always easier to get heavy if you can pretend you're not just doing it because it gets you off, and my tummy was already fluttering at the thought of what they might make me do. Dave spoke up, perhaps catching the calculating look on Pete's face.

'I ain't fucking doing it. I'm not a poof.'

Pete's face worked with emotion for an instant before he answered.

'Nor am I, mate, but don't you want to watch Fizz piss her knickers?'

'I . . . I don't know. That's a bit dirty, ain't it?'

'What then? Come on, it's not every day you get a chick saying she'll do anything you want, is it?'

Dave had his sulky face on, and as he put one tentative hand to the car key I was sure he was about to spoil everything. I leant quickly forward, nuzzling my face against his neck as I took hold of his cock. As I kissed him my hand had burrowed into his fly, pulling out his balls as I whispered the dirtiest things I could think of into his ear. He made a sort of strangled noise, but his cock was growing rapidly in my hand as I kept on.

'Come on, Dave, you want to do it, don't you? I don't mind, it turns me on, and I'll do anything, anything . . .'

Again he made an odd noise, then finally spoke.

'I . . . I want to put it up your bum.'

I rocked back, letting go of his cock.

'You dirty little pig!'

'Yeah, well, you want me to suck Pete's cock!'

For a long moment we were just staring at each other, perhaps both thinking the same thing: did we dare use each other's demands to fulfil dirty fantasies? I like to be touched between my cheeks, and I'd thought about how it would feel to take a cock up my bottom, but it always seemed too dirty to admit to. Now, maybe . . .

'OK, you little pervert, you suck Pete's cock and you can do what you want.'

Pete cut in immediately.

'Yeah, and I get mine too!'

I nodded, now trembling with excitement and apprehension too as Pete spoke again, to Dave.

'You tell anybody about this, Dave, and I'll fucking kill you.'

'Yeah, right, like I'm going to tell anyone!'

They went quiet, exchanging guilty glances. I leant close, craning forward between the seats. Both still had their cocks out, Pete's soft, Dave's rock hard with his balls bulging out of his fly. Pete spoke again, his voice now full of uncertainty.

'You going to get me hard, Fizz, or what?'

'Uh-uh, I want to see Dave do it.'

'You can be a real bitch, you know that?'

With those words he had swung around, offering his cock. Dave looked stunned, his face working in indecision, but he'd agreed to do it, and my heart was hammering at the thought. His eyes were fixed on Pete's cock, and he'd begun to go forward, only to stop. I reached out to take him gently by the neck, the way Steve holds me when he knows he needs to make me do it. He swore under his breath, then spoke, his voice thick with emotion.

'This is for you, Fizz, not because I . . .'

'Then suck his cock, Dave, now.'

I pushed his head down, right into Pete's lap, and he did it, his mouth open to take in the thick, flaccid penis. A powerful shiver ran through me at the sight, not sex so much as pure mischief, but he was only holding it in his mouth, not sucking, and already trying to pull back.

'No, you've got to suck it, like I do. Come on.'

The look of consternation on his face deepened as I pushed his head down, and then suddenly he was doing it, sucking on Pete's cock as if he'd been born to it, with his cheeks sucked in and eyes closed in what I'd have been willing to bet a thousand pounds was pleasure. Pete was silent, his eyes shut, his fists clenched. I wanted to laugh, I wanted to scream, I wanted to dance in sheer, wicked delight, but I wasn't going to spoil the moment. I kept Dave's head down, helping him get over his own feelings as he sucked on Pete's now growing cock. Again he tried to stop, again I held him in place, and at that he gave in completely, taking hold of Pete's cock as he sucked, quite obviously enjoying himself. Now it was sex, and I wanted to come. I let go, quickly tugging my skirt up as I spoke.

'Good boys. Just carry on, and you can watch me if you like, Pete.'

He turned around, opening his eyes. I don't think I've ever seen a man look so vulnerable, and in return I felt I could do as I liked in front of him, and for him. With my skirt around my waist and my blouse fully open, I began to play with myself, stroking my nipples and the front of my knickers. Pete was hard, his cock a stiff rod in Dave's mouth, a sight so deliciously dirty I was already feeling the first shivers of orgasm even as I pressed my fingers to my clit. I pushed my knickers down, letting my legs come wide to show everything. Pete spoke.

'This is worth it . . . yeah, Fizz, do it.'

I met his eyes, my back arched in pleasure as I teased my breasts and sex, my climax rising in my head. Dave was sucking harder now, a proper blow job, and on that thought I came, my body tight and my fingers busy between my open thighs as wave after wave of ecstasy swept over me, and as I finished Pete gave a sudden grunt and I knew he'd come in Dave's mouth. Before I'd even come down properly I was laughing, first at the sheer joy of what we'd done and then at the expression on Dave's face as he got his mouthful.

'Now you know what it's like!'

He didn't say anything, his face screwed up in disgust as he pulled back, but he'd swallowed, on purpose, and his own cock was rock hard in his hand. Obviously he'd enjoyed it, but it wouldn't have been fair to force an admission out of him, so I tousled his hair and kissed him as he sat up.

'Thanks, both of you.'

It was Pete who answered.

'Yeah, right, and now it's your turn.'

Dave agreed earnestly and I felt my tummy go tight in apprehension once more. I nodded, my feelings already shifting to that wonderful sense of helplessness Stephen provoked in me. They were going to make me be dirty, really dirty, and from the look on their faces I knew there would be no getting off. Pete glanced down to where my underwear was still in a tangle around my ankles.

'Pull your knickers back up, Fizz.'

Dave cut in immediately.

'What, you really going to make her pee in her panties?'

'Yeah.'

'Not in my car!'

'Don't be stupid, she can do it outside.'

I swallowed hard but did as I was told, wriggling my knickers back up my legs, but as I reached to open the door Pete spoke again.

'Tidy up, yeah, like you was in that office were you work. I want to see you do it like that.'

'Pervert.'

He was, but it made sense. If I had to do something so utterly dirty I should be as smart as possible first. I got out of the car, both of them watching me as I adjusted my clothing with trembling fingers. The interior light cast a dim yellowish pool on the ground, no more, but enough to illuminate me and leave the track and the woods behind me in utter darkness. Only when I looked almost as if I might just have stepped out of Black Knight Securities did Pete speak again.

'Nice and slow, and I want to see everything.'

'OK.'

The word came out as a whisper, showing my feelings, naughty but embarrassed too as I once more tugged my skirt up far enough to allow me to sink down into a squat. The front of my knickers were showing, their eyes glued firmly between my legs. I tried to let go, which should have been easy, but I couldn't. I closed my eyes, trying to concentrate, only to open them again at the sound of a car. Our own car shaded me, yet I waited, and just as well.

As the car passed I saw the all too familiar yellow and blue pattern on it side. Then it slowed. It stopped. It began to reverse. I was already running, over the bar that closed off the logging track and away. For a moment all I could see was the jagged tops of the trees, black against the stars. I was stumbling in my heels on the uneven ground, far too clumsy.

I stopped to duck in among the trees, my heart pounding as I felt my way between the pines in near total blackness, only to give in. They'd have torches, and I was helpless, unable to hide, unable to run properly in my stupid office clothes, surely caught. But what for? I'd just panicked, running by instinct, but I hadn't actually done anything, not obviously. I still didn't want to face the police and stayed where I was, ducked low behind a pine trunk as I looked back.

The police car had stopped, blocking in Dave's. Both the boys had got out, also two policemen, and while I couldn't make out their voices clearly it was easy to tell what was going on from their body language. Fortunately Dave had had time to put his cock away, and was doing his best to talk his way out of it. It was hopeless, with no tax disc, no insurance, his licence suspended and probably half a dozen things wrong with the car. I knew they wouldn't say I'd been there, and there was absolutely nothing I could do to help them, but I still felt guilty as I began to slink away through the trees.

8

I didn't feel too good on the Saturday morning, what with a slight hangover, aching muscles from my long walk home and a guilty feeling for abandoning Pete and Dave. As soon as I was properly awake I rang them both, to discover that the car had been impounded and Dave was up before the magistrates. Pete had been cautioned. My name had never come up, leaving me deeply grateful to them and guiltier still. I was cursing the police too, because we'd just been having some fun and they'd broken up the party just when everything was starting to focus on me.

There was quite a bit of explaining to do as well, as I'd left my muddy shoes by the door and my jacket was still covered in pine needles when Mum came in with a cup of tea in the morning. I admitted more or less what I'd been up to, leaving out only the filthy details, earning myself an exasperated lecture about growing up and finding more responsible company.

I took a long bath and spent the rest of the morning in my bedroom, reading magazines and slowly letting my body return to normal. Lunch made me feel a lot better, and my thoughts turned to my date with Stephen that evening. He was picking me up, so I had plenty of time and spent the afternoon slobbing about the house and playing cards with my sisters.

Eventually I decided it was time to get ready, but I wasn't at all sure how I should dress. My work suit was far too formal, not to mention in need of cleaning, although one of the white blouses I wore with it seemed a much better choice than the sort of top I normally wore, most of which advertised punk bands or were deliberately ripped up. Underwear was equally tricky, as I knew full well my clothes would be coming off and I'd probably be staying the night. Stephen seemed to like sensible knickers, but I wanted something a little daring, and in the end I decided on the matching dove-grey set Archie had given me for Christmas and which I'd never worn because I knew he'd only chosen it so he could perve over the thought of me wearing it. Using it specifically for the pleasure of another man at least diluted that feeling. That left a skirt or trousers, an even more difficult choice. Jeans didn't feel right and micro skirts held together with safety pins definitely weren't, which pretty well exhausted my wardrobe. In the end I borrowed a long blue and gold gypsy skirt from Mum.

A touch of make-up and I was ready, but as I waited for him I was feeling only marginally less conspicuous than I did in my work suit, which wasn't helped by my sisters who wouldn't stop teasing me. Fortunately it wasn't too long before he turned up, in a suit as usual, but a casual flannel one that made him look as if he was just off to watch the boat race or something. Mum was immediately fussing around him like an old hen, offering tea and biscuits and even telling me, in front of him, that I should behave myself properly during the evening. That showed just how much she knew, or maybe not, as I was sure Archie was an out-and-out pervert and she always seemed to pick men like that.

We finally managed to pull ourselves away, with Mum still cooing and ahing over Stephen's Saab, so that I couldn't get a word in edgeways until he'd actually turned the engine on.

'Sorry about Mum, she's always like that.'

'A charming woman, your mother.'

'Humph. So where do you live?'

'Brettenham.'

'That's on the far side of Thetford, isn't it?'

'Yes, but it's all right as long as the dual carriageway is clear.'

He'd let the clutch in as we spoke, and we turned into town, then east towards Thetford. As usual he was driving fast and slowing for the cameras, prompting me to tease him about his attitude.

'I don't suppose you're thinking of going into speed cameras too, from the way you treat the things?'

He laughed.

'I have considered it, actually. Digital units would be so much more efficient, and can even be co-ordinated with the ZX system.'

'But you don't like getting caught, do you?'

'Naturally not.'

'So how are you different from the scallies in Hockford?'

'Because my actions don't impose a cost on society. Yes, if I drove down Hockford High Street at seventy I would fully deserve to be caught and fined, even banned, but I don't. Did you know that the thirty mph limit was introduced in nineteen thirty-four? Brakes were far less efficient then, but of course there's always the chance of some idiot not looking where they're going. Here, on a straight road in a modern car with an experienced driver, fifty is frankly ridiculous.'

As if to illustrate his point he sped up, the needle already touching eighty as we passed the Sariton turning. I'd done the ton on the same road several times, so could hardly protest his point, but he did seem to have a pretty cavalier attitude. I thought of something else.

'So how about sex? What if the system catches a couple having a cuddle on the river path and they end up getting fined for indecent exposure or whatever it would be. They haven't imposed a cost on society, have they?'

'That's debatable. Personally, I agree, and I would drop all laws relating to public nudity and intimacy unless it is clearly intended to be threatening. Mrs Shelby, on the other hand, says ... what was it, "inappropriate behaviour for a family town" or something like that. I'm not quite sure what a family town is, as you would have thought all towns were family towns, but still. Mr Phelps is almost equally vehement, although his main concern is to discourage teenage sex.'

'He's one to talk. He reads dirty magazines.'

'He does?'

I back-peddled hastily.

'That's what I heard. I don't know, but sometimes I think the council go over the top.'

'Oh, absolutely, I couldn't agree more. In fact I, and you, we make our living because councils are inclined to go over the top.'

'That's true, I suppose, but what about the people who get fined when they're not really hurting anybody?'

He just shrugged, consummately indifferent, but spoke again once he'd overtaken a lorry.

'I have no sympathy at all with vandals and so forth, while people like that gay couple we saw will just have to learn not to do it anywhere they might cause offence. The Breckland is huge, after all, and not even Hockford Council could cover the whole of it with cameras. They have no right to anyway, as most of it's owned by the Forestry Commission.'

Again he went quiet, and I relaxed back in my seat, watching the numbers that mark the logging tracks sweep past. It was hard to pick a fault with his argument, but the whole thing still touched a raw nerve inside me. After a while he spoke again.

'Do I get the impression that my innocent little Felicity rather enjoys the idea of sex *al fresco*?'

'Perhaps she does.'

'I suspect rather more, and who knows, perhaps I can accommodate you one day.'

He finished with his dirty little chuckle, and I felt my sex tighten even as I thought of what a condescending bastard he was. I could picture it all too easily though, outdoors somewhere, first my bottom laid bare for a spanking, perhaps even in view of a path so there was a risk that somebody might see and think I was really being punished, which was a thought to set my stomach churning. Then, once my bottom was nice and hot he'd lead me deeper in among the trees, perhaps with my knickers still down, and there, he would fuck me.

Again he chuckled, as if he'd been reading my mind, and I found myself blushing. He really was a pig, but for some strange reason that turned me on, while the way he behaved towards me normally also seemed to make the dirty, humiliating sex more acceptable. In any event, I wanted it.

What I didn't want to do was talk, but he made me feel confused, so I turned the music up and tried to relax and not think about having my bottom smacked as we drove east, soon joining the A11 to get around Thetford. At Brettenham we turned off the main road immediately beyond the sign for the village, down a narrow but newly asphalted track which came to an end at a cluster of old red-brick and flint buildings set around a cobbled yard, obviously an old mill. There was even a great rotting wheel to one side, while the grind stone had been used to make a fountain at the centre of the courtyard. Stephen brought the Saab to a halt, and there was more than a little satisfaction in his voice as we got out.

'Here we are.'

'This is your flat?'

'I live in the upper part.'

He made a casual gesture to a long, red roof set with what were obviously new skylights. I'd expected a flat much like the ones I'd been into in Hockford, either the lower or upper storey of a house, or possibly within a modern block, and certainly nothing so expensive-looking. A wooden stair led up to the door, again new but made as if it was original, while there was a general air of understated wealth to the whole place. I didn't like to ask what it had cost, as Stephen didn't choose to tell me as we climbed the stair, instead gesturing out across the river to a jumble of woods and fields.

'We're a trust, and we've bought up both banks as well as the original plot of land, just in case the damn government decides to build all over it.'

The door swung open and I followed him inside. It was a single long room, all scrubbed brick, flint and polished wood, with chunky, cream-coloured furniture and bits of expensive-looking equipment scattered around. I went to the music system, hoping to find a bit of old-style punk in among his huge collection of CDs, but he immediately moved next to me, his voice more than a little nervous as he spoke.

'It's Sachs and Johansen, brand new and a bit complicated. What would you like, a touch of Vivaldi perhaps?'

I'd met enough men who were overprecious of their gear, Steve included, and stepped away.

'I don't know. Maybe something with a bit more ... a bit more guts?'

'Ah, ha, Wagner!'

'I was thinking more Stranglers, or maybe Scissor Girls?'

'I fear I have neither, although I did once possess a vinyl copy of Rattus Norvegicus passed down to me by my brother. They have a certain raw energy, I will admit, but as one matures so does one's appreciation in music.'

'Mine hasn't changed.'

'You're still young, of course, but weren't you listening to the latest boy band a few years ago?'

'No.'

'In that case you showed unusually good taste, and no doubt will come to appreciate Herr Wagner.'

'Wasn't he a bit of a Nazi?'

'Good heavens, no. He died in eighteen eighty-three, before Hitler was even born, I think. Don't they teach history at all in schools these days?'

I decided not to press the point and retreated to the sofa, which was huge and comfortable. There was no sign of a bed, and I was wondering where he slept, only to realise that what I'd taken for an alcove in the corner concealed a spiral staircase, presumably leading up to another level. The music started, at very low volume, but Stephen was pretending to conduct with one finger as he moved towards the kitchen area.

'We have music, now wine and food, and the evening will be complete.'

'Sex?'

'Patience, my dear. I hope you like gnocchi?'

'I don't know, I've never had them.'

'No? I'm surprised. Your mother has excellent taste.'

'Mum doesn't really go in for fancy cooking. She prefers to go out.'

'A shame. It is a rare chef who can equal what is possible at home, if only due to considerations of time and volume.'

As he spoke he had begun to set out implements and ingredients on his stone worktop, but suddenly stopped and ducked down to the fridge, speaking again as he removed a small brown bottle.

'I do apologise, I'm forgetting myself. A little manzanilla as an aperitif?'

'Thanks.'

He poured two glasses of pale sherry. It was dry and very cold, refreshing and with a slight burn of alcohol. I swallowed mine down, causing him to raise his eyebrows.

'One sips it, generally, and my preparations will take a while.'

I accepted a second glass, relaxing into the sofa and wondering about my own reactions as I sipped my sherry. He was so arrogant, and not me in so many ways, yet it was so easy to just let him take over. Then there was the sex, and the way something about him made me want to give in completely, to be down on my knees with my mouth full of cock, or over his knee with my bottom spanked hot.

All I'd had to eat was a packet of crisps at lunchtime, and I could already feel the sherry going to my head, making me feel mellow as he fussed over his preparations, talking all the while. He'd opened another bottle too, this one of an Italian red wine that looked strong. I knew I'd be drunk before the end of the evening, and I knew I'd be staying.

The gnocchi turned out to be little cheese-flavoured dumplings, which he served with smoked ham and spicy sausage, all delicious but not really very filling. By the time we'd finished I was hoping he'd produce some pudding, or preferably huge bowls of chocolate-chip ice cream, but he merely poured out the rest of the bottle into our glasses and moved from the table to the sofa, motioning me to join him. I followed, lying against him with my head nuzzled into the crook of his arm, quite relaxed, but wondering if he'd left me less than full so I'd be ready for sex. It seemed like just the sort of thing he'd do, but he was still talking about food.

'. . . the Italians immerse themselves in cooking in a way we British seldom if ever do, although it's peculiar, as we have if anything rather more of a variety of national styles. I suppose industrialisation was the death of British cooking, or very nearly so, but then again one could hardly classify the Italians as purely rustic.'

As he spoke his hand had moved to my breast, fondling me in a casual, possessive manner, first as if checking for quality, and then to make my nipple erect. I couldn't help but giggle and relaxed a little more, happy to have him toy with me. He was still talking as he began to unbutton my blouse, exposing my bra and tugging it gently up to leave my breasts bare and both nipples poking up in excitement. At the sight he gave the dirty little chuckle I was getting used to and went back to fondling me as he finally acknowledged what we were doing.

'You are truly beautiful, Felicity, and what is more important, sensual. So many women these days feel the need to make a production of their sexuality, but you know how to give into a man gracefully, which is infinitely more arousing.'

For him, maybe it was true. I certainly felt surrendered, lying against his body as he casually teased my naked breasts, and under his control as he guided my hand to his fly. I took him out, my eyes closed as I stroked his cock and balls, relaxing towards what I hoped would be a slow, intimate sexual encounter, quite willing for him to take the lead just so long as I reached orgasm and was given a certain little treat which was making my tummy flutter in anticipation.

'You are going to spank me, aren't you?'

'Say that again, would you?'

'You're a pervert, Stephen English. You are going to spank me, aren't you?'

'Naturally I shall spank you, but I am no pervert, simply a man, and any man with blood in his veins would want to spank you, Felicity.'

'You're the first.'

'Which merely shows what poor specimens of men you have found before, but I fear that is the general rule these days. Come along then.'

He moved as he spoke. I'd been quite happy where I was and about to crawl over his legs to have my bottom seen to while I played with his cock, but he had other ideas. He lifted me from the sofa with his normal lack of effort and I realised I was to be carried up to bed, squeaking in alarm as he slung me across his shoulder, leaving my bum the highest part of my body as he gave each cheek a single firm pat.

It was almost as undignified as getting into a spanking position, but I didn't mind, not even pretending to fight as he carried me up the stairs, removing his hand from my bottom only when he needed a grip on the banister. Only when he'd dumped me unceremoniously on his bed did I get to see his bedroom, a big, round chamber that had to be under the central, conical roof of the old mill. The walls were scrubbed brick, the furniture very plain and masculine, the bed huge and covered with a thick off-white spread. It was the perfect place for me to give in to his will. I rolled over, bottom up, and reached back to tug my skirt high, showing my legs and the seat of my knickers. He laughed as he sat down.

'Eager little thing, aren't you?'

I nodded, knowing it was true, however patronising his words. His hand found my bottom, squeezing one cheek through my knickers, applying a pat, and a second. I lifted my hips, my eyes now closed, wanting a slow, sensual spanking like the one he had first given me. He continued to smack, on my bottom and on my thighs too, using the tips of his fingers to make my skin sting and tingle. I reached back, taking hold of my knickers and pulling them up between my cheeks, deliberately showing off for him. Now he was smacking my bare bottom, still with his fingertips, and a moment later he had climbed on the bed, his voice curt as he pushed his half stiff cock at my face.

'Take me in your mouth. Suck me while I spank you.'

He didn't need to tell me. My mouth was already

open, and I took him in, sucking eagerly to make him swell as his hand continued to work on my bottom. I was still holding my knickers up between my cheeks, tight over my pussy, but he took over, tugging on them as he smacked me. He really was an utter pervert, getting off on playing with my knickers and spanking me while I sucked his cock, but knowing that just made it feel even better.

Soon he was hard in my mouth, while I was beginning to warm behind, my bottom flushed and my pussy ready to take him in. I hoped he'd put me on my knees and spank me while he fucked me, but he simply gave me a last, harder smack and moved back, looking down on my half-naked, aroused body with an amused, proprietorial air. He nodded.

'Yes, quite beautiful. Have you ever been caned, Felicity?'

'Caned? Like, with a stick?'

'Yes, essentially, but with a proper school cane.'

'I'd never been spanked before I met you. How much does it hurt?'

'A lot, I won't lie to you, but I think you might come to like it. Or rather, come to like it and hate it at the same time, which is the essence of accepting corporal punishment.'

I nodded, because I already understood what he meant, just as the spankings filled me with shame and resentment and fear at the same time as desire and longing. He had already taken my response as assent, tucking his cock carefully back inside his trousers and pulling up his fly as he climbed off the bed. There was a big chest of drawers on the far side of the room, and he crossed to it, opening the bottom one to extract a long, pale cane with a crook handle. I'd never seen one before except in cartoons and swallowed as I thought of having it put across my bottom.

'I'm not sure . . .'

'Shh, darling, just do as you're told, and you can stop any time you want. Now stand up.'

He had closed the drawer and now flexed the cane, every bit like a stern young headmaster except that his erection was making a hard bar in his trousers. I got up, shaking badly and biting my lip, but wanting it too, at least to try, and telling myself I should take one stroke at the very least. He gave a small, complacent nod as he saw that I was willing, and pointed to the exact centre of the room.

'Knickers down, Felicity, and touch your toes.'

As always when he gave me a command it sent a shock straight to my sex, and this time there was real fear too. My movements seemed mechanical as I got off the bed and adopted the exposed, pitiful position he had commanded, with my naked breasts hanging down between the open sides of my blouse, my skirt turned up at the back and my bottom pushed out in acceptance of what he was planning to do to me. As I pushed my knickers down to show him the target my fingers were shaking so hard I could barely control them, and yet I made a point of doing it properly, because I knew he would want the lips of my sex and the tiny star between my bottom cheeks to be showing. That was all part of my surrender, which was complete as I touched my fingers to the toes of my shoes. He gave a cluck of satisfaction and that same dirty chuckle, then spoke.

'Hmm, very good, Felicity, and may I compliment you on how sweet you look? I like a girl in punishment position to have her breasts showing. It adds a certain something. You have such a fine bottom too, and such a neatly turned cunt. You should be on display more often. Now, the cane. Six of the best is, I believe, traditional for naughty girls.'

Every word he spoke sent a fresh pang of shame-filled excitement through me. Part of me was screaming that he shouldn't be getting his perverted kicks out of my body, but still I held that awful pose as he tapped the cane across my bottom cheeks. Even that stung, the gentlest touch, making my muscles twitch, then he had lifted the cane and I was whimpering into my dress where it hung down to block my view.

For one eternal moment of terrified anticipation nothing happened, before I heard the swish and felt the hardness of the cane slap down across the bare, soft flesh of my bottom. It hurt so much, making me gasp and swear, calling him a pig and a bastard and a pervert, but I never broke my pose, holding myself ready in pain and indignity, because what he was doing to my body and my head was beyond anything I had experienced before short of actual orgasm.

'Good girl, and a nice, neat welt if I say so myself. Five more.'

As he spoke his words were soothing, but I could hear the mockery and the sadistic glee beneath, and let nobody tell you that it's a contradiction to hurt the one you love and to enjoy it. Stephen did, and I was enjoying being hurt, as once more I heard that awful swish and felt the cane cut across my naked cheeks, harder this time, to leave me dancing on my toes as well and gasping and wiggling my bum in a pointless attempt to make the pain go away. Again Stephen spoke.

'Very pretty, my dear. I do like a girl who responds well to punishment. Four more.'

I tried to answer him, but my words came as a broken sob and once more I'd put my fingertips to the toes of my shoes. The cane touched my bottom, a tap, lifted and swished down to lay a third line of fire across my cheeks. Again I cried out and again I gave my rude little wiggle, making him laugh once more.

'Perfect, you really are perfect in every way. You should be punished like this more often, preferably in front of a good-sized audience so that everybody can appreciate what a nice bottom you have, and how well you dance.'

'You bastard, you'd do it too, wouldn't you?'

'Certainly, it's only a shame the authorities take such a foolish view of such things.'

I screamed again as the cane bit in, completely unexpectedly and lower than before, to leave a fourth burning line across my flesh. My bottom was on fire, hotter even than when he'd given me my punishment spanking, but still I stayed in position, determined to take my full six, from pride and obstinacy, but most of all because only if I knew that I'd been properly beaten would I be able to give in completely once I was done. Again he spoke.

'Yes, I'd love to parade you naked in the High Street and cane you, just like this, only with a hundred people looking on. Two to go.'

Again the cane whipped down and again I screamed, this time losing control completely and jumping up to clutch at my hot bottom. He waited patiently while I went through my little act, his mouth set in a small, cruel smile, the horrible cane dangling negligently from his fingers. It was almost too much, but finally I managed to adopt my punishment pose once more, now gasping for breath even before he'd hit me.

'One to go, Felicity.'

He came close, to touch my bottom, running his fingers gently over the stinging welts that now decorated my flesh, five in all, which I knew would mark me for a week or more, mark me as his, mark me as a girl who got caned for kicks. After a moment his fingers pushed between my cheeks, spread them to show me off as he spoke.

'Ah, ha, your bottom hole has started to wink, always a sign that you're ready, I find.'

'You pig, you fucking pig . . .'

'Language, my dear, really. I can see you actually deserve this.'

As he spoke he'd let go of my bottom and lifted the cane above me, leaving me shaking my head and wiggling my toes in terrified anticipation for an instant before he brought it down, harder than ever and full across both cheeks, to leave me screaming and wiggling in frantic, pained reaction, but only for an instant before I dropped to my knees.

He came close, cool and easy as I scrabbled for his cock, the cane he'd beaten me with still hanging from his hand as I freed him into my mouth, then sucking urgently as I clutched at my hurt bottom. I could feel the welts, the welts he'd given me. A man had beaten me, used the cane on my bare bottom, humiliated me utterly, hurt me, and I was sucking on his cock in frenzied passion, completely subservient to him.

I'd have come, like that, sucking on his cock as I stroked my poor burning bottom and rubbed at my sex, but he had other ideas. He was barely fully hard in my mouth again before he lifted me and tossed me casually onto the bed. My ankles were taken in his hands, my body rolled up and opened, my skirt left like a huge flower with my welted bottom and my sex at the centre. He was looking down at me, admiring what he'd done as he entered me, pushing deep and setting up a steady rhythm that immediately had me gasping and shaking.

My hand went down, to touch myself, eager to come as I was fucked. He slapped it, just gently, and pulled out again, turning me onto my knees with my punished bottom stuck high as he took me from behind. Again I tried to get to myself, and again he stopped me, driving my frustration and need higher still as he eased himself in and out of my body.

I was begging for release, but he did it again, and yet again, manipulating my body as if I was a doll, and again and again taking my hand away from where it so badly needed to be. I was put on my back, my front, my side, on my knees and bent over the bed, mounted on him but still with my bottom showing, fucked deep and slow, his cock rubbed on my clitoris, his finger put in my bottom hole, my breasts fucked and my mouth, until at last he put me back on my knees and told me I could come.

Immediately I was babbling my thanks, with my fingers busy between my thighs even as he slid himself into me. My spare hand went back to touch my cane welts and I was masturbating as he fucked me, my head full of what he'd done, how he'd made me pose, how he'd beaten me, how he'd left me with my bottom decorated with the welts from his cane.

I have never come so hard, screaming and calling him every filthy name I could think of even as I wriggled on his cock, at once cursing him and telling him I loved him, calling him a bastard and demanding he spank me, yelling at him for using me so hard and begging him to come for me, which he did, driving my orgasm to a final blinding peak as the hot droplets spattered my upturned bottom cheeks.

9

It had been quite a weekend, the way a weekend should be, only distinctly weird. I'd made one male friend suck another's cock, and if that was bad, well then, my bottom was decorated with six neat, parallel red lines. That was the major experience. I'd been caned, beaten, punished. I'd allowed a man to put a stick across my bare bottom. You just do not do that nowadays, or if you do you end up on an assault charge. Stephen English had done it to me, and yet I could not find it in myself to be unhappy about it.

We slept together too, and when we had sex again, much later, it was very different, intimate and loving, cuddled close together in the warm darkness of his bedroom, and completely uninhibited. Even then I knew I could never have opened myself up to him so fully without my earlier caning.

I spent most of Sunday there, half of it just padding naked around his flat, which felt completely natural, while every time I caught a glimpse of my stripy bottom in the mirror it made me smile at my memories of the night before. Not that I really needed to see, because my welts still smarted, keeping me constantly in mind of the fact that I'd been caned. I even let him take a picture of me, to his personal direction, standing in the corner of his main room with my hands on my head and my face turned back towards the camera in a sulky pout, stark naked so that it was completely obvious what had been done to me.

He finally drove me back after lunch at the local pub, and I simply collapsed on my bed at home, face down. By the time I woke up it was nearly dark, and my memories of the night before seemed oddly hazy, as if none of it had ever happened. It was the same next morning, and I was actually feeling shy as I walked across the Hereward towards Black Knight Securities.

Stephen was the same as ever, almost, greeting me with a kiss and a pat to my bottom, but otherwise very much my boss rather than my lover. Paul was there too, and had apparently been told by Mr Phelps that the council had as good as accepted their system. It only needed to be rubber-stamped by the relevant committee and we would have the contract.

That meant updating the plans for installing the system throughout Hockford and the surrounding area, as Mr Phelps and his cronies wanted various changes and additions. It was all rather a rude shock to me, but there was nothing to be done but get on with my work and try to ignore the tender feeling every time I sat down. I'd lost, so it seemed, and all I could do was warn people and attempt to influence the final positioning of the cameras.

As it turned out, I could do better than that. I had the plans on my computer, and it was part of my job to print them out, which gave me the ideal opportunity. I made the changes while Stephen and Paul were sorting out which boxes we'd need in the warehouse; nothing major, hopefully nothing obvious, but just enough to allow Steve his short cut and make sure one or two crucial places weren't covered.

I felt bad as I did it, and repeatedly had to tell myself it made no difference to Black Knight Securities, let alone Stephen personally, but only to the council. That didn't stop my heart staying firmly in my mouth as I worked, or my worry once I'd done it and the sheets were squeezing out of the printer at what seemed a painfully slow speed. Neither Stephen nor Paul emerged from the warehouse, and as I soon as I was done I put one set into the file and the other into a big brown envelope. It was at least another ten minutes before Stephen came out.

'Are you finished, Felicity?'

'Yes, Mr English.'

He smiled at the way I said it, making my voice deliberately subservient, and allowed his hand to stray to the curve of my bottom as he came to stand by my chair, idly kneading one cheek even as he continued.

'Good. Would you mind running it over to the council offices? I'd prefer it delivered by hand, and if Paul or I go Phelps is sure to bombard us with questions.'

'Of course, Mr English.'

'Will you stop talking like that, or I might be tempted to put you across my knee right now.'

'Yes, please.'

His eyebrows rose and he wagged a finger at me, but I was already gathering up the envelope. I'd been play-acting, partly to hide my nervousness, but as I left the office I was reflecting that if I'd ever really deserved a spanking it was right now. But I wasn't going to get it, not for that anyway. I'd changed the master copy, and as Paul and Stephen had been so busy it was very unlikely they'd notice my changes unless the council complained, which again seemed unlikely.

It was only a short walk to the council offices, and

as luck would have it Mr Phelps was in the office car park, talking to Mr Burrows. They were standing next to a shiny red 4×4, and for once Phelps was smiling. I caught his voice as I approached.

'... won't be so easy to steal. The security system is top of the range.'

Mr Burrows gave a doubtful frown.

'I thought you left your keys in the car last time?'

'Well, yes, but ... What can I do for you, Miss Cotton?'

'I have the final proposal for the complete ZX system, Mr Phelps. Pardon me for eavesdropping, but had it already been installed, whoever stole your car would undoubtedly have been caught.'

'I know that, Miss Cotton. Good. I feel confident about this one, Geoffrey. It has the potential to make a real difference, both to crime rates and in terms of cost benefits ...'

He was talking to Mr Burrows, not even bothering to thank me as he walked away. I ignored the temptation to run a key along the side of his shiny new car, but only because I was right under one of the old cameras. Instead I started back, only to hesitate. It was lunch time, to all intents and purposes, and Stephen wasn't to know I'd delivered the plans so quickly. I might easily have been kept waiting to see Mr Phelps, for ten minutes, twenty minutes, perhaps even half an hour.

It had been a stressful morning, and the thought of a glass of cold vodka and lime in the Bull directly across the road was too much for me. With luck Stephen would arrive a few minutes after one and buy me lunch. I could tell him I'd only just left the council offices. To think was to act, and two minutes later I was sitting in a window alcove watching the world go by and sipping my drink.

I had done what I could, for the time being anyway, and I felt reasonably content, or at least resigned. I was telling myself that maybe Mum was right and it was time I began to behave with a bit more restraint, as she liked to put it. Not that bonking Archie Feltham was particularly restrained, but it did at least mean she could hardly complain about what I got up to with Stephen. I knew she might do anyway, especially if she discovered I got spanked, a thought that made me cringe with embarrassment. Evidently I'd have to be careful, especially walking around with a bruised bum.

My drink was only a little less than half full and it was still a few minutes before one when I saw Stephen approaching. He was alone, and I smiled and waved from the window, causing him to glance at his watch and lift one eyebrow. As soon as he came in he walked around to my alcove and I immediately found myself apologising.

'I'm sorry, I didn't think it would matter as . . .'

He raised a hand.

'Don't worry, not at all. Five minutes one way or the other is hardly the end of the world, and anyway, I think we both know the best way of dealing with minor infractions. What are you drinking?'

'Vodka and lime.'

He turned for the bar, leaving me with a now familiar sense of unease in my tummy. It was obvious what he meant, that my little piece of cheek was going to cost me a spanking. Soon he was back, and I pointed out something he seemed to have overlooked.

'I'm still a little sore.'

'I'm sure you are. But never mind, I prefer to start on pristine skin and it's fun to make you wait as well.'

'Sadist.'

'Absolutely. Now let me see. Going to lunch early without permission, not an especially serious offence. Let's just say a spanking, on the bare naturally. If you do it again, you'll get the cane.'

I nodded and swallowed. He was making no effort at all to conceal his delight, both in what he was going to do and in his power over me. Already my tummy was fluttering badly with the same mixture of resentment, apprehension and arousal welling up with astonishing speed. Stephen smiled as he sat back, took a moment to immerse his nose into his wine glass, then spoke again.

'Not bad at all, if rather young and a trifle oaky for my palate. Would you like some lunch?'

'Yes, thank you.'

He'd changed the subject casually and completely in his normal infuriating manner, as if the things that were so strong for me were of no more importance to him than what wine he happened to be drinking. Only as he went on did I realise that he was actually being anything but unemotional.

'Felicity ... I enjoyed our weekend immensely, and ... and I think I may fairly say that you possess a unique combination of innocence and, well, lewdness frankly, and please don't be offended when I say that.'

'I'm not, not at all.'

'Good. The thing is then, I mean to say, without being presumptuous, can I assume you're not in a serious relationship at all? You mentioned an American airman, I think?'

'Martin, yes. I doubt I'll be seeing him again. He was too possessive.'

'Ah ha, you dislike possessive men then?'

'If they think they can take me out on a couple of dates and then start ordering me around, yes.'

'Are you not interested in . . .'

He broke off as Paul appeared at his elbow, placing a large camera box on the table, the new ZX-6 he'd ordered, and within moments we were talking shop.

I was sure Stephen had been going to ask me if I wanted to make our relationship official, perhaps even exclusive. Unfortunately with the amount of work on and the council constantly wanting to check over a wealth of tiny details, we didn't get a chance to talk alone for the rest of the day. By the evening we were both exhausted, and while I'd have been happy to go for a drink after work he simply gave me his usual combination of a kiss and a pat and left.

The next day was the same, worse if anything, with Mr Phelps there half the day going over the plan. He'd written all over it, suggesting all sorts of changes, but in doing so completely obscuring the ones I'd already made. A few of mine were undone, but he'd missed the most important one completely, as did Stephen and Paul, leaving me as full of mischief and guilt as ever. Again I was hoping Stephen would suggest going out after work, but this time Paul wanted to talk to him and I ended up excusing myself.

I was feeling frustrated as I walked up the High Street, wondering exactly what he'd intended to say and how I should respond. He had brought out feelings in me like no other man, with the possible exception of Steve, who hardly counted. He had definitely done things to me like no other man, Steve included, and if they were distinctly kinky then I had to admit they were very nice too. On the other hand I wasn't really in love, because if I had been I was sure I'd have felt I wanted to be faithful to him for the sake of it, and I didn't. If I was faithful it would be for his sake, which again gave me mixed feelings.

My head was completely in the clouds, so much so that I didn't even notice the little knot of American servicemen gathered near the base of Town Bridge. I was almost on top of them before one spoke to me, and even then I had to do a double take before I realised who it was: Martin.

'Um . . . hi.'

'Hi, Fizz. You OK?'

His friends were exchanging knowing grins and quickly moved back to let us talk. I wasn't at all sure what to say, but he was being friendly and when he asked the crucial question there was no malice in his voice at all.

'What's this I've been hearing?'

'About what? No, I know. I suppose Billy's been telling you that I'm a cheating bitch, but it's not like that at all. I didn't know you wanted to be serious, and how was I to know you'd gone to Afghanistan, and . . .'

'Hey, cool down. I'm not pissed with you.'

'No?'

'No, that's just Billy. Where he comes from if you wink at a guy he'll probably decide you're his for life. That's not me.'

'Oh . . . good.'

'Since we're on the subject, what's the deal?'

I shrugged, not really sure. Stephen and I were getting serious, but I didn't want to commit myself when nothing had been said, or end up having either of them accusing me of being unfair to them. He spoke again before I could decide what to say.

'Do you want to see me again, or what?'

'I want to see you, yes ... of course I do, but it's all got rather complicated.'

'Tell me about it. Let's walk.'

He started down the steps to the river path. I hesitated, but we were already on camera. I followed, but when he tried to put his arm around me I detached it gently.

'What's the matter?'

'Nothing, except that we're being watched.'

He glanced back to the ZX-4 on the bridge.

'That's not covering us.'

'No, but at least two others are. My company's got a pilot scheme running right along this path.'

'But we ...'

'That was just before they were put up. If we did that now we'd be giving a live show, not just to my bosses either, but half the nosy bastards on the council, and the police.'

'Shit! Thanks for the warning.'

'The whole town will be covered in a few weeks, and all the local lay-bys and stuff.'

'You're kidding?'

'No. Look, Martin, I don't know what Billy told you, but this is how it stands. I'm seeing my boss, Stephen, but it's not official or anything, not yet.'

'You mean another guy might still get a look in?'

'Something like that.'

He laughed.

'You're honest, I'll give you that.'

'Not really. I just hate big emotional crises and stuff. I've never understood why people can't just have fun together, as friends, without getting jealous.'

'That's nature, I guess.'

'Do you think so? I think it's just the way we're brought up, like sex has to be such a big deal all the time. I've never felt I wanted to be faithful to one man, not ever.'

'Maybe you just haven't met the right man?'

'Maybe.'

We'd reached Foulds', out of sight of his mates but not the cameras. By the time we'd got to the bridge across towards the Blue Boar I'd made a decision, and took his arm as soon as we were safely into the fields. He didn't say anything or try to push it, accepting my gesture at face value. By then he was telling me what it had been like in Afghanistan, which was both fascinating and horrible, making me feel that my own concerns were really trivial.

I'd originally been meaning to go to the pub, but we crossed the road and walked up into the Breckland. It was a beautiful evening, soft and warm, making it very easy to relax after spending the whole day running around at work. When Martin finally decided to kiss me I gave in immediately, allowing him to take over. He'd steered me off the path, to a little glade where he laid me down among the long grass, still kissing me as he fumbled open the buttons of my blouse. I was enjoying being undressed, and much too into him to think of anything else, until he was easing my knickers down under my skirt. As he cupped one cheek in a massive hand I felt my bruises, my skin still ridged from the six cane welts. A moment later he'd sat up, quickly rolling me face down to inspect my bottom even as I gave a protesting squeak. My knickers were still down, and it was too late.

'Shit! What bastard did that to you?'

'It wasn't like that, Martin, it was ...'

I broke off, sure he wouldn't understand and with a horrible picture of him punching Stephen's lights out, which I was sure he could do, and easily. The next moment I was babbling, making it up as I went along and saying anything but the truth.

'... it was just a game, between me and ... and my friend Josie, you know, from the band. We got a bit drunk, and ... and she wanted to play forfeits, you know, when you have to tell a secret or do something ...'

'What, like truth or dare?'

'Yes, like that, and she ...'

'You played truth or dare and you got your butt whacked?'

His voice had changed completely, from aggression to amusement. Evidently it was all right for me to get caned, so long as it was from another girl. I managed a wry smile.

'Yes, six.'

'I can see that. Ouch! What was the truth?'

'Something really secret.'

'I guess it must have been.'

His hand was on my bottom, very gently touching my cane marks and shaking his head in astonishment for what I'd supposedly let Josie do to me. It felt quite nice, but from his initial tone it didn't seem likely that he'd be prepared to give me anything similar. Or so I thought, until he spoke again.

'So what, did she make you take your panties down?'

'Hey! I thought you were concerned about me?'

'Yeah, well ... if someone had done that to you when you didn't want it, I'd break his face, but seeing it was a game ...'

He trailed off, still stroking my bottom. I wasn't sure what to say for a moment, but it was probably obvious that I'd been done on the bare, while the thought seemed to turn him on.

'Yes, she made me take my knickers down.'

'She's a dyke, yeah?'

'Yes.'

It was true, although beyond touching my tits up on stage she'd never tried it on with me, and that was really just part of the act with Rubber Dollies. She'd never expressed the slightest interest in spanking or caning, to me or anyone else. Yet it obviously turned him on and I was enjoying the attention to my bottom. He was growing more intimate too, tickling me under my cheeks, and as I laid my chin on my hands I continued.

'You'd like to know, wouldn't you?'

'It's kind of horny, I guess, you know, two girls doing kinky stuff. I like that.'

'Yeah, you and every other man on this planet. OK, this is what she did. I had to bend over and touch my toes in front of her. She lifted my skirt up first, right up, then she took my knickers down, all the way, so everything showed. I had to stay like that while she fetched a cane ... a bamboo it was, out of a pot plant. She gave me six strokes, hard ones.'

'Looks it. I bet it hurt.'

'It stings like anything, but it's OK, afterwards at least, because it left my bum feeling sort of warm and glowy.'

'Yeah? So what, was that it, or did she hit on you?'

It was quite obvious that he wanted the answer to be yes, but it just didn't feel right and I decided to keep him guessing instead.

'Wouldn't you like to know?'

His eyes went round, obviously having reached his own conclusion. He blew his breath out as he rolled over into the grass. I too changed position, laughing at the thought of what would be going through his head and how easy it was to drive him wild. The bulge in his trousers was obvious to say the least, and I let my hand stray down, stroking him, which sent a little shock of pleasure through me. A moment later I'd unzipped him and he was bare in my hand, thick and dark and hot, his balls too, all of it protruding from the fly of his uniform. It's always my favourite, an otherwise fully dressed man with his cock and balls out, and what with airforce uniform and the sheer size of him, Martin was a perfect example. That was enough for me, the sheer physicality of it, but he had other ideas.

'Tell me about it while you do that.'

'You're a dirty old man, Martin, do you know that?'

As I spoke I began to masturbate him, trailing my fingers over the silky skin of his balls and up the shaft of his cock. He groaned in response, putting out one big arm to gather me in, his hand once more on my bottom, stroking my cheeks as he spoke again.

'Go on, Fizz, you can't leave me hanging like that.'

'Can't I?'

'Don't do this to me!'

I laughed again, amused by his urgency but still unsure. Josie was my friend and had always respected my sexuality, just as I respected hers. And yet it was only fantasy, just to get Martin even hotter.

'OK, but admit you're a dirty pig.'

'OK, OK, whatever.'

'Say it.'

'Jesus, Fizz! OK, I'm a dirty pig, now tell.'

'All right.'

I took hold of his cock, tugging firmly as he continued to fondle my behind. Not sure what to say, I decided to use my thoughts for how I liked to behave to Stephen after a punishment, only with Josie instead.

'When she beat me, it made me feel really horny, and sort of eager, like I wanted to do everything for her. She knew it too, and I reckon she set out to get me that way, because she started to give me orders. First she made me strip off, all the way, while she just sat back in her chair, watching me. Then I had to crawl across the floor to her, on my hands and knees, and turn around to show her my bum. She touched me up, just like you're doing, only putting her fingers everywhere, and I do mean everywhere.'

It was an invitation, and not one he was about to resist. Again he groaned, and his fingers were burrowing between my thighs, to cup my sex, masturbating me just as I was masturbating him. I gave a little wiggle against his hand as I went on, now thoroughly excited despite myself.

'She was really dirty with me, calling me her bitch and telling me how she would spank me regularly in future, always with my bum bare, and maybe in front of other people so everyone could see she was my boss. And when she'd had her fun with me she made me turn around again, and kneel at her feet while she took down her jeans and knickers. Then she made me lick her, Martin, she made me lick her pussy with my bum all hot behind where she'd caned me, all the way too, until she came . . .'

I broke off, my body tight in his grip from a spasm of pleasure like a mini orgasm. He was rubbing me hard, his thumb was on my bottom hole and I was wriggling into him, too high to care for anything but my pleasure. I was going to come, properly, and I couldn't get the images I'd made out of my head, of me crawling naked on the floor with six cane welts decorating my bottom as Josie pulled me in to make me lick her sex.

'You've made me do it, you bastard!'

With that I'd come, squirming myself onto Martin's busy hand as he brought me off, with my own hand squeezed tight on his cock. Before I'd even completely finished he was rolling on top of me, pushing my legs high and wrenching my half-lowered knickers further up, to hold me in place as he mounted me. For one moment I thought he was going to bugger me, because he seemed so obsessed with my bum, but he slid himself deep in the right hole, all the way, until his balls were pressed between my open cheeks.

He began to fuck me, fast and furious, setting me gasping and clutching at the grass, completely overwhelmed both mentally and physically, with my head full of shame and dirty thoughts just as my body was full of cock. I knew he'd be thinking the same too, of how my friend was supposed to have beaten me and made me crawl to her for a lick. It was just too dirty for me to hold back and, as he pulled out to finish himself off over my belly and thighs, my hand had gone back to my sex, rubbing hard to bring myself to my second orgasm within a minute or less.

My evening with Martin had been very good indeed, and not just the sex. Like Stephen, he could make me feel dirty and at ease with myself at the same time. That said, I was more than a little embarrassed at coming over the thought of Josie punishing me, which left me feeling seriously mixed up. Otherwise it had been great, and unlike Stephen, he treated me as fully equal.

On the other hand, he didn't and probably couldn't take me to that place I'd been when Stephen had punished me. That was an ecstasy beyond anything I'd experienced before, and which I'd been thinking about even as Martin made me come. I knew it was an addiction and maybe somewhere I shouldn't go, but I've never really been very good at making the sensible decision.

The very next afternoon, after a day's work only a little less trying than the one before, Stephen asked if I'd like to come to Cuatro Cortado with him. I accepted immediately, and was still trying to make up my mind what to say as we walked up the High Street together. He was as casual as ever, at least outwardly, discussing how he and Paul intended to use the camera system in Hockford as a showpiece for further sales and his hopes for company expansion. It had struck me before that if I had the sort of money he appeared to have I'd have taken it easy. This made me wonder what I might be getting myself into as we sat down with a bottle of a pale dry sherry between us. Unlike the dark stuff it was at least drinkable and had a good kick, while he assured me I'd eventually develop a taste for it. I decided to ask.

'How big do you want to get then? Wouldn't it be better to make enough money to be comfortable and then retire?'

'No, frankly, or at least not yet. I won't pretend money isn't important to me, but business is an end unto itself. If I wasn't involved with something I'd be climbing the walls in seconds. No, the knack is to build up a company until the major players in whatever market you've chosen start to take notice, when one of them is sure to try and buy me out. I always accept.'

'So you've done it before?'

'Twice now. The knack is to move with the times.'

He paused to fill our glasses and sat back, continuing with that same complacent certainty I always found so annoying and so compelling.

'I was at school in the eighties, when it was all about the stock market and business was actually seen as cool. I was too young to really benefit, but I did manage to get in right at the end of the yuppie boom and set enough aside to give me a start. When the housing market crashed I put everything into property, so that by the mid nineties I had a serious stake. Mobile phones were the big thing at the time, with the market growing at an astonishing rate. I teamed up with Paul, who as you know is far more technically minded than I am but has no real sense for business. We did very well, although with hindsight we could have pushed it a little further before selling up. That was the first time I used the magic formula, as my foray into the housing market doesn't really count.'

I was listening in fascination, amazed he could be so

casual, as if the whole thing was just a game. After a moment to savour his sherry he went on.

'That left us in a very healthy position. I invested enough to give myself a safety net, spent half a year in Europe just to soak up a little culture, and then had a crack at the new generation of computers – you know, flat-screen monitors and multi-gigabyte hard drives. Unfortunately there were just too many other people trying to do the same thing and it was hard to keep pace with the technology. We didn't actually make a loss, but it was hardly a great success. I then decided on security, which I think we can safely say will continue expanding for some years yet, and here I am.'

He smiled and lifted his glass once more. It sounded so easy, the way he said it, but I was thinking of one of Mum's exes, who'd always claimed to be on the verge of the next big thing but had ended up bankrupt. Evidently Stephen had a knack. I took a swallow of sherry, wondering how it would be to switch from employee to girlfriend. It would be an easy life, with no money worries, great sex and nothing to do but relax, or shop, or get drunk for the hell of it. Like him I might well be climbing the walls after a while, but there would surely be some way of keeping myself amused? He'd been fussing over his sherry, but began to talk again.

'Tell me about yourself then. How did you come to be living in Hockford?'

'There's not much to tell, really. My life's just been either boring or chaos.'

'Surely not? You're well spoken, well educated...'

'I was born in Hockford and I was at a really posh school when I was little, until I was eleven to be exact.

That's when Mum and Dad broke up after he lost his job as a manager at the shoe factory which used to be where the Hereward is now.'

'I fear such stresses are a frequent cause of divorce.'

'It was a bit more than that. Mum ... Mum likes her men, and she was already having an affair with a guy called Eddie French, only she kicked him out a few months after the divorce. It's been the same ever since, with one prat of a boyfriend after another. You've met Archie Feltham, haven't you?'

'He seems pleasant enough.'

'He's an idiot.'

'A little impractical, perhaps.'

'An idiot. And he's always leching after me, as if I'd go with a man his age!'

'I am somewhat older than you myself.'

'You're different. You don't seem old.'

'Hardly old.'

'Sorry. Older, anyway. Maybe it's just because Archie is Mum's boyfriend. Anyway, she's already starting to get bored of him, I know the signs. Sorry, I'm sure I'm boring you with my stupid life.'

'Not at all. I think you show remarkable strength of character in the circumstances. You're very much a free agent too. I admire that.'

He was right, in the sense that I don't let other people tell me what to do, although he was something of an exception. I'd finished my sherry and he refilled my glass, but not his own, explaining as he did so.

'Excellent though this fino is, I had better be careful. You, on the other hand, may drink as much as you please.'

'That depends how much work you expect to get out of me tomorrow morning.'

'If I get you drunk I can hardly complain if you have a hangover.'

'That's fair.'

He glanced at his watch.

'I should in fact be getting home. I have rather a fine escalope marinating in the fridge and it's calling to me.'

For one moment I thought he was going to avoid the crucial question yet again, only for him to continue.

'Quite a large escalope, in fact. I don't suppose you'd like to join me?'

'I'd like that very much.'

'Then perhaps if you would care to ring your mother, we shall be on our way. Bring the bottle.'

I did as I was told, cradling the still cold sherry bottle to my chest as he drove towards Brettenham at his normal high speed. He'd had his arm around me as we walked down to the car, and his conversation had begun to betray that same slight nervousness as he'd shown a few days before. Town had been thick with evening traffic as usual, and he had restricted his remarks to opinions of other drivers, but now he spoke to me again.

'Felicity, I shall say this now rather than later, because that way I can always drop you off by the roadside if the answer is no . . .'

He laughed, slightly strained, to show it was a joke.

'. . . but am I right in thinking you would like to stay more often, perhaps even every night?'

I'd made my decision already, and there was no hesitation in my answer.

'Yes, please, but you have to promise to spank me when I'm naughty.'

10

I woke the next morning with my future looking as rosy as my bottom. Stephen had made his promise and kept it, turning me across his knee after dinner for a long, sensuous spanking that had inevitably ended in sex. That had been the first time of several, both spankings and sex, although for me the two were now becoming inseparably intertwined. In the morning he'd asked if I would move in with him properly, and I'd agreed.

We hadn't bothered to thrash out the details, but I was sure that would all come with time. What mattered was that I was his girlfriend, I would be living with him, and I had decided I would also be faithful to him. After all, if we were living under the same roof it was hardly fair for me to spend my evenings joyriding or bonking American airmen. I still didn't feel he owned me, just that there ought to be a bit of give and take. Only one thing seemed to worry him at all, as he explained on the way into work.

'I still want you to work for us, of course, but inevitably this will change our day-to-day relationship.'

'I don't have to call you "Mr English" any more then?'

'Actually I'd rather you did, at least in front of these council types, and clients in general. You don't mind, do you?'

'No. It's fun really, because I'm calling you the same

thing in front of Mr Phelps and his lot as I do when you punish me.'

He laughed before answering me.

'Let's keep things more or less as they are then, only I'll bump up your salary a bit, of course.'

'That's very sweet of you, but it's really quite generous.'

Again he laughed, this time loudly.

'Felicity, darling, do you have any idea how much we're making?'

'I know the value of the council contract, yes, and how much the base units cost. Quite a bit, I suppose, but I haven't worked it out.'

'Quite a bit, yes, I suppose you could put it that way, and while your salary is perfectly fair it's hardly generous. You may as well have a car too while you're at it. You do drive, don't you?'

'Yes, but I'd rather buy one myself, if you don't mind. I'm a bit fussy, I suppose.'

'What did you have in mind?'

'I'm not sure. Something with style. A Morgan maybe, or an old-fashioned Jag.'

'Good heavens, you do have refined tastes!'

'I like cars, nice cars. I hate boxes on wheels.'

'Which is what you thought I was going to get you?'

'Oh ... no, sorry, I didn't mean to be rude ...'

'Tut, tut, Felicity, you really must mind your manners, but maybe a good spanking will help. That makes two I owe you, I believe.'

'What about last night?'

'Pure pleasure. However, we clearly need to distinguish between the two, so perhaps ... yes, that would be ideal. When we get home each evening we can settle any little matters of domestic discipline that may have come up.'

He finished with his characteristic chuckle, leaving me looking forward to a life of regular spankings with both apprehension and anticipation.

Things didn't really change much at all at work because there was simply too much going on to worry about the relationships between us, or even who was boss. If it was management, Stephen did it. If it was technical, Paul did it. Anything else, Fizz did it. I also seemed to have ended up as the one running backwards and forwards between the warehouse and the council offices, because while Mr Phelps was an ignorant pig, he was an ignorant pig to everybody, but Mr Burrows obviously fancied me and Mrs Shelby preferred dealing with a woman.

They seemed to want to speak to me every five minutes, and it was on one of my trips there and back that I ran into Pete and Dave, sitting together on a bench with cans of strong lager in their hands and a plastic carrier bag with yet more cans in it beside them. I'd spoken to them several times, but I hadn't seen them since they got arrested, and immediately found myself smiling in a mixture of embarrassment and sympathy.

'Hi, boys.'

It was Dave who answered, grinning.

'Hey, Fizz, you owe us, big time.'

I shrugged, hardly able to deny it outright but knowing I was going to have to turn them down. Pete added his opinion.

'Yeah, big, big time. The works, I reckon.'

'Sorry, boys, no can do.'

Dave looked hurt.

'What do you mean, no can do? You said you would, and I got nicked!'

'You got nicked for driving a car without tax and insurance or anything, Dave, not for being dirty with me.'

'Yeah, but you still owe us. For fuck's sake, I . . .'

He trailed off, unwilling to say it. I found myself trying not to laugh, but he did have a point and at the very least I owed them an explanation.

'I'm sorry, really, and I would have gone through with it, only my boyfriend has asked me to move in with him so I can hardly go around getting kinky with you two, can I?'

'Why not?'

'Because . . . because I've decided to be faithful to him, that's why. It's only right, when I'm living in his house.'

He did not look happy, but he couldn't find an answer. Nor could Pete. I did feel bad and ducked down to kiss them both, saying the only thing I could think of to cheer them up.

'I'm sorry, but I'm not saying never, OK?'

That brightened them up, and although I knew that I was very, very unlikely ever to do it, I at least felt better as I walked away. I was glad I'd had the conversation, and got it over so quickly. Now they knew I was no longer up for kicks, and that only left Martin, who deserved an explanation, and Steve, but Steve was Steve and didn't really count.

Steve was also going to get his way with the council, as I discovered that afternoon. Mr Phelps himself called to say that they had finally approved the camera sites, although there were still various committees and so forth to get through before we actually got the go-ahead to put the things up. The main camera on the Bury Road would allow Steve to sneak in and out of town by going through the park, creating an instant alibi for his trips to Calais, should one ever be needed.

I still wasn't completely happy, but there didn't seem to be anything else I could do, except of course for moving to Brettenham, which didn't have any cameras at all. My scally friends, sadly, would just have to take their chances, and all I could do was watch the process roll on towards completion.

Friday came around again, but instead of heading back to Brettenham for dinner and what was to be my first punishment spanking, Stephen stopped the car in the mouth of one of the logging tracks on the Thetford Road. I immediately wondered what he was up to. Sure enough, no sooner had we stepped out into the warm evening sunlight than he confirmed my hopes and my fears too.

'This is a pretty place, and I seem to remember promising you a spanking *al fresco*.'

'Sort of . . .'

'Let us not nit-pick. You are about to get one.'

He'd swung his leg over the barrier, and drew in a deep breath of air as he started down the track. We were only just outside town, really rather too close for comfort, making me even more nervous than usual as I followed him. He was already looking around, as if trying to select a suitable place to sit while he spanked me, even though we were in full view of the passing traffic.

'Um . . . Stephen, shouldn't we go a little further into the woods?'

He gave a solemn nod.

'A few paces, perhaps. I wouldn't want to be responsible for causing a crash.'

'How about a few hundred paces, and right in among the trees?'

'Oh, I don't think that will be necessary, but I do need somewhere to sit. Hmm, perhaps this pile of logs?'

'You're not suppose to climb on the log piles, in case they collapse, and anyway, you'll get pine resin all over your trousers.'

'Ah, yes, I hadn't thought of that. Thank you.'

He walked on, but only a little way, stopping where a footpath cut across the track. The stile was perfect, at least for sitting on. He turned to me.

'OK. A little variation this time, I think. Take your knickers down, not off, just to the tops of your thighs.'

'What, here?'

'Of course.'

I couldn't help but look sulky as I obeyed him, reaching up under my skirt to push my thumbs into my knickers and lowering them to the tops of my thighs. Nothing was showing, but I felt intensely self-conscious with my bottom bare under my skirt. It was risky too, with every chance that somebody might come by, and if they did they would see me getting my bare bottom warmed. Or so I thought, but Stephen had other ideas.

'Let's walk a little further, shall we? Leave your knickers as they are.'

He wagged his finger at me, his face full of amusement at the state he'd put me in. I found myself pulling a face, but there was no denying my rising arousal, and I knew only too well how high he could take me with a little time and a little cruelty. He took my hand

and we walked on along the track. I could feel my bare skin moving against the inside of my skirt, keeping me constantly aware of my exposure. My knickers had also begun to work their way down my thighs as I walked, until I was sure they were showing.

'Hang on, Stephen.'

'What's the matter?'

'My knickers are falling down!'

He laughed, his eyes full of mischief, and watched me in open delight as I adjusted myself, pulling my knickers up but not all the way, so my bottom remained bare, the way he wanted me. It was perverse, pure and simple, real dirty old man stuff. Before I could never have imagined myself getting off on it. Now I was already wet and wondering how high he'd take me this time.

We moved on, deep into the woods. Twice we passed people walking their dogs, both women, and each time we exchanged nods and brief, polite remarks. I was already shaking and sure that anybody else who passed would notice, and guess. We'd crossed the Sariton Road before it happened: an elderly man with an Alsatian appearing around the corner at the exact moment I'd stopped to adjust my knickers for maybe the fifth or sixth time. I was sure he'd seen, and although it was absurd I was equally sure he'd guess what was going on. When we drew level his dog began to sniff around me, putting me into a state of agonising embarrassment. Stephen merely chuckled, but I was fit to burst and found the words tumbling out as soon as the man was safely out of sight.

'I can't take this. If you're going to spank me, do it.'

'If you insist.'

He immediately pulled me towards the trees. They

were big pines, fully mature, with a lot of open space beneath their trunks, only thinly grown with ferns. There was nowhere to sit either, and the ground was damp, making Stephen consider.

'Hmm, how awkward. Still, one must always oblige a lady. Hold onto that branch.'

The one he meant was sticking out from the nearest pine trunk, well above my head height. It was dead and broken off short, with only about half a metre of barkless wood sticking out. I reached up, on tiptoe before I could take hold, and it felt anything but secure, forcing me to brace myself as he came up beside me.

'Perfect, although I do like to feel your body as you lie across my knee. I suppose a little variety won't do any harm.'

As he'd spoken he'd pulled up my skirt, tucking it into the waistband along with the tail of my jacket. My bottom was now completely bare, showing behind in a frame of my dishevelled clothing, and very much vulnerable. He began to touch, stroking my skin, and then to spank, slapping upwards to make my cheeks bounce. I clung on, wriggling just a little, my mouth pursed against the stinging pain, mild but very rapidly making my flesh warm.

I knew there was a chance of being seen too, the path not so very far away between the big trees. I heard the slap of Stephen's fingers on my cheeks loud in the still evening air, although I was doing my very best not to make too much fuss about it and risk drawing attention to myself. Even then I wasn't sure if I wanted to be seen or not. The thought was alarming, deeply embarrassing, but compelling too, bringing me all those strange mixed-up feelings that come with a smacked bottom.

Stephen was simply having fun, enjoying my nudity and enjoying my reaction, but very cool about it, applying accurate, methodical slaps to my quivering bottom even as I wriggled and gasped my way through the punishment. In no time I was hot and ready, not just happy to make myself available to him, but eager, even if he laid me down on the wet ground and took me like that.

The spanking stopped finally, leaving me glowing and badly in need, too excited even to cover myself, and still clinging to the low branch with my now red bottom pushed out for his attention. Stephen gave his cock a brief squeeze through his trousers, but that was it. He had folded his arms across his chest as he stepped away from the tree.

'Very pretty, and I do like the way you respond, so much emotion. Now, food time.'

'Don't you want me?'

'Naturally, but the ground is a little wet. I tell you what: you can walk back to the car like that if you like, to keep you in the mood. With your skirt down, that is, unless you'd rather go bare?'

'You are such a bastard, Stephen.'

He merely chuckled, obviously fully aware of what he was doing to me. The thought of walking all the way back to the car with my red bottom showing was immensely powerful, but just too embarrassing for me to cope with. I pulled my skirt down, but left my knickers as they were, knowing that he'd manipulated me into doing it, and liking it.

Every step of the way back I was aware of the condition I was in, from the feel of my knickers around my thighs and the heat in my bottom, keeping me in a constant, jittery state of arousal. We passed several people, and I was sure they'd realise how badly I was shaking, or even smell my excitement, making my feelings stronger still. On reaching the car and safety I was filled with as much regret as relief, and I stayed as I was for the journey to Brettenham, which seemed to take minutes.

Stephen was as cool as ever throughout, chatting casually about this and that, but with the occasional remark thrown in about my spanking to keep me on edge. Even back at the mill he remained calm, even though I was ready to be had on the doormat, merely going to the fridge and extracting a bottle of wine as he spoke.

'How's your cooking?'

'I . . . I don't really.'

'Then you must learn. It is the most civilised of skills. I shall show you how to chop garlic. Come here.'

I came to stand beside him where he had laid out a thick chopping board and a large cook's knife. There was a string of garlic bulbs hanging above us and he carefully cut one off, explaining as he began to prepare it.

'First, you top and tail the clove, like so, then squeeze gently, which loosens the skin, making it easier to get off. Once the clove is bare, you then slice it as finely as possible, pile up the slices and chop, like this.'

He demonstrated, holding the knife lengthways across the board by both handle and blade so that he could make little brisk cutting motions, dividing the garlic into tiny pieces.

'You try.'

I took the knife, and after a couple of false starts

managed to get the hang of it. Meanwhile he was washing his hands, and spoke again as he shook the water free.

'Why don't you do the rest?'

'If you like. What are you going to do?'

'We can't do anything else until the garlic's chopped, so I shall have a glass of wine.'

He'd come close, taking hold of my skirt. I managed a sigh of mock protest, imagining I was about to be taken over the work surface, but he merely tucked everything up as he had before, leaving my bottom bare to the room.

'That's better.'

'Pig!'

'Now, now.'

He chuckled and turned to attend to the wine bottle, opening it and pouring out two large glasses. I was given mine and he took his to the sofa, relaxing back into one corner with his legs crossed as he sipped the wine and watched me work. There was no denying what he was doing to me, but I imagined with mixed feelings a future of doing his cooking and housework while dressed in nothing but a pinny. Barefoot in the kitchen was bad enough, but bare bottom in the kitchen was something else.

At least it was sexual, and not genuine chauvinism, or not entirely. When he'd had his fill of watching me he came back to the work surface, quickly preparing some tiny onions in a saucepan of hot olive oil, then adding tomatoes and my garlic, all done with precise, fussy movements. I was clearly only there for decoration, so stepped back and tried to lay the table, only to discover that there was a right way to do that as well: his way.

Dinner was delicious, veal that melted in my mouth and a sauce packed with flavour. I even forgot about the state of arousal he'd put me in but it came back as we lay together on the sofa afterwards, sipping wine as he gently caressed my neck and stroked my hair. So few men are ever patient, always too eager to get started and finished too soon. Not Stephen. He had put some soothing classical music on, the only illumination from the slowly gathering dusk. I let myself slip into a pleasant, erotic haze which he could have taken advantage of at any time, but didn't.

In the end it was me who broke the spell, my need simply too strong to hold back. I was cuddled into him, and it was simply more than I could resist not to reach out and ease his fly down, but his hand closed on top of mine before his zip was half open.

'Tut, tut, aren't we forgetting something?'

'No, I don't think so. I'm more than ready, believe me.'

'No doubt, but a treat is always better if you have to wait for it, don't you think?'

'Who's getting the treat here? I was going to give you a suck.'

'A great pleasure, no question, but I want you to learn to look on being allowed to touch me as a privilege, which I assure you will make it far more worthwhile.'

I really wasn't having that.

'No way! It's touching me that's the privilege, that's just the way it works.'

'I rather think not.'

I'd sat up as I spoke, a big mistake. His arm was already around me, and before I could even react I'd been flipped across his legs, bottom up, with his arm tight around my waist. I managed a single squeal of shock and surprise as my skirt was hauled up, he jerked my knickers down with one quick motion and I was being spanked again.

'Ow! Stephen, this isn't fair!'

'Yes it is. You agreed to be punished, did you not?'

'Yes, but ... ow! Ow! What about in the ... ow, woods?'

'Merely an amusing diversion, now do be quiet.'

Despite myself I shut up, although I was far from quiet as he completed my spanking, applying maybe a couple of hundred firm swats to my bottom, which left me hot and red and blazing with resentment, but more in need than ever. Finally it stopped and he let go, sending me tumbling to the floor, where I sat, kneeling, with my hands back to caress my cheeks and completely unable to stop pouting. Stephen gave his little chuckle as he opened his legs and casually peeled down his fly to extract his cock and balls.

'Now you may have your treat.'

I called him a bastard even as I leant forward to take him in my mouth, and as I began to suck I was wondering if I would ever be able to come to terms with the way he handled me. Nobody made me feel the way he did, not even Martin. Nobody could make me grovel on my knees, grateful for the privilege of taking his cock in my mouth, not even Steve. Nobody, but nobody, could spank me and shame me and make me like every second of it, except him.

He knew too, as if he could read my mind, his face set in easy bliss as he watched me suck his penis and lick his balls, all the while stroking my hair and tickling me behind my ears and at the back of my neck. I knew I couldn't hold back for long. It wasn't even worth trying. I was already holding my smacked bottom, and more for the pleasure of touching my hot, roughened skin than to soothe myself. In just moments I'd slipped a hand around to the front and down my half-lowered panties, to touch myself.

Stephen merely gave a knowing chuckle as he saw what I was doing. I didn't care. I wanted him to know, wanted him to realise what he did to me, how he took me to places I'd never been and could never even have imagined. He was hard, and as I used my tongue and lips and mouth it was true worship, his cock and balls godlike to me as I knelt at his feet, masturbating.

I thought of how he'd treated me, flipping me over his knee for a punishment spanking, so casually, and I hoped he'd do it again, many times. I thought of how he'd made me work with my red bottom showing to the room and I hoped it would become part of a daily routine. I thought of how he'd made me walk through the woods with my knickers down under my office skirt, and I was hoping he'd make me go like that all day. I thought of how he'd made me cling onto the branch above my head and spanked me in the open where there was a chance of being seen, and I wished we had been seen, not just seen, but watched, with me held tight across his knee as he sat on the stile and spanked my bare bottom in front of half the population of Hockford.

With that I came, an orgasm so long, so glorious that I seemed to be floating, and all the while sucking on his beautiful cock and holding the image of myself being spanked in public in my head. He came too, just as I was finishing, adding a final perfect touch both to my climax and to my worship.

* * * *

That was only the beginning. The rest of the evening and most of the night passed in a golden haze of sex and wine until at last I was drifting towards sleep in a state of blissful exhaustion, still cradled into Stephen's arms.

Saturday was much the same, padding naked around his flat, walking in the local woods and beside the river, lunching on the lawn beside the mill, and being kept in a permanent state of sexual readiness. I stayed the night again, now content that it was where I would be living, but decided that I really ought to go home on the Sunday, to give Mum the good news and figure out how I was going to move all my stuff.

For all his sexual dominance, Stephen was doing his best to be accommodating, only voicing concern when I asked if I could set up my drum kit in his flat. I'd always been banned from keeping it at home, meaning I had to practise in Josie's garage and pick it up from there when we played. Fortunately, the state Josie's dad was in most of the time he wouldn't have noticed if we'd let a bomb off under his chair, and Stephen eventually managed to persuade me it was best to keep things that way.

Otherwise there wasn't much I needed. Stephen still didn't know how I usually dressed, but that wasn't really a problem, more an excuse for a huge shopping spree, which I could now afford. Mum was going to be delighted about that too, because she'd been expecting me to grow out of my punk phase for years and getting increasingly exasperated when I didn't.

I wanted some time to sort things out by myself as well, so I asked Stephen if he'd drop me off and collect me in the late afternoon. He agreed readily enough, and I ended up at home, or rather what had been home for so many years, with the smell of roast beef and Yorkshire pudding drifting from the open kitchen window. Inside, they were getting ready to eat, Mum fussing around, my sisters squabbling over who was sitting where, Steve teasing my baby brother by pretending we were eating roast dog. I immediately felt deeply lonely at the thought of leaving, but I wasn't given a minute to reflect, Mum immediately thrusting an oven cloth into my hands.

'There you are, Felicity, just on time as usual. Could you drain the vegetables, please.'

I drained the vegetables, helped put out the plates, put some new butter in the dish and finally managed to sit down as Steve began to carve. There was no sign of Archie Feltham, slightly to my surprise, as he was always keen to freeload Mum's Sunday roasts. Mum seemed a little stressed too, so I posed a careful question.

'No Archie?'

Her answer left no room for doubt.

'I am no longer seeing Mr Feltham.'

'Oh. Sorry.'

'Never mind. I know you didn't like him anyway. Could you pass the pepper please?'

I passed the pepper, and waited until the complicated little ritual of getting all the right food on all the right plates had been completed before speaking again.

'I've got something very important to tell you. Stephen has asked me to move in with him and I've said I will.'

I could see the mixed emotions on Mum's face even before she answered.

'Oh, that's lovely. I am glad. He seems such a nice man. He lives in Brettenham, doesn't he?'

'Yes, in a converted mill. How did you know?'

'We often talk, at Cuatro Cortado.'

'Oh. Anyway, I'm going.'

Only Mum seemed even vaguely interested, making me feel even more sorry for myself. Steve was doing his best to get his dinner in his mouth, but finally found the time to say something.

'D'you want to borrow the van?'

'No thanks. There's not really that much I want to take. I'm leaving my drums at Josie's.'

'Best place for 'em. She wants to see you, got a gig, I think.'

'Oh, right. Where, Hockwold Airbase?'

'Nah, your show was a bit dirty for them. Billy got torn off a right strip. It's someplace called the Flying Fortress, a club I think.'

'Thanks, I'll go over later.'

I settled down to eat, now wondering how I should broach the subject of Rubber Dollies with Stephen. He knew I played the drums, he knew I played venues occasionally, but he had no idea of the details. I could hardly see our brand of retro punk gelling with his tastes, but so far at least he'd been tolerant save in his conviction that his opinion was always definitive.

By the time we'd finished lunch I was feeling pleasantly full and more than a little sleepy, with the excesses of the previous two nights finally catching up with me. I went up to my room to sort my things out but simply sat down on the bed, suddenly overcome with melancholy. All my life I'd been in that same room, and it was very much me: my bed, my things strewn all over the place, my posters on the walls, all of it very much me and very much not Stephen. He was tidy, almost obsessively so, while I loved to live in chaos. His flat was intensely masculine, and while that was sure to change I couldn't quite see myself in his room blending together different colours of eye shadow to try to get the perfect purple. Then there was the row of dolls and bears who'd sat along the top of my wardrobe, untouched for nearly ten years, but still mine and I couldn't imagine bringing them. They'd seen enough, God knows, and it was the most ridiculous thought, but I didn't want them to watch while I was being spanked.

For a good ten minutes I just sat there staring into space, feeling deeply homesick. Reminding myself of how good I'd felt that morning didn't help at all, and I only managed a wan smile when Mum called upstairs for me to help with the washing-up. That at least would change, as Stephen had a dishwasher and to judge by his performance so far was too precious about his things to let me anywhere near them. I hadn't even been allowed to polish his wine glasses because he was scared I might snap the stems.

When I'd finished I went out, having decided that all I really needed to take with me was a bag of clothes and a few obvious basics from the bathroom. I would start shopping in my lunch break on Monday and keep going until I had a decent wardrobe again, only in a completely different style, what Mum would have considered a grown-up style.

I'd put on jeans and a sloppy top, which was just as well as I was getting close to Josie's house when she pulled up beside me and motioned that I should get on the back of her bike. She started off the instant I was mounted up, forcing me to cling on tight to her waist. After what I'd been thinking about, and saying, with Martin I couldn't help but feel self-conscious but at least she didn't know. Or so I thought. Her first words as she took off her helmet sending blood rushing to my face.

'What's with the kinky fantasies, you little perve?'

There was only one thing it could be, as I was very sure indeed nobody else knew about what I'd been getting up to with Stephen. I immediately felt bad for Josie, embarrassed for myself and angry at Martin.

'Jesus, can't anybody keep their mouth shut around here? Sorry, Josie, I . . .'

She stepped forward and hugged me, a purely friendly gesture, but she couldn't resist giving me a swat on my bum as she moved back.

'Don't worry about it. I know you, and I know what men are like. He wanted to get off on some fake lezzie fantasy, right?'

'Something like that, yes.'

She shook her head, grinning, and I let myself relax, only to have the blood rush back to my face, hotter than ever as she spoke again.

'So how'd you really get the marks on your bum then?'

I didn't know what to say, whether to claim Martin had been lying or that I'd been playing about with somebody. From the small, sly smile on Josie's face I knew she wasn't going to be fooled. I shrugged, my face the colour of beetroot as I answered.

'My . . . my new boyfriend, he's a bit kinky.'

'A bit?'

'OK, seriously kinky. Look, please don't tell anyone, Josie, you know what they're like. Please?'

She was trying not to laugh as she answered.

'OK, I promise. So what's the deal, he hit you with a

cane? I know you, Fizz, so how come he's not wearing his balls as an extra pair of tonsils?'

'I don't know, I honestly don't. He just makes me feel different, like I want to be ... to be punished. Not nastily, there's nothing nasty about it ... not really. I don't know, Josie ...'

I trailed off, close to tears. She reached out to put a hand on my shoulder and I gave in to my emotions, the tears streaming down my face even as I continued to attempt to explain.

'He likes to be in control of me, and to punish me when I'm bad ... naughty, and I love it. I don't love it, I crave it. It's like an addiction, and I really, really do not want everybody to know. You understand, don't you?'

'Hey, come on, Fizz. You know I understand. What do you think it's like being the only dyke in town?'

I managed a smile.

'Tough, I suppose.'

'Yeah, it's tough, and you've always stuck up for me. Now stop crying or you'll set me off, you big baby.'

She took me in her arms, hugging me close to her, but only for a moment before she broke away.

'Better watch it, or we'll set the curtains twitching.'

'We do that anyway. Steve says you've got a gig?'

'Yeah, another one from Billy. There's this club in Norwich, the Flying Fortress, which is really popular with the Yanks. It's a jazz place, but they've managed to get us in, or else they don't know what we play. We even get paid!'

'Shit! Great, so when is it?'

'Next Saturday.'

'Brilliant, only it's going to take a bit of explaining to Stephen. He doesn't even know about Rubber Dollies, and he thinks I'm this sweet, innocent little thing . . . well, maybe not so innocent.'

'Why tell him?'

'Because I'm going to be living with him. I can't just bugger off with no explanation, can I?'

'You could say it was a girls' night out or something. You can change here.'

'I'm going to have to tell him some time.'

'Your call.'

11

Josie was right that it was my call, and it was not an easy one. I'd have far preferred to just carry on as before, but as Rubber Dollies still seemed to be alive despite all our difficulties I wasn't going to be the one to break it up. I was going to have to tell Stephen, but the thought of him attending a gig was hideously embarrassing, so I could only hope he'd accept it as part of my life that didn't involve him.

When he came to pick me up he was astonished to find that I had only one bag, and admitted it.

'I had visions of you standing on the pavement surrounded by furniture and piles of knick-knacks.'

'Not me. I travel light.'

'So I see. I'm sorry about the drums too, but maybe we could sort something out.'

'Don't worry, they're better off where they are, as long as you don't mind me going off to practise now and then.'

'Not at all. I don't want to tie you down.'

'Oh, I was rather hoping . . .'

'Very funny. No doubt something can be arranged, if you insist, although it's not really my thing. Seriously, you're to come and go as you please, and not to feel I'm in any way holding you back. I do realise there's quite an age gap between us.'

'Thanks, and talking about drums, my friend Sam

203

has set up a gig for our band next Saturday, in a jazz club in Norwich.'

'Jazz? Jazz has a certain style, I'll admit.'

'We're not playing jazz, we're playing retro punk.'

'Ah, I suppose I might have guessed from your taste in music. In that case, I hope you won't be offended if I don't attend?'

'Not at all. I know you'd hate it. Thanks.'

I kissed him, thoroughly happy with the outcome. It was surprising to find him so accommodating when he was such a control freak in the bedroom and the office, but I wasn't complaining. He'd started the car, and spoke again as we pulled out into the road.

'Will you want to come back late, or stay here?'

'Um ... I don't know. It might be really late and we'll all be together in the van, so it might be best if I crashed here. Sorry, I don't mean to spoil the weekend, especially when there's so much work on during the week.'

'Don't worry, we can make up for it on Friday night.'

I knew how, and answered his big dirty grin with a smile. Maybe life was going to be good after all.

We drove south and east by the now familiar route. Once back at Stephen's I quickly found myself in the same state of bliss I'd been enjoying before and wondering why I'd felt so upset. It wasn't even the wrong time of the month. The evening was also warm and dry, so we ate outside, on the strip of lawn between the mill and the river, sipping cold white wine with smoked salmon and a potato salad.

Once we'd watched the sun set behind the row of tall poplars on the opposite bank of the river we went indoors and to bed. This time our sex was slow and loving and equal which, while beautiful in its way, failed to bring out the full agonising intensity of being under his command and his hand.

We were up early on Monday and work was absolutely frantic, with endless comings and goings from the council, who seemed to have an infinite capacity for detail and an infinite number of committees, all of which wanted to stick their oar in. Stephen seemed to regard it all as some great game, and I tried to take the same attitude.

I did at least manage to get my shopping done, using most of my first pay cheque to buy myself two more smart skirt suits and a lot of the very feminine casual wear Stephen seemed to like, particularly long, loose skirts and girlie blouses. Hockford being Hockford, that sort of thing was far easier to buy than punk gear, most of which I'd got on the Net.

Tuesday was much the same. I'd gone up to the council offices to explain to Mr Phelps that if we placed a camera in the position his committee had decided on it would actually be mounted in the centre of a plate glass window. Their receptionist and I were getting quite friendly, hardly surprising when I was seeing more of her than my family, and she greeted me with a smile and nodded me through security. Mr Phelps wasn't in his office, but as I passed the committee room next door I saw that he was at the table, along with Mrs Shelby, Mr Burrows and various others I recognised. I waited, unsure what to do, but they had seen me and Mr Burrows beckoned for me to come in, speaking immediately.

'Ah, Felicity, I was hoping Mr English and Mr Minter would be coming up?'

'It's only a minor detail, surely?'

'Far from it, I assure you. Do sit down anyway.'

Puzzled, I took a seat. Mr Phelps began to speak, only to stop immediately as both Stephen and Paul appeared at the door, obviously summoned almost immediately after I'd left the warehouse. Mr Phelps began again, in his usual curt manner.

'I regret to say that a serious difficulty has arisen.'

It was Stephen who answered him, with the same blend of energy and optimism he always used when facing the council.

'Nothing too disastrous, I trust? We are now fully ready to begin installation, saving the matter Miss Cotton was here to discuss and one or two other minor details.'

He cast me a questioning glance, but I could only shrug in return as Mr Phelps went on.

'This is more than a minor detail. In fact, we will be unable to go ahead with the installation.'

Stephen looked genuinely astonished.

'Unable to go ahead? But, Mr Phelps, we have the contracts signed and agreement on –'

'Nevertheless we are unable to go ahead. I have a direct instruction from the Home Office to that effect.'

'The Home Office?'

I could see Mr Phelps swelling slightly as his sense of importance rose.

'The Home Office, who in turn have received a communication from the American Embassy to the effect that nobody in Hockford, public or private, may erect or use any system of security cameras that employs facial recognition technology.'

Both Stephen and Paul now looked completely stunned.

'What has the American Embassy got to do with it? This is hardly their jurisdiction, and –'

Mr Phelps broke in again.

'It is a matter of military security. The Commander at Hockwold Airbase has made a specific request that we do not store facial recognition data on his personnel, nor any other American personnel.'

Mr Burrows added a remark.

'I fear your system has become the victim of its own efficiency, Stephen, and unfortunately we have no choice but to comply.'

I really thought Stephen was going to swear, but he managed to remain calm as he answered.

'Can I assume that the contract will be honoured as it stands?'

'Certainly.'

That was that essentially, although they went on for quite a bit. Eventually we left, crossing the road directly to the Bull by unspoken consent. As soon as he'd put a bottle of white wine and three glasses on the table Stephen spoke again.

'How in hell's name did the Yanks get wind of it?'

I could guess but I wasn't saying anything. It was only then that it really sank in. I'd done it, maybe not on purpose, maybe not by some bold and clever scheme, but I'd done it anyway, simply by warning a boyfriend not to get horny with me unless he wanted us to be on public record. Quite possibly I'd also made myself redundant, but that no longer mattered. I was the boss's girlfriend.

Paul shook his head.

'Bloody Yanks. So what now?'

Stephen considered for a moment before answering.

'Well, we still have our stock. The basic principle is still sound, so I suggest we start up again somewhere else, somewhere that isn't crawling with Americans.'

'Not East Anglia then?'

'No. Hmm ... you didn't tell any of your American friends about the system did you, Felicity?'

'No, no, absolutely not. I'm not surprised they heard about it though. Everybody who works for the council knew, just about. One of the women there probably has a boyfriend on the base or something.'

'No doubt you're right. Damn.'

He broke off to take a swallow of wine, then spoke again.

'That leaves us at a bit of a loose end then, except for deciding where we go next. You will be staying with us, won't you, Felicity?'

'Yes, of course, if you want me?'

'Absolutely. You know how everything works, and I don't suppose it would be much fun for you playing house in a strange town?'

'No, that's true. Do you have any idea where we'll be going?'

'Not really, no. We need a small town or the logistics become impractical, and it has to have a high crime rate for the sort of thing the ZX is good at stopping. I told you Hockford had the highest per capita rate of taking and driving in the country, didn't I, which is why we chose to set up here in the first place. The second was somewhere in South Wales, if I remember rightly.'

Paul frowned.

'Wasn't it that place outside Manchester?'

I didn't really care either way. They were equally remote, giving me a touch of fear and homesickness at the thought of breaking off my ties with Hockford and even Suffolk so completely. Before, I'd always felt tied down, but suddenly my past life seemed idyllic, at least compared to starting again in another small town where I didn't even know anybody. I'd be completely dependent on Stephen, both financially and emotionally. The only other person I'd even know, at least at first, would be Paul, and while he was a nice enough guy we really didn't have much in common.

Yet I'd be earning money, and I told myself I'd soon make new friends. What sort of friends was a different matter. At best it seemed likely I'd always have to keep a part of myself secret, and while that had been part of the thrill when I was first with Stephen it didn't seem so appealing in the long term.

They'd begun to discuss the relocation, leaving me to sip my wine and deal with my mixed emotions. I did want to be with Stephen, badly, but the cost of doing so seemed to keep rising. Was I even in love with him? I wasn't sure. I wasn't even sure if I understood what love was. It was supposed to mean that he was the sole object of my affection, wasn't it? All other men should have been beneath my notice, but I still had affection for my friends. Maybe it was just the sex I was in love with, and particularly the spankings. Stephen alone brought out those feelings in me, but as Martin and I had lain together in the long grass with his huge hand cupping my bottom I'd been wondering how it would feel from him, and from Josie too, who wasn't even a man.

I was going to get drunk if I didn't leave the wine bottle alone, and I swallowed what remained in my glass before putting it down. Paul and Stephen were now discussing the rival virtues of graffiti and car crime for pissing off town councils, but I at last managed to get a word in.

'Do you mind if I go shopping?'

Stephen responded with a casual gesture.

'Go ahead. There are a few things I'll need you to do in the office, but there's no rush any more.'

'Thanks.'

I kissed him and left the pub, feeling slightly tipsy and very mixed up. Even shopping didn't help, because all the things I needed meant one more step towards the new me, and I wasn't sure how well I got on with her. After spending ten minutes staring into windows I changed my mind and decided to take a walk instead, only to stop as I saw that Martin, Billy and several of their friends were seated in Buzz Shack.

Eventually I was going to have to tell Martin that I was now with Stephen, but I really didn't want to do it in front of a group of his friends. I walked past, only to reconsider. It was hard to bear the thought of how they'd look at me if I simply said I'd chosen Stephen over Martin and that was that. On the other hand, I now had an excuse.

As far as he was aware I was a loyal employee of Black Knight Securities but simply didn't fancy being caught on camera while he fondled my buttocks. By passing on what I'd told him about the cameras he had put my job at risk, and I was hardly likely to be happy about it. Still I hesitated. I liked Martin and I really didn't want to cut him off. Then again I'd told myself I'd be faithful to Stephen and it was better to let Martin think I was angry with him and so make a clean break of it. Finally I turned on my heel, determined to go through with it, but still unsure if I was being an angel or a total bitch.

I put on a deliberately angry expression as I walked into Buzz Shack. Martin had seen me, and stopped with his bottle of beer raised in a frozen salute as he saw my face.

'Hi, Fizz, what's the matter?'

'You know perfectly well what the matter is, or if you don't you should do.'

'I don't. What am I supposed to have done?'

His friends had begun to exchange looks and snigger, except for Billy, who was already looking aggressive. I forced myself to go on.

'You told everybody about the cameras, didn't you?'

It wasn't what he'd been expecting at all, and it took him a moment to change gear.

'The cameras? Yeah ... sure I did. I had to, Fizz, it was a matter of base security. Sorry.'

I just melted. He sounded so genuinely apologetic and yet confident about his decision, while I knew I wasn't being truthful. Instead of telling him how he'd lost Black Knight Securities their contract and nearly cost me my job, I found myself stammering.

'Oh ... I suppose so, but still ...'

'Hey, I'm really sorry, Fizz, but it had to be done. Have a mixer, yeah?'

'No, thanks ... I ... I'll see you around, Martin. Bye.'

I'd failed utterly, unable to tell him what I needed to. As I walked away up the High Street I was wishing he didn't have to be so nice about everything, because I'd have to let him down eventually, and when I did it would be all the more painful. Stephen was now the only man who had any claim on me, and that was how it should be, or so I kept telling myself as I walked rapidly up to Town Bridge and down the steps. I needed to walk, to get away from people and be alone for a while, but I didn't want to take the route Martin and I had walked before.

The other way was better anyway, along the river and out of town past the Hattersley Estate. Our cameras were still there, making me intensely self-conscious until I could cross the river. I slowed as I started across the fields, on absolutely flat land, the same route Pete and I had come into town on after burning out Mr Phelps' car.

I walked right out to the edge of the fens, and turned back only when I realised that my smart shoes weren't really suitable for walking in. After a life spent mostly in trainers I simply hadn't realised how much heels could rub, and how physically inefficient that made me, another black mark against suits. In the end I took a bus back into town, arriving at the warehouse to find Stephen drinking coffee in front of his computer screen and no sign of Paul.

'Sorry I was so long.'

'Don't mention it ... actually, do.'

He'd pushed his chair back as he spoke, making a lap. I knew exactly what that meant.

'I ... I'm not really in the mood.'

'Ah, but you soon will be. Come along, let's not have any nonsense.'

I made a face.

'What about Paul?'

'He's at the council offices, dismantling the system.'

'Oh.'

'Over my knee, Felicity.'

I was still pulling a face, but I went, draping myself across his lap in the now familiar position with my head hung down over the orange carpet squares. After all, I was due a punishment for failing to cut Martin off and it was so easy to obey Stephen, as my boss and as my lover. Everything about him and something about the office made it appropriate for me to be spanked.

His fingers found the hem of my skirt and I closed my eyes as I was put through the little ritual of exposure: skirt up, knickers down, the way he liked to say it, savouring every word. As my bottom came bare my lips had parted in a quiet sigh, quite involuntary. All my cares seemed to be slipping away in the face of my rising excitement, and despite my vulnerability I'd never felt so protected.

Stephen began to spank me, my body limp and surrendered across his knees, my bottom bare, as a bad girl's should be while she's punished. And what better way to punish me, for taking too long a lunch break, for anything he pleased, over his knee in the office and smack, smack, smack on my bare bottom.

It began to get harder, stinging my flesh and making me kick a little. Stephen changed his grip, holding me in place and lifting one knee to bring my bottom up and make my cheeks come open. Now it hurt, and he could see every intimate detail of my body, as was his right. He knew what he was talking about too, because he'd taken me from a fit of the sulks to ecstasy in a couple of minutes. I needed to be spanked. I really, genuinely needed to be spanked. He stopped.

'Hmm, perhaps a little addition, as you're such a bad girl.'

He was playing, but I felt it was real, because of my emotions and because I'd lied to him, because I'd told Martin about the cameras and implied I'd see him again, and because of a thousand other things I'd done. Oh, yes, I really deserved to be spanked, and more, which was exactly what I was going to get.

One of the cameras they'd been experimenting with was on the desk, a jumble of wires hanging from the end. As I twisted my head around I could just about see as he detached a length of cable, his face set in the calm, cruel smile I knew so well. He adjusted himself a little, leaving me more evenly balanced across his knees as he spoke.

'Put your hands behind your back, Felicity.'

I obeyed without hesitation. He immediately caught my wrists, crossing them in the small of my back and looping the piece of wire around them. A couple of twists, a knot, and I was helpless, not merely surrendered to him, but dependent on him. I'd begun to sob as he tucked my office skirt up under my bound wrists, hoping and dreading that with me now completely helpless he would spank me hard.

He wasn't finished. Instead of going back to my punishment, he began to hum one of his favourite tunes, and to lever my knickers further down my legs, and off. As they came free of my ankles I was left nude from the waist down but for stay-ups and shoes, leaving my legs free to come wide and expose my sex more fully then ever. That wasn't why he'd done it.

'Open wide, Felicity.'

As he spoke he'd offered my knickers to my mouth. For one horrified second I could only stare at the little bundle of white cotton, and then I'd obeyed him, opening my mouth and allowing him to feed me my own knickers. Now I was bound and gagged, in the most humiliating way, taking me higher still as I waited for my punishment to start again.

I could still see, and my bottom tightened involuntarily as he picked up Paul's design ruler, a heavy plastic thing half a metre long. It was really going to hurt, and I didn't know whether to be more scared than grateful as he tapped it down on my bottom, cold against my already heated skin.

Then he'd begun to spank again, applying the ruler hard across my bottom, and fast too, never giving me a chance to recover myself as I was smacked into a squirming, wriggling mess, my bottom bucking up and down in my pain, my legs scissored wide to show everything between, my wrists jerking in the wire noose that held them together. It hurt so much, taking me completely out of myself, completely out of control.

I have no idea how long it went on. I was in a haze of pain, my burning bottom the focus of my entire existence, and the only even vaguely rational thought that remained in my head was that I was being punished, well and truly punished. I'd begun to cry long before he stopped, but it was what I needed, to let all my bad feelings out until I was clean.

When he did stop I begged for more, mumbling through my now soggy knickers. I got it, the ruler applied to my bare cheeks in a furious crescendo of smacks at a faster rhythm than the craziest drum beat and every bit as hard. Finally something inside me seemed to break and I was in that same heavenly state he'd put me in before, properly beaten, eager and submissive to his will, eager to serve him. He seemed to know, and gave me a last few firm swats before stopping.

'Now that's how an office girl should be spanked, and this is what she should do afterwards. On your knees, Felicity.'

He helped me down, guiding me to the floor and into a kneeling position, my hands still tied behind my back, my bottom stuck out behind me, hot and bare. I knew what he was going to make me do, the obvious thing for a well-spanked office girl to say thank you to her boss for punishing her. My knickers were pulled out of my mouth, his fly came down and his cock and balls came out, offered to me to suck.

I paused just a moment to take in the way he looked, a perfect image, sat on his office chair in immaculate suit and tie save for his already engorged cock and the heavy sack of his balls thrusting rudely from his open fly. All I could do was shuffle forward on my knees to take him in, and he immediately took me by my hair, controlling the motion of my sucking.

My head was spinning with arousal, my pussy in urgent need of attention, but there was nothing I could do, only kneel there as he fucked my mouth, completely subservient to his pleasure. I still trusted him. I knew he'd let me come, maybe make me come, but he was going to be first and he was going to do it in my mouth.

Just knowing that was ecstasy, and when he did it an instant later I nearly came. I swallowed as best I could, an act of worship in itself, and I kept him in as long as possible, until he had to gently detach me by pulling on my hair. I looked up, my vision hazy as I met his eyes. He was smiling.

'Good girl. You're learning. Now turn around.'

I obeyed, shuffling around on my knees as quickly as I could despite not knowing what he was going to do. My bottom was already ablaze, my punishment complete, but if he wanted to beat me he could. That was his right.

'Stick your bottom out, right out. That's my girl, back in so your cheeks open properly.'

I'd adopted the position he'd ordered, my bum pushed out with my back in as tight as it would go. My cheeks were wide open, my bottom hole on show to him as well as my sex, nothing hidden, just as it should be. I craned back over my shoulder to find him smiling down at the view I was providing him. He'd just come, his pleasure more control than sexual, which made it even stronger for me as he spoke.

'Now, I'm going to masturbate you.'

His words drew a sob from my throat, and another as he reached back, picking something up from the desk. My eyes went wide as I saw what he'd got, two thick marker pens, one red, one black, the rounded tips ideal for insertion into a woman's body. He laughed to see the expression on my face, and spoke as he leant down.

'Keep it well out, Felicity, one in each hole, I think.'

I was sobbing as I was penetrated, one pen slid deep in up my pussy before being put to my bumhole and up, the other eased into my sex. I was imagining how I'd look as he gave his low, dirty chuckle, kneeling in front of him, my hands tied tight behind me back, my skirt turned high, my bare spanked bottom thrust out, the ends of the pens protruding from my sex and bottom.

His arms came around me and he spoke again.

'One last detail.'

I felt his fingers on my blouse. One button was eased open, a second, a third and he'd pulled my blouse wide across my breasts. A quick tug and my bra was up, depriving me of my last scrap of decency. He spent a moment fondling my breasts, which brought my shivering up to an uncontrollable peak, then he had sat back, and a moment later applied the rounded toe of his shoe to my sex.

It was a truly awful thing to do. I'd thought he would use his hand, but no, I was to be brought off on his shoe, and I couldn't have stopped him if I'd wanted to. I was already whimpering with pleasure even as he began to rub, with what he had done to me running through my head, every awful, wonderful detail sending a fresh shiver through my body as I was brought towards orgasm. I thought of how he'd told me I was going to be spanked, not asked me if he could, but told me he was going to do it. I thought of how he'd bared my bottom, of how big his hand felt as it rose and fell on my cheeks, of how he'd tied my hands behind my back with wire, of how he'd pulled my knickers off and used them to gag me, of how he'd beaten me with the ruler, of how he made me grovel at his feet while he fucked my head, and lastly how I was kneeling for him with every single intimate detail of my body bare in his office while he brought me off on his shoe.

How I screamed when I came. They must have heard me in the other warehouses on the estate. They probably heard me in Norwich. I couldn't help it though, and by the time he tried to jam my knickers back in my mouth it was too late. My entire body was wracked by spasm after spasm of ecstasy, unbearably strong but completely unstoppable.

I almost fainted, and when I finished I just collapsed, little shivers still running through my body, but as I came slowly down I knew that I was definitely staying with Stephen. Whatever the sacrifice, it was worth it.

12

Stephen and Paul had decided on Burston, a town to the north of Manchester. It was hardly appealing, although neither of them had any intention of actually living there, which was something. I still found myself constantly having to think back to the way Stephen handled me sexually and the amount of money I'd be earning in order to cope with the idea of leaving Hockford. It meant the end of so much, my entire life really.

The plan was for Stephen to sound out the council and, if things looked promising, to rent out the house in Brettenham and use some of his surplus cash to buy another in the Pennines to the north and west of Burston. I'd never been there, but I had images of rain-swept moors cut by valleys full of terraced houses and factories with enormous chimneys, so different to the woods and fens I was used to.

It also looked certain that the Flying Fortress would be the Rubber Dollies' farewell gig. We'd always been on shaky ground, stumbling from one venue to the next, and getting banned so often I'd lost count, either for public nudity, being too noisy or general mayhem. Never once had we compromised, refusing to accept restrictions even if it meant not being able to play. I was proud of that, but with me gone the band was almost certain to fall apart, and that felt like a betrayal.

I was up and down all week, on a high when I was

with Stephen, fed up when I wasn't. The only thing which remained constant was that I was determined to go out in style. I'd play better, I'd dress better, and I'd be more outrageous. The dressing part meant setting off from Hockford, so Stephen drove me in on the Saturday morning. Unfortunately he didn't leave, but accepted Mum's invitation to drink coffee in the garden. I didn't feel right getting dolled up with him around, so I shoved what clothes and make-up I needed into a bag and left them discussing cheese.

At Josie's I gave myself a one-hundred-per-cent make-over, first stripping off to shower and do my hair, which she helped me tease into stiff blonde spikes, tipped in different colours: vivid green, scarlet, turquoise and black. It looked great, completely transforming me from sweet, neatly dressed office girl to naked, snarling punk. Even Josie was impressed.

'That's my Fizz. Safety pins?'

'Sure, why not?'

I'd already taken my earrings out and substituted them for two chains of safety pins. Josie watched, apparently as oblivious as ever to me being stark naked, although it was hard not to think about what she knew. Determined not to change my behaviour in any way, I made a point of not putting anything on as I made up at her dressing table. She sat on the edge of her bed, explaining the order of songs to me.

'... then *Pretty Vacant* and when I get to "oh so pretty" you can start stripping off if you want to.'

'Count on it. It's our last time, Josie, so I want to go all the way.'

'What, strip naked?'

'Yeah, why not?'

'No reason. You go for it. But who says it's our last time?'

I took a deep breath.

'Stephen's moving the company to Burston, near Manchester. I'm going with them.'

'Shit! You're not!'

'I am. Sorry.'

'Oh fuck, Fizz, what about the band? And you're my only decent friend, now Sam spends her every waking minute with Billy.'

'I'm sorry, I really am. It's not an easy choice, believe me, and I'll miss you.'

She drew a heavy sigh and went silent, staring at the floor. There was a huge lump in my throat and I was struggling not to cry, but she suddenly stood up.

'Fuck it! Let's make it a good one then. You do your strip. Tell you what, we'll do "God Save the Queen", and before you stand up and salute at the end, rip your skirt off.'

'I'll take it off first. Nobody will see, behind my kit.'

'Yeah, cool, that'll shock them!'

'And ... um, you can touch me up, if you want, like at the Dog and Duck that time.'

'Slut!'

I'd sat up a little to get the outline of my lippy exactly right, lifting my bum off the stool. As she spoke she planted a smack across my cheeks, hard enough to make me squeak and leave a stinging spot as I quickly sat down again.

'Ow! Josie!'

She just laughed and began to rummage in her wardrobe. I carried on making up, not sure whether to go for red and black or rainbow colours to match my hair. She went into the bathroom to shower, leaving me to it. With my warpaint complete I started on my fingernails, painting each one a different colour. Only when I'd finished did I realise that I'd pretty well have to stay naked until they were dry. Briefly I wondered if there was some subconscious motivation, only to dismiss the idea as silly.

Having said I'd strip there was no way I could back out. What I didn't want to do was end up stark naked on stage with nothing handy, so I packed a pair of knickers, a skirt and a long, loose top into a bag. I'd already decided on clumpy boots instead of heels and fishnets, not only because it was easier to play, but it would be a much stronger image to be strutting around stark naked except for knee-high boots. One of my little black skirts was ideal, because all I had to do was take down the zip at the side and I could slip it off, while a couple of careful snips with Josie's nail scissors set my top up to be ripped off. There was no point in wearing a bra, and after a moment's hesitation I decided to do without knickers either.

By the time Steve arrived with the van we were both ready, Josie looking tough in her leathers, and sexy too, with nothing under her jacket. We certainly had Steve staring, and he cheekily lifted the back of my skirt as we were loading things into the van. I slapped his hand away, just gently, as I would have done in any case, still unwilling to cut off that particular strand of my old life. He simply laughed.

'No knickers, huh?'

'No. You'll see why later.'

'Sounds tempting, but I'm not coming with you.'

'No, why not?'

'I'm doing the booze for an all-nighter at Lingfield Farm.'

I hadn't even heard about it, which showed how out of touch I'd been. He went on.

'So I need the van dropped there. Anytime will do, but keep it down on the booze, yeah?'

'Who says I'm driving?'

Josie shrugged.

'It's you or me, girl.'

'How about Sam?'

'She's going with Billy.'

'Oh shit, he's not going to be there, is he? And Martin too, I suppose?'

'Martin's on duty, she says.'

'That's a relief. Things are ... a bit difficult with Martin and I suppose I can just ignore Billy. But look, I hate playing when I'm sober. Couldn't you drive, Josie?'

'I'm on ten points, Fizz. You're on what, none?'

'Yes, but ...'

'But nothing. Anyway, you've driven this heap loads of times, so you're driving. What's the problem? You can have a couple, and we'll get coffee somewhere after.'

'All right, if I have to.'

There really wasn't much choice, and she was right. Even a speed camera bust and she'd get her licence suspended, not that it would stop her riding, but then there was the chance of more fines and more hassle. My own licence was clean, if only because every time the cameras had caught me I'd been in stolen cars.

Steve helped us pack our gear in and make sure it wasn't going to rattle around, then drove as far as Lingfield Farm. I took over, driving out through the

Breckland and onto the A11. It felt odd to be passing the turning to Brettenham, and I wondered if Stephen was home yet, perhaps making a careful selection from his collection of fancy wines for whatever would go best with his equally fancy cooking. All I'd had was a sausage sandwich, which had left me in need of repairs to my lippy.

By the time we got to Norwich it was beginning to get dark, with the lights going up, which made the club look all the more spectacular when we got there. There was a big hangar, just like the one we'd played in at Hockwold, only instead of just a door, the front was an aeroplane, a huge Second World War bomber with four engines and silver livery, even a half-naked Vargas-style pin-up beside a wooden staircase. Some of it may even have been real, but the fuselage was a corridor leading back into the hangar, with no tail to the aircraft at all, just a flight of steps down to the main floor.

The decor was straight out of the 40s, or at least it looked that way. All the tables were very neat, round and covered by cloths, well spaced around the floor with a central area open for dancing. Silhouettes decorated the walls, black on pastel green, of jazz musicians playing various implements, and all lit by mellow-toned bulbs beneath green and yellow shades. It had atmosphere, plenty of it, just not ours.

Sam was already there, and got Billy and several of his mates to help us set up. I could tell I was unpopular, presumably because they thought I should be Martin's plaything, with several of them casting me sour glances as if I was the scarlet woman of Babylon. Total bullshit, of course, because that was exactly the way they wanted me to be, except when they weren't the ones getting the nookie. I did my best to ignore them, but it was impossible not to get a bit wound up by their attitude.

The bar was in keeping with the rest of the place, with two guys in monkey suits doing the serving, three different beers and a huge range of cocktails. It was seriously tempting to start in on the cocktails, but I contented myself with a beer while Josie watched the barman put together something called a Manhattan. Not many other people were there, and with no wish to talk to the Americans I went up on stage, seating myself behind my kit to practise and get the feel for how it would be to play.

We had lights in our eyes, like on a lot of stages, so I couldn't really see the main space, only my drums and the brightly lit crescent of floor where Josie and Sam would be playing. I didn't mind, because it's often easier to get lost in the music if you can't see the crowd, especially when the crowd doesn't look right or isn't really into the music.

Josie and I had been listening to the Buzzcocks on the way, and I began to tap out the rhythm to *Ever Fallen In Love With Someone*, which had stuck in my head because I couldn't stop myself from connecting the lyrics with my situation with Stephen. I badly needed to get all of that out of my head, and bagged myself another beer before starting to practise again. There were too many niggles in my head, and I wanted to be drunk, really drunk, so that the drumming was all that mattered.

We were opening with *Barbed Wire Love*, which is tricky because of all the changes, and I began to practise that, only to find the lyrics made me think of Stephen yet again. I just had to get out of myself, and went back to the bar for a third beer, sure I could sweat the alcohol out while I played and promising myself I wouldn't bring anything up on stage.

People had begun to arrive, a mixed crowd of American servicemen, older men and women who shared a laid-back look and were evidently the regulars, along with plenty of our own crowd. I switched to *Homicide* as Josie joined me on stage, and began to feel a bit better. She was facing me, playing together the way we did in her garage, full of attitude and raw, sexual power, which helped to lift me and make me feel the same way. We went right through the song just on instruments, which left our own mob and some of the Americans calling for more. Some of the jazz crowd approved, more just looked bemused, and nobody left.

We were ready to go, and Josie climbed down to haul Sam out of Billy's close embrace. Her hands were full of beers as she climbed onstage, and she gave two to me, ducking down to speak as she put them on the floor. I just kept playing, now on my high, as she gave me a last few instructions. The footlights came right up as she stepped away and I was in my own cocoon of light and sound as Sam began to pick out the bass line.

Josie screamed out a welcome, defying the jazz crowd to like us or fuck off, and we had begun. I crashed into the song and hit the beat immediately, without even thinking, and it stayed that way, my emotions building with the song, and with the next, until I was oblivious to everything but the music and a tiny voice deep in my head telling me it was the last time, over and over.

I had to play, and play like I'd never played before. *Ever Fallen In Love With Someone* had me in tears, my vision now no more than a haze of coloured light. Still I beat the drums with every ounce of my strength, to set the club shaking and draw screams and stamping from the crowd. The tracks had become a blur, each fading into the next, and I'd forgotten the order completely, just picking up each beat as Josie yelled out the title: *My Way* Sex Pistols-style, and *Teenage Kicks*, and *Homicide*, and *Pretty Vacant*.

My limbs were already wet with sweat, my muscles hot from playing, my brain buzzing. I was going to do it, to strip naked in front of all of them and play naked, defying them to stop the music and throw us out. All I needed was my cue, but Josie had come right back behind me, dropping her guitar but still singing with Sam, carrying the song on the bass alone in true chaotic punk style. She put the microphone to my mouth and I was yelling out the words, in wild excitement as she tore my top wide open, spilling my breasts out for all to see.

She'd snatched the microphone back, jiggling my breasts to taunt the crowd, with me still trying to play, but as the chorus finished she had pressed her mouth to mine, kissing me hard, only to suddenly pull back, give my tits a final bounce and stride back to the front of the stage. I managed to pick up the beat again, just as she retrieved her guitar and we were back into the song, only now with the crowd screaming their heads off and my ruined top wide open at the front.

As the song ended I simply peeled my top right off. My skin was wet with sweat, my mouth still tingling from Josie's kiss, my nipples hard. I was going all the way, no question. Josie was taunting the crowd, demanding to know if they wanted to see more. Suddenly she'd spun Sam around, jerking up her skirt to show off twin, fishnet-clad cheeks, and with everybody's attention on them I slipped my own skirt down and off.

I was stark naked except for my boots and revelling in it, so dirty and so free, and about to be on display to the entire audience. *God Save the Queen* kicked off and I was playing nude, and not knowing if they'd seen or they hadn't, if they'd be into it or we were about to get closed down. Josie seemed to be off her head, improvising lyrics far worse than anything the Sex Pistols had come up with, and I could only guess when she was nearing the end, beating out a final crescendo on the drums, kicking out to send my kit flying and making absolutely sure everybody in the room got a good view, standing up to attention and snapping out a smart salute, in boots and not another stitch.

Josie had dropped her guitar. Sam's died with a whine, leaving only the delighted whoops of the punks in the crowd, clapping and wolf whistles from the Americans and a few of the others. I raised my hands, waving cheerfully as I wondered what to do if they demanded an encore, just as the lights came up. A man was walking towards us, the miserable, killjoy expression on his face all too familiar, although his words were lost in the din. It was over.

My bag was right next to me, the fire exit just a few paces away. I grabbed the first and kicked the second open, setting off an alarm. I didn't care, even if they confiscated my drum kit. I didn't need it any more, but I had finished on one hell of a high. Hidden behind a box van, I quickly pulled on my spare knickers, skirt and top, rendering myself legal and decent.

Nobody seemed to have followed me, and before

long people were spilling out of the front of the club, Josie included, holding her guitar and the microphone. I joined her at the van, unable to stop myself grinning.

'What's happening?'

'The usual shit, but he wants to keep it quiet.'

'We're banned?'

'What do you think?'

I just laughed. It felt good, like it always felt good, but this time, instead of the drawback being one more venue that wouldn't have us, it was that I'd never do it again. As I climbed into the van I was telling myself I'd had my run, but it wouldn't make the feeling go away. I heard Billy's voice, and stayed where I was as our gear was loaded into the back, my eyes closed as I thought of how it had felt to go nude in front of so many people, to have my top ripped wide, to be kissed on my open mouth by another girl . . .

'Wake up, Fizz. You are fit to drive, aren't you?'

'Yeah, sure, no problem. Just thinking how good that was.'

I felt OK, but unsure how much of that was adrenalin. Josie lit a cigarette and offered me one. I took it, despite having given up long before, and the matches, an old-style box from the Flying Fortress. For once I felt I needed to smoke, and finished two before letting the clutch in and moving cautiously out of the club car park. All the way out of Norwich I was expecting to get stopped, but nothing happened, and on the main road I gradually began to relax. I began to get tired too and pulled in at an all-night garage to pick up big frothy coffees with sugar on top and jam doughnuts. We ate them in a lay-by, Josie speaking between mouthfuls, the same thing she'd said maybe six or seven times since we'd left the club.

'It was good, wasn't it, the best.'

There was something wistful in her voice, immediately making me feel bad for being the one who'd brought it all to an end.

'Sorry, Josie, I . . .'

'Don't be. You made my night.'

She paused, staring out of the window with her coffee cup held in her lap as if she was unable to look at me. I felt worse than ever, knowing she had to blame me. Rubber Dollies was her band, and always had been. It was so much a part of her image too, the thing that had made her popular at school and so cool hardly anyone had minded when she came out as a lesbian. I was struggling for something to say, but she spoke first.

'I should be the one saying sorry.'

'What for?'

I was genuinely puzzled, but she didn't answer, making me insist.

'What for, Josie?'

'Pushing you, touching you up . . . kissing you like that.'

'That's all right. I said you could.'

'Yeah, but I shouldn't have done it. I know you're not into me and . . .'

'I didn't mind, Josie, really.'

'I know, but . . . oh shit, you're going to hate me for this, but it was OK when you were there, but now you're going away, and I had to. I'm sorry, I just need you so badly, I always have, Fizz . . . and just to kiss you, just once . . . oh fuck!'

She'd burst into tears, sobbing her heart out with her face turned away and her hands shaking so badly I thought she'd drop her coffee. I still didn't know what to say, completely taken aback by her admission and feeling stupid for not realising.

'Hey, come on, Josie, don't cry. You never cry!'

'You'd be surprised. Sorry, Fizz.'

As she spoke she'd wiped her eyes with the back of her hand, smearing her make-up across her face. I struggled for something to say, anything to make her feel better.

'It was nice, Josie. I liked it, really, especially when you... you know, jiggled me a bit. You got my nipples hard, and in front of all those jazz types!'

It was half true but I was also trying to make her laugh, and I did manage to raise a weak smile but as I reached out to hug her she pushed my arms away.

'No, Fizz, don't. I can't bear it.'

'Don't be silly, Josie, just hug me, will you?'

I wasn't taking no for an answer, taking her coffee cup out of her hands and gathering her into my arms. She didn't respond, still crying, and she wasn't even very drunk. I took her arm and put it around my waist, trying to get her to respond, feeling bad for her and asking myself why I shouldn't give her what she wanted the way I did for Steve and other friends too. What difference did it make? I like to give. Still I was full of confusion, not sure what I wanted at all, but with a rising excitement inside I didn't want to push down. At last I spoke, desperately trying to pretend to myself it was purely to be nice to her.

'Josie? Come on, you can touch if you like. I don't mind, really.'

'Not out of sympathy, Fizz.'

I hesitated, still holding her, forcing me to admit what I realised had been building up in me ever since I'd fantasised about her, maybe longer.

'It won't be out of sympathy. It will be because I'm your friend, and ... and I like it. Do you really think I'd have let you if I didn't like it? Do you really think I'd have got off with Martin over you beating me if there hadn't been at least a little something in my head? Now kiss me, you silly bitch.'

She was going to speak again but I'd lifted her head and pressed my lips to hers. I could taste the sugar from the doughnuts, and coffee, the sweet taste making it easier to kiss harder, and suddenly she had given in, and more. Her mouth wasn't just open under mine; she was returning my kiss, more forcefully than I'd given it. I let myself relax, telling myself I'd let her do as she pleased as she mashed her mouth against mine, with her arms tight around my back.

I'd never felt that anybody needed me so badly, emotionally and physically too. She was trembling as we kissed, and pulling me onto her across the wide seat. Momentarily we broke apart as I scrambled across to her, straddling her body on the seat. Her hands found the hem of my top and our eyes met, hers full of uncertainty. I nodded and my top had been pulled up. I closed my eyes, letting her touch me as she pleased and unable to deny the pleasure of the sensation as she quickly pulled my bra up and took my breasts in her hands.

She had my nipples hard, just as hard as any man, and I couldn't help but respond. Still trying to tell myself I was doing it for her sake but knowing full well it was a lie, I returned the favour, jerking her top high. She was bare underneath, and as my hands found her breasts a powerful shiver ran through me. It felt weird, but it felt good, sexy, and far more than that, naughty, so naughty, to be playing with each other's breasts, and kissing, and maybe more.

'Anything you like, Josie, anything at all . . . I mean it.'

Her answer was to let her hands slip lower, around my back to take hold of my bottom. I rose up, kneeling across her on the seat, my eyes shut in bliss as my skirt was eased up over my hips and around my waist. Now I was really being naughty, with just my knickers to cover me, then not even that. She'd pulled them down, baring my bottom and my pussy even as she pulled me forward. Her mouth found one breast and her hands were on my bottom, holding me open, sliding between my cheeks and deeper still.

I cried out as she penetrated me, pushing two fingers deep into my body with ease. Now she knew how wet she'd made me, and there were no more lies any more. I began to struggle out of my clothes, stripping everything off except my boots, to go the same way I'd been on stage, only not in front of an audience this time, but with my lover, my female lover.

The moment I was nude I came back into her arms, her hands now exploring without restraint, eager to enjoy every part of my body. It wasn't easy in the cramped cab, but we were both too eager to care, kissing and touching until I was high enough to want to give her that most intimate act, to make her come under my tongue. I knew from experience I could get down in the well with the seat pushed right back, and I did, slipping down from her grip to kneel between her thighs. She looked me full in the face.

'Do you want to?'

I nodded and immediately she was tugging her skirt

up and pushing her knickers down and off to present me with her open sex. I'd seen her naked a hundred times, but this was different, her thighs open to show herself off for the attention of my tongue. For a moment I hesitated, wondering if I could really do it, and then I had, my face buried between her thighs, my tongue lapping between her lips as she gave a deep, soft sigh and called my name.

Her hand found the back of my head, holding me gently but firmly in place as I licked her, and with that gesture my feelings grew stronger still. Now I was really doing it, beyond naughty, into that realm of surrender where only Stephen had ever taken me. I wanted to please her, any way she liked, to be hers to enjoy, to strip me, to touch me where she pleased, to have me lick her, maybe even to spank my bottom if she wanted to.

With that my hand went back to find my sex, only to stop. I had to come, but not yet, because I had to get what I'd thought of before and the chance would never come again. I licked harder, and faster, right on her clitoris. She groaned, called my name, and a moment later she'd come, rubbing my face into her sex as spasm after spasm ran through her body.

I stopped only when she pulled my head back. She was smiling down at me, content yet sad. Her arms came open to hug me as she spoke.

'Thanks, Fizz . . .'

'Sure, only I need the same favour. I want you to spank me, Josie . . . to spank my bottom, nice and hard.'

She looked surprised, but moved aside as I scrambled up on the seat, my knees wide and my bum stuck well out. My hand went back and I was masturbating, even as she knelt up beside me, to take me firmly around the waist. Her hand found my bottom, first squeezing, then giving me the gentlest of smacks.

'Harder, Josie, punish me.'

She didn't need telling twice, tightening her grip on my waist and laying into my bottom. As I felt the warmth start to spread I was completely lost, rubbing hard at myself with the same rude thought running around and around in my head, that I was being spanked by another woman, Josie, who'd always been so strong, so tough. It was better than having a man do it, far better, naughtier, more humiliating, better for bringing out that awful wonderful sense of resentment, and as my cheeks bounced I was screaming her name and begging her to spank me harder, and to make me lick her again afterwards as I remembered how she'd had me grovelling on my knees, nude but for my boots, kneeling to her in worship with my tongue busy on her pussy.

With that I came, an orgasm that seemed to last forever, and she never once paused in my spanking as I shook and shivered and told her over and over again how much I loved her and how good it felt to be under her control. She never questioned me either, but just held on, as I came. Afterwards, neither of us spoke as we cuddled and kissed for what seemed like an age. Finally it was she who pulled away, her voice a sigh as she spoke.

'I've wanted you for so long, Fizz ... thank you.'

'You don't need to thank me. That was lovely, and I'd do it again, anytime.'

Her answer was a weak smile, but I knew what she was thinking. We could have been enjoying ourselves for years. If only she'd told me, perhaps teased me into it one night when we'd been drunk together. Once I'd given in to the feelings of submission she brought out in me I'd have been OK. After that it would have been a regular thing, our naughty, dirty, delicious secret. Now it would never be.

It was nearly one in the morning by the time we'd got dressed and tidied ourselves up. I was getting tired and she agreed to drive, guiding the van back onto the main road. As we went we had one of those soft, sensible conversations, when you both know you're putting your emotions second. We agreed that if we'd both been living in Hockford we wouldn't be able to leave each other alone, that there might have been all sorts of consequences and so it was probably best that I was leaving. I told her everything about Stephen, and as I did so I felt increasingly guilty and confused, until it had become almost a physical pain. At last I could bear it no longer. I needed to see him and reaffirm my feelings.

'Could you drop me at the Brettenham turning?'

'Yeah? I thought . . . nah, it's probably best.'

I nodded, the lump in my throat suddenly too big to let me speak. For maybe a minute we drove on in silence, before the sign for my turning appeared in the headlights. Josie slowed the van and stopped where the minor road came off, biting her lip as she turned to me.

'Thanks again, Fizz. I needed that so badly.'

'That's OK.'

'Now fuck off before I start to cry again.'

I kissed her and got down from the van. Our eyes met for one last moment and she was gone, leaving me standing by the road with my head a mess of emotions: lingering excitement and arousal, joy and yet sadness too, mischievousness and guilt, but above

all a bitter sense of loss. After all those years of freedom, and when I'd finally decided to give it up I almost
immediately found something so good I could hardly
bear to go without.

Yet I knew the cure, for all that the tears were
beginning to well up in my eyes as I walked the
moonlit road. Once I was under Stephen's firm, loving
control I would be OK again. That was what I needed,
to be held tight and have him tell me that he loved
me, which he'd not yet done. Then he could spank me
rosy and all would be well again.

My thoughts were going round and round as I
walked, but always coming back to the same conclusion. That was what I needed, and I needed it now.
My heart was in my throat as I climbed the wooden
stair to his flat. His car was there, so he was in. I would
wake him and ask him to cuddle me and then to spank
me, taking my well-deserved punishment for all that
he didn't know I'd done. Or maybe I should tell him?
Maybe I should tell him I'd been with another girl,
apologise and beg for him to punish me.

Yes, that was best. I would admit it and beg forgive-
ness. I would tell him he could punish me any way he
pleased, spank me, cane me and, afterwards, have me
naked on my knees, penetrated from behind with my
punished bottom lifted to him. Maybe he should even
sodomise me. Yes, that was what I deserved, to be
spanked and sodomised as a punishment. I knew he'd
do it.

I turned the key in the lock as carefully as I could,
sliding the door open with only the slightest noise.
Inside it was dark, save for a faint light from the
stairwell up to his bedroom. It was not quiet, the first
sound I heard the unmistakable smack of a hard male

hand applied to a soft female bottom, then a little gasp and a giggle. I froze, my mouth coming slowly open as the all too familiar noises continued. Without the slightest doubt Stephen had another woman in his bedroom, our bedroom. He was spanking her, and she was thoroughly enjoying it.

Anger welled up inside me, only to die as I thought of what I'd just done, and rise again. Maybe I'd been with Josie, but not in the bed where I'd given so much. It just wasn't fair, not behind my back, and it could hardly be somebody he'd just chanced to pick up for the night, or almost certainly not. How many women get straight into heavy spanking on a first date?

I stepped forward, knowing only that I was going to confront him, and that I wanted to catch him red-handed, with no possibility of talking his way out of it. Walking on tiptoe, I crossed the floor, all the while the smacks growing louder and her response more openly sexual, only to stop, and as I heard Stephen sigh I knew he'd stopped her mouth with his cock, exactly the way he liked to do to me. I reached the spiral stair and started up, step by careful step, until I could poke my head up out of the well and see what was going on.

Stephen knelt on the bed, turned slightly away from me, still in his shirt and suit trousers, but with his cock and balls protruding from the fly, the way I enjoyed so much. He was erect, and his shaft was half hidden in the mouth of the woman who was sucking his cock. She was naked, on her hands and knees with her tummy supported on a pile of pillows. Her bottom was lifted towards me, pushed up high and well open, her full cheeks red with spanking and open to show every intimate detail between, while his big hand rose and fell to make her cheeks quiver and bounce. She was wet, and a small carrot had been inserted up her bottom.

None of that mattered, not in the least. There could have been a thousand more details, just as dirty as you please, and still none of them would have mattered. Only one thing mattered, the identity of the woman he was with, who was sucking his cock, who he was spanking. My mother.

I walked back down those stairs and away, numb with shock, not knowing what to think or what to do, my mind simply unable to take it in. His car keys were on the telephone table and I picked them up by instinct, closing the door behind me. I climbed down to ground level and got into his gleaming silver Saab, knowing only that I wanted to go, to get as far away as possible as fast as possible.

They hadn't noticed me, too lost in each other to realise, and I left unhindered, driving out onto the main road with some vague idea of catching up with Josie, only to change my mind. I put my foot down, hitting eighty, ninety, one hundred, wondering if I should just ram the car into another and put an end to everything, and with that awful thought my emotions burst. The tears were streaming from my eyes as I tore through the night, anger welling up to push everything else aside, but I had to slow, or crash.

I slowed, enough sense left to me for that, and pulled off the fast road towards Hockford. Deep in the woods I stopped at the mouth of a logging track and got out of the car, trying to think. It wasn't too late. I could still go back, leave the car and somehow get home on foot, pretend nothing had happened. Or I could set light to the bastard's car and leave it to burn as a beacon to his betrayal. I could be his again, meek and subservient, going over his knee to have my knickers pulled down and my bottom spanked but all the while knowing he had neither loyalty nor respect for me. Or I could keep my pride and sacrifice my relationship and my job as well, maybe take up with Martin, maybe steal Mr Phelps' new car, maybe go out with Pete and afterwards pee in my knickers for him somewhere deep in the wood, maybe surrender my bottom to Dave Shaw, definitely play with Josie again. I could be me.

The matches from the Flying Fortress were still in my pocket. I took them out, looking at the little aeroplane in the dim light from inside the car. All it would take was one strike, or I could drive back to Brettenham and continue to be Stephen's little dolly bird. No, I was going to be me.

I lit the match.

LOOK OUT FOR THE ALL-NEW BLACK LACE BOOKS – AVAILABLE NOW!

All books priced £7.99 in the UK. Please note publication dates apply to the UK only. For other territories, please contact your retailer.

GOTHIC BLUE
Portia Da Costa
ISBN 978 0 352 33075 8

At an archduke's reception, a handsome young nobleman falls under the spell of a malevolent but irresistible sorceress. Two hundred years later, Belinda Seward also falls prey to sensual forces she can neither understand nor control. Stranded by a thunderstorm at a remote Gothic priory, Belinda and her boyfriend are drawn into an enclosed world of luxurious decadence and sexual alchemy. Their host is the courteous but melancholic André von Kastel, a beautiful aristocrat who mourns his lost love. He has plans for Belinda – plans that will take her into the realms of obsessive love and the erotic paranormal.

Coming in March 2007

FLOOD
Anna Clare
ISBN 978 0 352 34094 8

London, 1877. Phoebe Flood, a watch mender's daughter from Blackfriars, is hired as lady's maid to the glamorous Louisa LeClerk, a high class tart with connections to the underworld of gentlemen pornographers. Fascinated by her new mistress and troubled by strange dreams, Phoebe receives an extraordinary education in all matters sensual. And her destiny and secret self gradually reveals itself when she meets Garou, a freak show attraction, The Boy Who Was Raised by Wolves.

MÉNAGE
Emma Holly
ISBN 978 0 352 34118 1

Bookstore owner Kate comes home from work one day to find her two flatmates in bed . . . together. Joe – a sensitive composer – is mortified. Sean – an irrepressible bad boy – asks her to join in. Kate's been fantasising about her hunky new houseshares since they moved in, but she was convinced they were both gay. Realising that pleasure is a multi-faceted thing, she sets her cares aside and embarks on a ménage à trois with the wild duo. Kate wants nothing more than to keep both her admirers happy, but inevitably things become complicated, especially at work. Kate has told her colleagues that Joe and Sean are gay but the gossip begins when she's caught snogging one of them in her lunch hour! To add to this, one of Kate's more conservative suitors is showing interest again, but she's hooked on the different kind of loving that she enjoys with her boys – even though she knows it cannot last. Or can it?

COOKING UP A STORM
Emma Holly
ISBN 978 0 352 34114 3

The Coates Inn restaurant in Cape Cod is about to go out of business when its striking owner, Abby, jumps at a stranger's offer of help – both in her kitchen and her bedroom. Storm, a handsome chef, claims to have a secret weapon: an aphrodisiac menu that her patrons won't be able to resist. It certainly works on Abby – who gives in to the passions she has denied herself for years.

But can this playboy chef really be Abby's hero if her body means more to him than her heart, and his initial plan was to steal the restaurant from under her nose? Storm soon turns the restaurant around, but Abby's insatiable desires have taken over her life. She's never known a guy into crazy sex like him before, and she wants to spend every spare moment getting as much intense erotic pleasure as she can. Meanwhile, her best friend Marissa becomes suspicious of the new wonder-boy in the kitchen. Before things get really out of control, someone has to assume responsibility. But can Abby tear herself away from the object of her lustful attention long enough to see what's really going on?

Coming in April 2007

WING OF MADNESS
Mae Nixon
ISBN 978 0 352 34099 3

As a university academic, Claire has always sought safety in facts and information. But then she meets Jim and he becomes her guide on a sensual journey with no limits except their own imagination – and Claire's has always been overactive. She learns to submit to a man totally, to be his to use for pleasure or sensual punishment. Together they begin to explore the dark, forbidden places inside her and she quickly learns how little she really knows about her own erotic nature. The only thing she knows with absolute certainty is that she never wants it to stop . . .

THE TOP OF HER GAME
Emma Holly
ISBN 978 0 352 34116 7

It's not only Julia's professional acumen that has men quaking in their shoes – she also has a taste for keeping men in line after office hours. With an impressive collection of whips and high heels to her name, she sure has some kinky ways of showing affection. But Julia's been searching all her life for a man who won't be tamed too quickly – and when she meets rugged dude rancher Zach on a business get-together in Montana, she thinks she might have found him.

He may be a simple countryman, but he's not about to take any nonsense from uppity city women like Julia. Zach's full of surprises: where she thinks he's tough, he turns out to be gentle; she's confident she's got this particular cowboy broken in, he turns the tables on her. Has she locked horns with an animal too wild even for her? When it comes to sex, Zach doesn't go for half measures. Underneath the big sky of Montana, has the steely Ms Mueller finally met her match?

Black Lace Booklist

Information is correct at time of printing. To avoid disappointment, check availability before ordering. Go to www.blacklace-books.co.uk. All books are priced £7.99 unless another price is given.

BLACK LACE BOOKS WITH A CONTEMPORARY SETTING

☐ ALWAYS THE BRIDEGROOM Tesni Morgan	ISBN 978 0 352 33855 6	£6.99
☐ THE ANGELS' SHARE Maya Hess	ISBN 978 0 352 34043 6	
☐ ARIA APPASSIONATA Julie Hastings	ISBN 978 0 352 33056 7	£6.99
☐ ASKING FOR TROUBLE Kristina Lloyd	ISBN 978 0 352 33362 9	
☐ BLACK LIPSTICK KISSES Monica Belle	ISBN 978 0 352 33885 3	£6.99
☐ BONDED Fleur Reynolds	ISBN 978 0 352 33192 2	£6.99
☐ THE BOSS Monica Belle	ISBN 978 0 352 34088 7	£6.99
☐ BOUND IN BLUE Monica Belle	ISBN 978 0 352 34012 2	
☐ CAMPAIGN HEAT Gabrielle Marcola	ISBN 978 0 352 33941 6	
☐ CAT SCRATCH FEVER Sophie Mouette	ISBN 978 0 352 34021 4	
☐ CIRCUS EXCITE Nikki Magennis	ISBN 978 0 352 34033 7	
☐ CLUB CRÈME Primula Bond	ISBN 978 0 352 33907 2	£6.99
☐ COMING ROUND THE MOUNTAIN Tabitha Flyte	ISBN 978 0 352 33873 0	£6.99
☐ CONFESSIONAL Judith Roycroft	ISBN 978 0 352 33421 3	
☐ CONTINUUM Portia Da Costa	ISBN 978 0 352 33120 5	
☐ DANGEROUS CONSEQUENCES Pamela Rochford	ISBN 978 0 352 33185 4	
☐ DARK DESIGNS Madelynne Ellis	ISBN 978 0 352 34075 7	
☐ THE DEVIL INSIDE Portia Da Costa	ISBN 978 0 352 32993 6	
☐ EDEN'S FLESH Robyn Russell	ISBN 978 0 352 33923 2	£6.99
☐ ENTERTAINING MR STONE Portia Da Costa	ISBN 978 0 352 34029 0	
☐ EQUAL OPPORTUNITIES Mathilde Madden	ISBN 978 0 352 34070 2	
☐ FEMININE WILES Karina Moore	ISBN 978 0 352 33874 7	£6.99
☐ FIRE AND ICE Laura Hamilton	ISBN 978 0 352 33486 2	
☐ GOING DEEP Kimberly Dean	ISBN 978 0 352 33876 1	£6.99
☐ GOING TOO FAR Laura Hamilton	ISBN 978 0 352 33657 6	£6.99
☐ GONE WILD Maria Eppie	ISBN 978 0 352 33670 5	

☐ IN PURSUIT OF ANNA Natasha Rostova   ISBN 978 0 352 34060 3

☐ MAD ABOUT THE BOY Mathilde Madden   ISBN 978 0 352 34001 6

☐ MAKE YOU A MAN Anna Clare   ISBN 978 0 352 34006 1

☐ MAN HUNT Cathleen Ross   ISBN 978 0 352 33583 8

☐ MIXED DOUBLES Zoe le Verdier   ISBN 978 0 352 33312 4   £6.99

☐ MIXED SIGNALS Anna Clare   ISBN 978 0 352 33889 1   £6.99

☐ MS BEHAVIOUR Mini Lee   ISBN 978 0 352 33962 1

☐ A MULTITUDE OF SINS Kit Mason   ISBN 978 0 352 33737 5   £6.99

☐ PACKING HEAT Karina Moore   ISBN 978 0 352 33356 8   £6.99

☐ PAGAN HEAT Monica Belle   ISBN 978 0 352 33974 4

☐ PASSION OF ISIS Madelynne Ellis   ISBN 978 0 352 33993 5

☐ PEEP SHOW Mathilde Madden   ISBN 978 0 352 33924 9

☐ THE POWER GAME Carrera Devonshire   ISBN 978 0 352 33990 4

☐ THE PRIVATE UNDOING OF A PUBLIC SERVANT   ISBN 978 0 352 34066 5
    Leonie Martel

☐ RELEASE ME Suki Cunningham   ISBN 978 0 352 33671 2   £6.99

☐ RUDE AWAKENING Pamela Kyle   ISBN 978 0 352 33036 9

☐ SAUCE FOR THE GOOSE Mary Rose Maxwell   ISBN 978 0 352 33492 3

☐ SIN.NET Helena Ravenscroft   ISBN 978 0 352 33598 2   £6.99

☐ SLAVE TO SUCCESS Kimberley Raines   ISBN 978 0 352 33687 3   £6.99

☐ SLEAZY RIDER Karen S. Smith   ISBN 978 0 352 33964 5

☐ STELLA DOES HOLLYWOOD Stella Black   ISBN 978 0 352 33588 3

☐ THE STRANGER Portia Da Costa   ISBN 978 0 352 33211 0

☐ SUMMER FEVER Anna Ricci   ISBN 978 0 352 33625 5   £6.99

☐ SWITCHING HANDS Alaine Hood   ISBN 978 0 352 33896 9   £6.99

☐ SYMPHONY X Jasmine Stone   ISBN 978 0 352 33629 3   £6.99

☐ TONGUE IN CHEEK Tabitha Flyte   ISBN 978 0 352 33484 8

☐ TWO WEEKS IN TANGIER Annabel Lee   ISBN 978 0 352 33599 9   £6.99

☐ UNNATURAL SELECTION Alaine Hood   ISBN 978 0 352 33963 8

☐ UP TO NO GOOD Karen S. Smith   ISBN 978 0 352 33589 0   £6.99

☐ VILLAGE OF SECRETS Mercedes Kelly   ISBN 978 0 352 33344 5

☐ WILD BY NATURE Monica Belle   ISBN 978 0 352 33915 7   £6.99

☐ WILD CARD Madeline Moore   ISBN 978 0 352 34038 2

BLACK LACE BOOKS WITH AN HISTORICAL SETTING

- [ ] THE AMULET Lisette Allen — ISBN 978 0 352 33019 2 £6.99
- [ ] THE BARBARIAN GEISHA Charlotte Royal — ISBN 978 0 352 33267 7
- [ ] BARBARIAN PRIZE Deanna Ashford — ISBN 978 0 352 34017 7
- [ ] DANCE OF OBSESSION Olivia Christie — ISBN 978 0 352 33101 4
- [ ] DARKER THAN LOVE Kristina Lloyd — ISBN 978 0 352 33279 0
- [ ] ELENA'S DESTINY Lisette Allen — ISBN 978 0 352 33218 9
- [ ] FRENCH MANNERS Olivia Christie — ISBN 978 0 352 33214 1
- [ ] THE HAND OF AMUN Juliet Hastings — ISBN 978 0 352 33144 1 £6.99
- [ ] LORD WRAXALL'S FANCY Anna Lieff Saxby — ISBN 978 0 352 33080 2
- [ ] THE MASTER OF SHILDEN Lucinda Carrington — ISBN 978 0 352 33140 3
- [ ] NICOLE'S REVENGE Lisette Allen — ISBN 978 0 352 32984 4
- [ ] THE SENSES BEJEWELLED Cleo Cordell — ISBN 978 0 352 32904 2 £6.99
- [ ] THE SOCIETY OF SIN Sian Lacey Taylder — ISBN 978 0 352 34080 1
- [ ] UNDRESSING THE DEVIL Angel Strand — ISBN 978 0 352 33938 6
- [ ] WHITE ROSE ENSNARED Juliet Hastings — ISBN 978 0 352 33052 9 £6.99

BLACK LACE BOOKS WITH A PARANORMAL THEME

- [ ] BURNING BRIGHT Janine Ashbless — ISBN 978 0 352 34085 6
- [ ] CRUEL ENCHANTMENT Janine Ashbless — ISBN 978 0 352 33483 1
- [ ] THE PRIDE Edie Bingham — ISBN 978 0 352 33997 3
- [ ] GOTHIC BLUE Portia Da Costa — ISBN 978 0 352 33075 8

BLACK LACE ANTHOLOGIES

- [ ] MORE WICKED WORDS Various — ISBN 978 0 352 33487 9 £6.99
- [ ] WICKED WORDS 3 Various — ISBN 978 0 352 33522 7 £6.99
- [ ] WICKED WORDS 4 Various — ISBN 978 0 352 33603 3 £6.99
- [ ] WICKED WORDS 5 Various — ISBN 978 0 352 33642 2 £6.99
- [ ] WICKED WORDS 6 Various — ISBN 978 0 352 33690 3 £6.99
- [ ] WICKED WORDS 7 Various — ISBN 978 0 352 33743 6 £6.99
- [ ] WICKED WORDS 8 Various — ISBN 978 0 352 33787 0 £6.99
- [ ] WICKED WORDS 9 Various — ISBN 978 0 352 33860 0
- [ ] WICKED WORDS 10 Various — ISBN 978 0 352 33893 8
- [ ] THE BEST OF BLACK LACE 2 Various — ISBN 978 0 352 33718 4
- [ ] WICKED WORDS: SEX IN THE OFFICE Various — ISBN 978 0 352 39944 7

☐ WICKED WORDS: SEX AT THE SPORTS CLUB   ISBN 978 0 352 33991 1
   Various
☐ WICKED WORDS: SEX ON HOLIDAY Various   ISBN 978 0 352 33961 4
☐ WICKED WORDS: SEX IN UNIFORM Various   ISBN 978 0 352 34002 3
☐ WICKED WORDS: SEX IN THE KITCHEN Various ISBN 978 0 352 34018 4
☐ WICKED WORDS: SEX ON THE MOVE Various   ISBN 978 0 352 34034 4
☐ WICKED WORDS: SEX AND MUSIC Various   ISBN 978 0 352 34061 0
☐ WICKED WORDS: SEX AND SHOPPING Various   ISBN 978 0 352 34076 4
☐ SEX IN PUBLIC Various   ISBN 978 0 352 34089 4

BLACK LACE NON-FICTION
☐ THE BLACK LACE BOOK OF WOMEN'S SEXUAL   ISBN 978 0 352 33793 1   £6.99
   FANTASIES Edited by Kerri Sharp

To find out the latest information about Black Lace titles, check out the website: www.blacklace-books.co.uk or send for a booklist with complete synopses by writing to:

> Black Lace Booklist, Virgin Books Ltd
> Thames Wharf Studios
> Rainville Road
> London W6 9HA

Please include an SAE of decent size. Please note only British stamps are valid.

Our privacy policy
We will not disclose information you supply us to any other parties. We will not disclose any information which identifies you personally to any person without your express consent.

From time to time we may send out information about Black Lace books and special offers. Please tick here if you do not wish to receive Black Lace information.   ☐